A FORCE TO BE RECKONED WITH

Sterling Young

ISBN-13: 978-1493634101

ISBN-10: 1493634100

ACKNOWLEDGEMENTS

Many of my friends have helped make the release of Delayed Reckoning a success. I will undoubtedly seek their help again with my 2nd book in the Tom Padgett series, A Force to Be Reckoned With. Getting a book established in today's market is no easy task. I will once again reach out to the people that helped me in the past. I hope that doing so doesn't aggravate them. I really dislike being a pest, but if I don't promote myself, nobody else will either.

I don't plan to list various individuals that were instrumental in getting Delayed Reckoning off the ground, like many well known authors do. Frankly, the people that have helped me might not appreciate seeing their names in a book. And besides that, I can't possibly remember everybody's names. That's enough about that.

I do greatly appreciate the assistance that various newspapers have given me. They have printed press releases, written book reviews, and interviewed me for articles in the paper. All of these efforts have been most helpful at getting the word out about Tom Padgett. I will be contacting the newspapers again about this second book, and if all goes well, maybe the popularity of the Padgett series will continue to grow.

Next on my list are the libraries, for not only seeing that Delayed Reckoning was available to check out, but for also hosting book signings. Both of these events helped to get the word out about Padgett. The libraries even went further, doing their own press releases. Every little bit helps. Thank you to the library personnel for taking time to help me out.

And, I can't forget the bars that have helped. They are in the Tom Padgett books and my wife and I have been known to frequent them. They have helped promote my book in various ways, and I am grateful. Sometimes when I sell books while I'm in a bar, the sales suffer, because I, like Tom Padgett, enjoy a Budweiser every now and again. Thanks to the bars and pubs. You guys know who you are.

And last, but certainly not least, I wish to thank my wife, Cindy. She has once again struggled through another one of my novels. I can't thank her enough. Also, thanks to my father-in-law. He double checks the editing and offers good editorial suggestions.

Thanks to everyone who bought my first book and who plan to buy more. Your support is truly appreciated.

CHAPTER 1

Thanksgiving was history now; it was two days behind him. It was a crisp Saturday morning, the last one of November. It was early, really cold, and Shane Miller knew it was bound to get even colder. It was only five-thirty. Unfortunately for Shane, he was already in the woods, and he wasn't happy about being there. He would have preferred to be at home curled up in a warm bed, but he'd blown that chance on opening day. Shane was disgusted with himself. He remembered having heard that if you didn't produce on opening weekend, this was what would happen. If all went well this morning, he'd be home by noon to enjoy some leftover turkey.

He leaned back against a tree and reached into his pocket, pulling out his cigarettes and lighter. He knew better than to light-up while deer hunting. Today, he just didn't care. He felt that his chances of getting a buck this morning were slight, at best. As he lit his cigarette he smirked, *Kentucky's Best.* Shane wasn't sure about them being the best, but for his money, the price was right. He closed his eyes and inhaled deeply. One of the only benefits to being in the woods early in the morning freezing your ass off was a good smoke. He knew the scent from the smoke would waft away in the breeze and that was ok, because he'd be finished soon. Besides that, it was at least an hour before the deer would be moving.

Moments later, while he stubbed his smoke out in the dirt, he thought he heard movement. He was puzzled because he wondered why the deer didn't smell the smoke; maybe because they were upwind. Very slowly, he reached down and gripped his shotgun. Shane was well aware that legal hunting hours were a half-hour before sunrise and a half-hour after sunset. It was well before sunrise, but if the buck showed himself, it was all over. He squinted, trying to focus on the dark woods as the noise continued. He thought about the area that he strained to see. He recalled that it was surrounded by a heavy thicket. When he had arrived earlier, he shone his light into the thicket as he made his way around it. Maybe the deer were hidden within it, and were just waking.

Shane heard another noise. It surprised him because it almost sounded like a man's cough. He was convinced that he was the only person hunting in the area. He assured himself that the noise he'd heard was a grunt, and based on the loudness of it, it must have been made by a good-sized buck. Seconds ticked by. Shane was able to make out more of the shapes around him. He felt that he could almost see the buck move around in the thicket. He wasn't going to blow this chance; no way. He wasn't going to let that buck wander off and leave him without a trophy. He raised the gun to his shoulder and concentrated on the noise coming from the thicket. He held his breath, squeezed off a shot just as the buck began to move.

Though it was still quite dark Shane felt extremely good about the shot he'd made. Unfortunately, the buck continued to thrash around. He chambered a slug and pumped another shot into the thicket. Silence; that was a sound Shane really appreciated. Now, all he needed to do was lean back against the tree and wait for the sunrise. He thought about how good the microwaved turkey and leftover dressing would taste. He lit up another cigarette. Oh yes, this was what hunting was all about; the uncertainty of the hunt. He chuckled to himself, *sometimes you get the bear, and sometimes the bear gets you.*

Shane took another drag on his smoke and peered into the lingering shadows of the thicket. There was no movement within; not a sound to be heard. The buck had to be dead. But, to be on the safe side, Shane decided he'd better wait for daylight. He fantasized about the buck, wondering how many points it had. Sometimes, it was hard to determine the number of points a buck had, even in broad daylight. Shane was getting excited as he thought about the size of the buck's rack. He recalled a mistake he'd made a few years back when he shot a doe that he'd mistaken for a buck. That was such a stupid mistake. He'd never make a mistake like that again.

Shane was getting more anxious. It would be daylight soon. He had smoked a bunch of cigarettes and he was still cold. Shane knew that the buck would have had plenty of time to expire by now. He needed to wrap things up. He got up and stretched. His joints ached and were stiff. He moved slowly, carefully approaching the thicket and chambered another round, just in case the monster buck wasn't dead. He didn't want to be unprepared and have a run-in with a wounded buck.

Shane was alarmed when he saw the amount of blood, there was plenty of it. Usually, a lot of blood was a good sign, meaning the shot had done its job. Shane's kill hadn't produced the trophy buck he'd expected. He was in a state of shock as he realized there were no antlers. The dead man at Shane's feet was no trophy. On this cold Saturday morning, the last one of November, Shane Miller had made the mother of all stupid mistakes.

Shane shook as he stared at the unbelievable mess that lay at his feet. He understood what had happened, but knowing how didn't help him any. The dead man must have gotten lost and then tangled in the briars. It had been so dark. He must not have been able to make his way out of the thicket. Why hadn't he had a flashlight? Who would wander into the woods in the middle of the night without a light?

Shane tried to convince himself that the shooting could be justified. *I thought the man was a buck and shot him. It was as simple as that. Shot him not just once, but twice. I killed a man because I was so damned anxious to mount a head on his wall.* Shane knelt down on the ground next to the man and studied him, willing him to move, even though he knew it wouldn't happen. Shane was disoriented, wrestling with what he had done. He acknowledged that he didn't have many options. He understood the serious consequences of his actions. Even though it had been a mistake, Shane had made the mistake twice. The fact that he'd shot well before legal hunting hours was insignificant when compared to murder. He just couldn't believe what had happened. It was an accident but who would believe that? He was certain it meant jail time. He had just turned twenty-five; too young to go to jail. Even if his sentence wasn't long, it would still include some sort of probation. Shane needed to think it all through, but first, he needed to get out of there fast. He absolutely had to find a way out of this mess.

Shane looked down at the body one last time before he made up his mind. He would leave the Clay Wildlife Management Area and act as if he hadn't been there today. He'd pretend that he had never been to the Clay WMA ever before. He snatched up his gun from the ground and quickly made his way out of the woods and noticed two other trucks parked in the lot next to his. He hoped that their owners had paid his vehicle little attention. That was one thing Shane felt was definitely in his favor; his truck was far from memorable. It was a rusty, beat up 2000 Ford Ranger. Not the kind of truck anyone was likely to remember. He jumped in, fired up the Ranger, and quickly as he dared, drove out of the Reserve.

He felt fortunate about two things; one was that it had only been his second visit to Clay WMA; the other was that he had been hunting in Nicholas County. Shane lived in Fleming County. He hoped no one had recognized him or his truck. As he made the left turn onto Mt. Tabor Road, he breathed a welcome sigh of relief. Shane was almost home. He pulled his truck into the detached garage and pushed the button that lowered the garage door. He rarely parked in the garage, but today Shane felt it necessary. He removed his hunting gear and carefully laid it on the workbench, pulled the door closed and slowly made his way to the house and hesitantly climbed the steps. Shane opened the back door of his modular, into the kitchen. Joanne, his wife, stood at the sink doing dishes.

He hesitated and watched her rinse a plate. Joanne looked up. She asked curiously, "Why'd you park in the garage, Shane? You never park in there."

Shane didn't have a very good answer. "Oh, I don't know, I felt like doing something different."

She studied him for a second longer. "How'd you do today? I bet you're starved. How about some turkey and dressing?"

Shane wasn't hungry, he wasn't hungry at all. But, knew

6

he'd better act like he was. He knew he was behaving weirdly and was sure that Joanne would be able to tell. If he didn't want to be plied with a bunch of questions, he'd better eat.

Monday Morning

Bill Wilson felt more and more comfortable being Sheriff. He had over a half year under his belt, seven months actually, as Sheriff of Nicholas County, Kentucky. He felt he had a pretty good handle on things in *his county*. He combed his dark brown hair and noticed a few new gray ones. He paused to contemplate them and proceeded to put his hat on. He methodically adjusted the hat to make sure it was just right. He turned sideways, looked at himself in the mirror, and then attempted to tighten his holster another notch, but not today. Wilson hadn't started to work out yet, like he'd planned on doing. But, he'd get around to it soon. He looked approvingly at his reflection. Wilson had some tough times early on as Sheriff. Now, he felt as if he'd finally turned a corner.

Wilson was glad that Thanksgiving was over. He had spent the holiday weekend alone. Fortunately, his days off had been quite restful. Now, he was ready to get back to work. He had some big issues to deal with. He smiled to himself as he thought about some of them. First and foremost, he needed to look into the events which led to Jimmy Fugate's death. Jimmy had been killed by a twelve gauge slug. He'd been shot in the back. Fugate was found with his pants down to his ankles, evidently in the middle of raping a young Mexican girl. Wilson considered that maybe he got what he deserved. Justice still needed to be served; right from wrong had to be determined. Wilson glanced at his cell phone, noticed he had no messages or missed calls. Good, no emergencies; that was the way it should be on a Monday morning.

Wilson carried his coffee out onto the back porch. He ventured a glance to his neighbor's house. Thank God, the nosy old biddy wasn't outside. He couldn't believe the number of people that had been at her house on Thanksgiving Day. Who in their right mind would want to visit that busy body? The kids probably felt obligated. He stepped to the far end of the porch as he studied the

7

exterior of her house. Suddenly her door flew open and she stepped outside. She moved surprisingly quickly for a woman of her age. Wilson obviously hadn't moved quickly enough. He had barely reached his door, when he heard her yell, "Wilson, I'm glad you didn't do anything stupid over the weekend."

He slammed the door behind him, walked over to the sink, and poured out the remains of his coffee. Now, Wilson wasn't happy. Doesn't that nosy-ass old woman have anything better to do than worry about me? He brushed his teeth, combed his hair again, and then put his hat back on. He needed to go to Carlisle. It would likely be a busy day. He put on his coat, walked out the front door, fired up his truck and backed down the drive. As he was about to put the Dodge into gear, he sensed something and glanced to his left. The nosy neighbor was standing at her front door watching him. "Damned old woman," Wilson spat.

This was definitely his favorite time of day. Tom Padgett smiled in disbelief as he read the latest CNN news on-line; some things will never change. He also read the local weekly papers. It kept him abreast of events around Nicholas and surrounding counties. He also followed the news of the world. Sometimes, he wasn't sure which of the events were funniest; things that happened in the county or what happened elsewhere in the world. Maybe he was being cynical, but tragic world events were sometimes ridiculous. Bella, his golden/lab mix, lay at his feet. She didn't understand what was up. She intently watched Tom. She wondered what was so funny. Tom poured himself another cup of coffee and resumed reading.

After he finished reading, he looked at Bella. "OK girl, I'm through messing. Would you like to go on a walk?" Tom already knew the answer to that question, but he enjoyed asking it, just to see her reaction. Her response was as expected. She sprung to her feet and ran to the trailer door. Tom wondered, *when will she start to slow down? She's nearly four years old.* He laughed to himself as he put on his blaze orange vest. The day he bought his vest he also bought one for Bella. She hated her vest. During hunting season, it could be dangerous not to wear blaze orange in the

8

woods. Tom had to play a game with Bella in order to get her to cooperate. First, he had to slip the vest over her head; that could be tough to do, because she'd lower her chin to the floor. Once Bella's vest was on, Tom would snap the straps between her legs.

Now that they both had on their vests, Tom had to give Bella further assurance that everything was okay. "Papa has his vest on and Bella has her vest on." He patted his chest and said, "Papa's vest," and then he patted her chest, "Bella's vest." This seemed to placate her for the moment. The first morning she'd worn her vest, Bella acted as if it was hard for her to walk. The straps must have made her feel confined. She was smart, but sometimes she could be a big baby. He put on his hat and gloves and walked out into the morning chill. It was cold, only eighteen according to the Weather Channel. Cold weather had no effect on Bella; no effect at all, especially when she wore her vest.

Tom was at ease this morning as they walked along the trail because gun season had ended yesterday. Now, presumably only bow hunters should be about. Tom thought that the chance of seeing a bow hunter this morning unlikely; especially after the pressure of the past two weeks with all the gun hunters in the woods. He also doubted that they'd see any deer. Bella didn't care, there were still other animals to chase. She frantically tried to sniff out a field mouse. Tom watched her dig as she attempted to find the mouse. He wished she'd do that back at the trailer.

Wilson was in his office busy scribbling notes to himself. He hated writing and he hated the fact that his position didn't warrant a secretary. Why didn't it? After all, he had seven thousand citizens to take care of. Carlisle's Police Department had a force of seven officers. Hell, Carlisle was technically a town with a population of under two-thousand. Why did they have a secretary? To Wilson, this didn't seem fair. All the help he had was his deputy, Leland, and he surely wasn't a secretary. Wilson eventually tired of complaining to himself. He needed to focus and get organized. He summarized the notes that he had taken when he and Sheriff Davis had jointly investigated the murder of Jimmy Fugate.

Wilson considered the sequence of events that had happened. Fugate had been shot to death in a doublewide trailer, which was located on the Fleming/Nicholas County line. Why had Fugate been there? Fugate had a Maysville address. That would require some additional checking. He continued to ponder. The doublewide had been lived in by a bunch of Mexican migrant workers. There was one young girl in the group, at least that's what the landlord, Harold Ricks, had mentioned. The Mexicans were most likely illegal, probably the reason that they ran. That would have been the only reason to have run, especially since the young girl had been raped. He scribbled again on the pad. Sheriff Davis, of Fleming County, didn't believe that the Mexicans would have shot Fugate. He believed that if one of the Mexicans had doled out the punishment, it would have been far more severe. Wilson agreed with this assessment. He cringed as he thought about his privates being cut off. He'd seen this in a Mexican movie, years back.

Wilson chewed on his pencil, deep in thought. *Jimmy had broken into the doublewide, obviously to get the girl. Did they know one another? Did Fugate just happen to be driving by? Not likely. Assuming Fugate knew the girl, he probably knew the group. Maybe he worked with them.* Wilson remembered he had seen a group of Mexicans at the Gyp Joint a while back. *There was one white guy in that group. He appeared to be a Mexican wannabe, or trying to blend in. Maybe that had been Fugate. But, who would have shot Fugate if it hadn't been the Mexicans? How would anyone else know what was happening inside that doublewide?* Wilson suddenly realized he had more questions than answers. He didn't like that. He liked answers and he knew where he might find some; at Tom Padgett's. Padgett seemed to know a lot about things that happened in his neck of the woods.

Tom reluctantly pulled the box out from under his bed. He really didn't feel up to it today, but he knew it needed to be done. He stared at the carton. He knew this would be a lot of work. But, there were trees that needed to come down. Was he getting lazy? He had ordered the chainsaw months ago. Now, after all this time, he was finally going to put it to use. He thought back to his younger days. Back then, as soon as he would have received the delivery, he would have immediately gone right to work. Now, he seemed content to push the box farther and farther under the bed. Today, this was going to change. He had wrestled with the decision about which chainsaw to buy for days; did he want a Stihl or a Husqvarna? He read all the reviews and found that they were quite similar. He finally decided on the Husqvarna, because he got more saw for less money. Tom was frugal and price was usually the determining factor in most decisions.

Now, he'd find out if he had made the right choice. Time to assemble the saw. First, he put the bar and chain on. Next, he added the bar oil and then the fuel. The saw was lighter than the Homelite he'd had all those years ago. He'd cut one hell of a lot of wood with that old XL-12. He laughed to himself and wondered whether his ex-wife, Darlene, was using the chainsaw now. Tom put on gloves, glasses, ear muffs, and then primed and choked the saw and gave the cord a pull. It fired on the first pull. That was great. He let the machine warm for a moment while he got comfortable with it. It was fast, much faster than he remembered the Homelite had been. He had some trees in mind and went after them. He cut down a couple of honey locusts. The thorny things had bothered him ever since he'd moved into his trailer.

He was surprised to find that he made short work of the trees. Tom had nearly forgotten what hard work felt like. After a while, he had piles of wood scattered everywhere. He wasn't sure what he'd do with all the wood. Should he buy a wood stove? Surely someone manufactures a decent wood stove that's suitable for an old trailer with paper-thin walls? Tom shut off the saw. It was time for a break. Bella had been content to watch him from a safe distance. She wasn't so sure about the noisy screaming machine. Tom pulled a beer from the fridge and sat on the wheelchair ramp to relax. Then, he heard a familiar-sounding truck. Tom knew the sound well. He didn't even bother to turn around, as the truck came to a stop.

He waited patiently while Wilson climbed from the cab. He knew exactly what Wilson would do. First, he would hike up his pants and then he'd adjust his gun belt. Next, he would reach inside the truck's cab and grab his hat. Then, he would slowly place his hat on his head and make sure that it was in perfect alignment, all while Wilson stared in Tom's direction. When Wilson finished, he would begin his slow methodical strut over to Tom. Tom still sipped his beer, but for some reason, it had lost its appeal.

Wilson cleared his throat and said, "Padgett."

Tom feigned surprise, "Oh, Wilson. I didn't hear you pull in. It's probably because of all the ringing in my head, you know, from the chainsaw. I'd offer you coffee, but I'm out. Would you care for a beer?"

"No thanks, Padgett. I don't drink when I'm on duty."

"Oh, so you're on duty. Don't tell me, you're here for one of your social visits?"

"You wouldn't happen to have a chair, would you? Maybe if we were both sitting, we'd be able to have a decent conversation."

Tom reluctantly walked to the storage shed and grabbed a chair. He handed it to Wilson and watched as he struggled to unfold it. When it snapped open, Wilson quickly plopped down on it. He was red in the face from messing with the chair, but managed to stay calm. "Padgett, I assume you've heard about the shooting that took place over near the county line?"

Tom smiled as he sensed the familiarity of Wilson's approach, "Yes, I do recall hearing something about it. Have you found the shooter?"

"No, we haven't found the shooter. But, we're working some leads."

"That sounds promising; I hope you find whoever did it, soon. That way Bella and I will be able to sleep easier at night."

"You know what? The shooting happened less than three miles from here. Hell, maybe only about two miles if a person took a short cut through the woods."

Tom had an idea where Wilson was heading with this line

of bullshit. He decided not to interrupt.

"You've still been deer hunting haven't you, Padgett? I know that you hunt over at Clay WMA. But I'm curious; do you ever hunt around here?"

Tom slowly nodded. "Yes, I hunt around here sometimes. So what's on your mind, Wilson?"

"I'm curious about what type of gun you hunt with?"

"I use a twelve gauge slug; the same type everyone else uses around here."

"Were you hunting around here last Saturday?"

"Last Saturday, you mean the Saturday after Thanksgiving?

"No, the one prior to that."

Tom considered the question. He had been hunting on that day, but telling Wilson might be a mistake.

Wilson's phone rang. He stood and slipped off toward his truck, out of earshot.

"This is Wilson. Uh huh, I'm only about fifteen minutes out, I'll be right over." After ending the call, he walked back to where Padgett was seated. "Well, Padgett, it seems we'll have to finish our conversation later. It appears there's been another shooting, and it's in another of your stomping grounds, over at the Clay WMA." Wilson started to leave, but stopped. "Padgett, just because I'm being summoned, doesn't mean I'm going to stay away. I'll be back. You can count on that."

Wilson's accusations were beginning to get under his skin. He realized Wilson meant what he said, the part about 'he'd be back'. Tom knew that in police work, many of the things you reacted to were based on instinct. He didn't believe Wilson necessarily worked that way. Wilson's reactions seemed to be based on his utter dislike of Tom. Tom got up from the ramp and walked to the trailer. He needed a beer. One more beer, why not?

Wilson had given him something new to think about. After he finished his beer, he would need to get to work. He knocked the thorns from the honey locust logs and then loaded them into the wheelbarrow. He stacked the firewood in a tree row, not far from the trailer's back door. When and if he found a woodstove, he didn't want to move the wood pile again. When the last wheelbarrow load was empty, Tom stared at a spot in the drive where Wilson's truck had been parked, thinking about what Wilson had said.

Ever since Tom had moved into Nicholas County, Wilson had been dogging him. Wilson had been on his case for months. When would it stop? He had accused Tom of being involved in most of the crime that had happened around here. Tom wasn't sure why. Was it because he'd been Chief of the Mt. Sterling Police? Was Wilson jealous of him? Tom knew all about jealous behavior. The Mayor of Mt. Sterling, Bud Blankenship, had been jealous of him, too. Wilson was different though. It was more than just jealousy. There was something else, something that seemed to be driving him. Did Wilson have a basis for his suspicions? He shook his head and called Bella, "Come on girl, I need a shower."

As he pulled out the drive and onto the road, Wilson watched Padgett in his rear view mirror. He must have gotten to Padgett. It looked like he finally had his attention, which was extremely satisfying. He followed Abners Mill Road toward Route 32, and thought about what he'd learned. Another dead person in the county; two people had been shot in a little over a week. What are the chances of that, especially in this county with a population of 7,000? Interestingly enough, both places where the shootings occurred were part of Padgett's hunting territory. Wilson gloated at this thought; maybe Padgett has finally screwed up. If he has, it will give me extreme pleasure to be the one that brings the big guy down.

Wilson turned left into Clay Reserve and pulled his truck alongside the Fish and Wildlife vehicle. He climbed from his truck and shook the Conservation Officer's hand. The officer explained that a body had been discovered earlier that morning. It had been discovered by a hunter, as he was walking through the woods. The hunter had come across the body as he was on his way to the parking lot. Deputy Leland arrived as Wilson and the Conservation Officer were about to head into the woods. The officer led while Wilson and his deputy followed. Once at the scene, it was Wilson's turn to take over. He informed the officer that he and his deputy would take it from here. The officer was happy to oblige and left. Wilson glanced down at the dead hunter. He was actually getting accustomed to seeing dead people, but he still didn't like it. Now, at least he no longer felt squeamish. It helped that the cold weather had helped to preserve the body, although some animals had visited.

Wilson looked the body over as he thought about his next step. He noticed that Leland was getting antsy. The deputy kicked around a pile of dry leaves. "Leland, don't be kicking stuff around. Do you want to compromise the crime scene?"

Leland shook his head. "What makes you think it's a crime scene, Sheriff? Maybe it was a hunting accident."

"Leland, from the look of things, there appears to be two holes in the body. I'm pretty sure that makes it a crime. Besides, if it were an accident, don't you think the shooter would have turned himself in?"

For once Leland was silent. Maybe he was confused by something that Wilson had said. Wilson took this opportunity to explain what they needed to do. "OK, Leland, here's what we need to do. First, let's do a careful scan of the area. We're looking for evidence, something like a slug casing. If you happen to find a casing don't touch it. Just let me know, and then I'll bag it. You got any questions, Deputy?"

"No, Sheriff."

Wilson attempted to figure out where the shot had been fired from. He studied the position of the body. Wilson needed to explain some more things to Leland. The primary reason for this was to show the Deputy his investigative knowledge.

"Deputy, what do we know about the body? Is there

anything obvious, something that might shed some light about where the shooter might have stood when he took the shot?"

Leland looked at the body and scratched under his cap. "I don't know Sheriff. What makes you think it's a he?"

"Damn it, Leland, almost all crimes are committed by men, and since it appears that a twelve gauge slug gun was used, I'm fairly confident that the shooter was a man."

"But, I have a cousin named Sue, who hunts all the time with a slug gun, and she uses a twelve gauge."

Wilson glared at his deputy, "Alright, Leland, where do you think the shooter, male or female, might have been standing when they took the shot? What do the entry wound and exit wounds tell us? Do they give us any clue as to where the shot came from?"

"Maybe, Sheriff, but how do you know that the body didn't spin around before it hit the ground?"

Wilson considered this. Maybe his deputy wasn't as dumb as he'd originally thought. The more Wilson thought about this, the more likely it seemed that the entry wounds could have originated from different directions, maybe there were two shooters?

Wilson had a plan. He wasn't sure if it was the best plan, but at least it was a plan. Wilson should be able to control the pattern; he would keep Leland to his left. He planned to walk clockwise around the body. He was going to start at a distance of five feet from the body, while Leland was positioned ten feet out. After they made a complete revolution, they'd each move ten feet further out and start the process again. That might take a while. Wilson hoped that the shooter hadn't been a hundred yards out. After two complete revolutions, Wilson moved twenty-five feet from the body while Leland was thirty-feet. The plan seemed to be working well, but when they were fifty and fifty-five feet from the body, Wilson realized the circles were getting much larger and much more difficult to control.

Wilson was frustrated. He heard Leland yell, "Sheriff, I

found a shell."

"Good, Leland. Don't touch it!"

Wilson walked over to Leland and then bent down to pick up the shell, using the end of a stick. He looked at the casing for a moment before he placed it in a baggy. Wilson was quite impressed with his stick maneuver. He had seen that move on a cop show a while back. They continued to search for the second shell casing.

Leland had wandered a few feet onwards. "Sheriff, I found where the shooter was sitting."

Wilson joined Leland and together they looked down. There were cigarette butts stuck in the dirt, a bunch of them. Wilson wondered, *what kind of hunter would be in the woods smoking? Obviously, not the smartest one.* With gloved hands, he carefully put the butts into another baggy.

On the drive back to Carlisle, Wilson got angrier by the minute. He was extremely pissed off about the cigarette butts they'd found at the scene. He was pretty sure that Padgett didn't smoke. Damn it, he was positive the guy didn't smoke. He was also angry because this new development put an unwelcome wrinkle in his plans. If Leland hadn't been there, he could have buried that piece of evidence. But, Leland's presence forced him to follow procedure. Bill Wilson always preferred to dictate his own actions. So, now he had two shootings; both of them involved the use of twelve gauge shotguns. Both of the shootings were in places that Padgett frequented. Yes, there are the cigarettes, but that doesn't mean the shooter smoked them.

Wilson would have to send the evidence off to the lab and see what the results would yield. He would have those results soon, which would help to explain some things. Wilson was confident that with a little tampering, he could make the evidence against Padgett airtight. Not even Padgett and all his slick maneuvering would be able to slip this net. He allowed himself a mischievous grin; yeah, maybe it hadn't been such a bad morning after all. He pulled over to the shoulder of the road and made a phone call. When he finished the call, he quickly accelerated back onto Route 32. He was excited. Maybe he could kill two birds with one stone. He could get rid of Padgett and solve both murders.

Keith Poole, the Nicholas County Coroner, hung up the phone. He muttered to himself, the Sheriff could really be a pain in the backside sometimes. Keith had told him, "Yes, I look forward to getting the body, and yes, I will work on it right away." Keith failed to tell Wilson that he hadn't even gotten in touch with Woozy Fugate yet. She knew nothing of her husband, Jimmy's, death. Keith had the body for nearly a week, but he'd been busy. Besides, he was the Coroner, and how he did his job was his business. Keith thought about the two men both dying of gunshot wounds. They had both been shot in rural parts of the county in the past week. Keith wondered, what were the chances of that?

CHAPTER 2

Monday Afternoon

Shane Miller held his end of the sheet of drywall. In the background, Kenny Chesney sang on the radio. Today, Shane worked for his neighbor who was building a house on Mt. Tabor Road. Shane helped him whenever he needed an extra laborer. Although Shane was physically there, his mind was elsewhere. He had much to be thankful for, mainly his wife Joanne. She had a good job. She worked at Fleming County Hospital as a shift nurse. Her job made up for the lack of money Shane earned. Shane worked odd jobs here and there which didn't actually pay many of the bills. He helped hold the sheet, while another guy ran screws into the four by twelve piece of drywall. It was pretty cold to be hanging drywall, but it was a job. It brought in some extra cash, and besides that, it was close to home.

Shane was preoccupied. He couldn't stop thinking about the hunter he'd shot at Clay WMA. He still couldn't believe it had happened. He'd been sure that what he'd heard was a buck, because of the way it thrashed around and grunted. Shane remembered what had happened to his first cousin, Jim. He lived over in Pike County. Jim had accidentally shot a hunter a few years back. Because of this, he had to spend time in jail. But the man Jim had shot hadn't died. Shane was convinced that if he turned himself in, he would get more than a short jail sentence. Shane's workmate mumbled something and Shane snapped back to reality. He helped him grab another piece of sheet rock.

Together, they lifted the next sheet into place. His neighbor told Shane he needed help all week. That was good news for Shane. He could leave his truck where it was, parked in the garage, hidden out of sight. His neighbor's job site was only a half mile walk from his house. His wife might wonder why he was suddenly worried about getting exercise or going green. But, he'd come up with some excuse. He bent down to score the sheet which lay at his feet. He pulled the knife across the sheet, then stood it on end and snapped it. Then, he finished it by cutting the back side. Working here close to home was good as he'd be able to stay out of sight for the next five days. Over the coming weekend, maybe his truck could remain parked in the garage. If Joanne wanted to go anywhere or do anything, he'd insist that they drive her car.

Tom walked into Walmart. He didn't see Nick, so he asked if Nick was working and was told that Nick was on a break. Tom found him in the break area doing what he did best, talking. Tom listened while Nick entertained a group of extremely bored fellow employees. They had heard many of Nick's stories before. The oldest employee seemed slightly interested in what Nick was going on about, the younger two not so much. When Nick paused for breath, the younger employees stood up from the table and left. Next, the older gentleman came up with an excuse to leave. Nick watched as they walked away. His surprised expression said it all.

Tom laughed, "Not everyone has the patience that I have, Nick."

Nick sighed, "Yeah, I guess you're right, Tom. What's going on?"

"Oh, I was in the neighborhood. I thought I'd stop in and visit my favorite greeter. What time do you get off?"

"I'm off in another hour. You feel up to O'Rourke's?"

"Yeah, that sounds good. But, I need to pick up a few things first. I need some dog food. Bella seems to have found her long lost appetite."

Tom grabbed a cart and headed toward the dog food isle. Since he was there, he might as well grab a few other things. After Tom paid and just walked out the door, someone grabbed him by the elbow.

"Can I see your receipt, sir?"

"Ever the joker, my friend. Nick, I owe you one."

Woozy was getting ready for work when she heard the phone rang. She didn't get many phone calls. She ran to the kitchen and snatched up her phone, which lay on the counter. The caller was the Nicholas County Coroner. She was relieved after she finished her conversation with the man. He had asked her to come to Carlisle, to identify a body. He told her that the remains were thought to be that of her husband. After Woozy ended the call, she sat down at the kitchen table and began to cry. She didn't shed tears of sorrow. They were tears of relief, maybe even tears of joy. A huge pressure had just been lifted, and now Woozy could get on with her life. She was positive that she hadn't sounded upset when the Coroner told her the reason for the call. That was okay. If the Coroner knew what she'd been through, he would understand.

Woozy walked down the hall to the bathroom. She needed to finish putting on her makeup. Woozy finally felt that she was free. She felt liberated. The last time Jimmy had beaten her up and put her in the hospital, she knew that the likelihood of him returning to Maysville was remote, since he'd already served a thirty day stint, and he wouldn't want to go back. Most likely, he had hidden in a nearby county to keep from going back to jail. Now, she realized he'd never return.

She dabbed her eyes with a tissue, attempting to dry them, so that she could finish applying her eye liner. She wondered what Jimmy did and who he had made mad, mad enough to kill him. She knew the list of people that Jimmy could have pissed off in the weeks since he'd left, could have been long, extremely long.

Keith Poole closed his phone; he had been talking to Woozy Fugate. Keith was the Nicholas County Coroner. Whenever a death occurred in the county, it was one of his responsibilities to notify the next of kin. The remains of Jimmy Fugate had been delivered to the funeral home on the Tuesday prior to

21

Thanksgiving. Keith could have attempted to notify Mrs. Fugate before the Thanksgiving holiday. But, he had prior plans. In addition to his duties as Coroner, he also ran two funeral homes. He had already planned on taking Wednesday off, and then Jimmy's death occurred. He hadn't had two days off in over a year, and he was determined to stick to his plans. He hadn't been able to reach Mrs. Fugate on Friday, but today he managed to get hold of her. He was relieved that Mrs. Fugate didn't appear upset or bothered with the late notification. Woozy was going to come to Carlisle to identify her husband's remains on Wednesday morning.

Keith Poole had multiple responsibilities as Coroner. Besides notifying the next of kin, he also performed autopsies, if necessary. He had resources available from Frankfort, the state capitol, for situations that were beyond his capabilities. He wouldn't need Frankfort's assistance with Fugate. He had already made the determination that the deceased had died from a single gunshot wound. Jimmy had been shot through the back. The twelve gauge slug had severed his spine and exited through his heart. Keith was certain that Woozy Fugate's husband had died immediately. If there had been anything unusual about the circumstances surrounding Fugate's death, Keith might have felt compelled to work with the experts in Frankfort. But in this case, it wasn't necessary.

Keith thought about the young girl that Jimmy had raped. He wondered where the Mexicans might have run off to. When Wilson had Jimmy Fugate's body delivered to the cold storage unit, Wilson mentioned something about his reason why the Mexicans wouldn't have killed Fugate. Keith wasn't sure Wilson's assumptions had any foundation.

Keith was tired. It had been a very long day and he was ready to call it a night. As he turned the lights out to the viewing room, he thought of Woozy Fugate. He was sure she wasn't upset when she heard about the death of her husband. Based on Woozy's reaction, could she have been involved with his death? Why was her husband down in Nicholas County, anyway? Why was he in the trailer that a group of Mexican migrant workers lived in? These questions were above his pay grade. He'd leave them for Wilson to sort out.

22

Tom had been at O'Rourke's for ten minutes. He was enjoying a beer when the doors burst open and Nick rolled in. As usual, Nick was all smiles.

Nick animatedly yelled, "Hey Woozy, long time no see. Well, hello Tom. Fancy meeting you here."

Tom shook his head in amusement as he watched him complete the circuit. He shook peoples' hands and slapped them on the back. Nick needed to run for political office; that was for sure. He definitely had the gift of politicking. Woozy placed Nick's beer on the counter and handed Tom another one.

Woozy leaned on the bar and whispered to Tom, "The Coroner from Nicholas County phoned me today. He said he has a body that needs to be identified. He said that it's Jimmy. I'm going to Carlisle on Wednesday morning for the identification."

Tom just listened. He didn't bother to say he was sorry, because he wasn't. He could see that Woozy was relieved.

Nick came back. He'd managed to work up a thirst. He nearly drained his beer in one chug, and then took a breath, "Why are you two looking so glum?"

Woozy walked toward the other end of the bar and called over her shoulder, "You can tell him if want to, Tom."

Tom relayed the story about Jimmy to Nick. Nick was sad for Woozy and fretted about what he should say to Woozy.

Tom could sense Nick's dilemma. "Nick, you don't need to say you're sorry or anything like that to Woozy. This is a good thing."

Nick was shocked. "How is losing your husband ever a good thing?"

"Come on, Nick, you can't be serious. He was a wife beater. Woozy is lucky to be alive."

"I hadn't thought of it in that way. How about another beer? Hey, Woozy could we get another round? And, we'd like a pizza, too."

Nick was always thirsty and usually hungry. He'd never lose the weight that he dreamt about losing.

Tom drove more slowly than usual on the way home from O'Rourke's. He thought about Woozy. She looked better tonight. Her bruises were healing nicely and they were barely visible. He was looking forward to having lunch with her on Wednesday. Maybe they'd be able to have a decent conversation. Conversations with Woozy, when she tended bar, were always short. It would be nice to learn more about her and find out what she's really like. Tom looked out the passenger window and noticed smoke curling into the sky from one of the Amish's chimney. They had no electricity, unless it was produced by solar power or a generator. They used some gas powered devices, but not all. He couldn't understand some aspects of the culture, or why they chose to live that way, but their way of life seemed to work for them. He figured that's all that mattered.

CHAPTER 3

Wednesday Morning

As she looked through her closet, Woozy was beginning to feel excited. Strange, she thought, that she felt this way, especially in light of the fact that she was going to identify her husband's remains. But, didn't she have the right to be callous? She really didn't want to see Jimmy's remains, but she realized it had to be done. She thought about some of the beatings he had given her. She remembered how he always told her that her actions were the primary reason he beat her. It had always been her fault. Through the years and all the beatings, she had actually begun to believe him. Woozy felt sure about one thing, she was never going to allow another man to hit her again, never. She pulled out an outfit, a matching top and pants. It was one she hadn't worn in years. She held it up in front of her as she studied herself in the full length mirror.

She was quite pleased. It was a nice choice. Woozy didn't need to hide beneath conservative clothing any longer; she was free to express herself. She looked closely at her bruises. She smiled; they were fading and barely visible. The scars on her lips might never go away. But, Woozy found strength in knowing that she'd never receive another one. Today, she was worried about what she might do when she saw Jimmy's body. She hoped she could control herself and be able to be composed. She buttoned her blouse, turned to the left, then to the right and noticed it still fit nicely. She would have preferred wearing a skirt, but she had to work this evening. Woozy found that it was hard serving drinks with a skirt on. She preferred to wear pants. Woozy let out a sigh, she was anxious about the visit to the funeral home, but she was looking forward to seeing Tom afterward.

He sat down and gently petted Bella while he sipped his coffee. Tom knew that his ever-faithful companion wasn't going to be happy with just being petted. She wanted to go for a romp in the woods. He didn't blame her. He loved wandering the woods, too. He quickly skimmed over the news articles on the web; not much was going on. Fox News always had its spin and CNN, of course, had an opposing one. Tom wondered which news organizations embellished their stories the most. Bella didn't care at all about the news. At the moment, she was interested in one thing and one thing only. She wanted to know when her master was going to get up off his butt and do his job. To Bella, Tom's only job was that of taking care of her.

He closed the laptop and Bella alertly lifted her head. She thought that closing the computer was an indicator, or some kind a sign of things to come. Tom began to lace his boots. This was definitely a sign, one that Bella knew well. He strapped Bella's blaze orange vest on before doing the same for himself. Bella had finally gotten comfortable wearing her vest. She no longer threw a fit. For this, he was glad. He opened the door and Bella took off. She hardly allowed him to get the screen open before she squeezed out. She still hadn't developed patience. He watched as Bella chased a squirrel. She loved these woods. Tom smiled as he followed along. He felt good, and content as he thought about lunch with Woozy.

Wilson carefully placed the cup down into the crowded sink; he would finish that pile of dishes later. Wilson was anxious to hear what the lab had found out. Hopefully, the lab tech would be older and more experienced than the ones he'd dealt with recently. Most of them had been useless and wet behind the ears as far as Wilson was concerned. But, he needed to hold his tongue, especially if he expected any cooperation. Last night he had a restful evening. He relaxed out on the back porch until the evening chill had set in. The old nosy neighbor hadn't even stuck her head out of her door. Wilson opened the front door and looked at his truck, which was parked in the drive. Damn, there's frost on the windows.

Wilson hated many things, and wasting time scraping ice from his windows was one of them. He walked outside, opened the truck's door, then reached in and fired it up. He carefully laid his hat on the seat and pulled the scraper from its slot in the door. The ice was thick. Wilson wondered, *how cold is it?* He was having difficulty with the last patch of ice when he heard a dreaded noise, the neighbor's door opening. Wilson had no place to hide. He acted as if he hadn't heard anything and continued to scrape. Suddenly, he sensed her. He could feel the old lady's presence. She had stopped a few feet away. He glanced up, noticed that she was standing on the sidewalk, staring at him. Surprisingly, she was even smiling. Wilson thought this was very unusual.

She spoke quietly, "Wilson, you've got a garage. Why don't you use it?"

Woozy had never been to Carlisle, but Tom had told her about it. Woozy passed the courthouse as she headed east and saw Garrett's Restaurant on the corner. She was going to meet Tom there after she finished with the Coroner. She found the funeral home without a problem. She parked and before getting out, checked her reflection in the mirror. She reminded herself, Woozy just relax. Woozy knocked and a few moments later, a man opened the door. He led her down a hallway into a parlor and told her to have a seat. She glanced around the room. It was full of antiques. Another man appeared and introduced himself as Keith Poole, the Nicholas County Coroner.

After the introduction, Keith sat down behind his desk. He studied the woman before him. In Keith's line of business, he'd gotten quite good at applying make-up. Evidently, Mrs. Fugate was skilled, also. Keith placed some paperwork on the desk and arranged a few items before he proceeded.

He spoke quite softly, "Mrs. Fugate, this is one of the most difficult parts of my job as Coroner. First, we are going to view the remains, then afterward we will return to this room, because, naturally, there is paperwork that must be completed. Ma'am, are you ready?"

Woozy replied nervously, "Yes, I guess I'm as ready as I'll ever be."

They stepped into a large room which was surprisingly cool. The room was nearly empty, except for a gurney that had a sheet draped over it. Woozy stood to one side as the Coroner pulled back the sheet.

Keith dropped his voice for the next question, "Mrs. Fugate, are these the remains of your husband, Jimmy Fugate?"

Woozy had to really concentrate; she didn't want to betray her sense of relief, "Yes, Mr. Poole, that's Jimmy."

Keith asked if she needed some time alone with her husband.

"No thank you, Mr. Poole, this has been quite long enough."

Keith led Woozy back to the office, where they'd initially talked to complete the paperwork. He showed her what to fill out and where to sign. Keith stood off to the side and discreetly observed Woozy as she filled in the forms. He was positive that she had hidden bruises under the make-up around her eyes. He could easily see the scars around her lips. He noticed that Mrs. Fugate seemed quite eager to be done with all the paperwork. Maybe she had good reason.

Keith still had some additional business with Woozy. "Ma'am, would you prefer to have the funeral proceeding elsewhere, possibly in a place of your choosing? Or, we would be more than happy to take care of everything for you, right here."

"I appreciate that Mr. Poole, but I have no plans of doing anything with Jimmy's remains. As far as I'm concerned they can stay in that freezer of yours for the rest of time."

"Excuse me, Ma'am. Does that mean you'd like us to handle the arrangements?"

"No, it does not, Mr. Poole. My husband spent time in the military. Doesn't that entitle him to some sort of military funeral?"

"Mrs. Fugate, was your husband honorably discharged?

"No, does that matter?"

"Well, yes as an honorably discharged veteran, he would be entitled to things one that was dishonorably discharged wouldn't be. But, if you are unable or unwilling to provide for the cost of burial, I will assist in finding what funding is available to you."

Woozy had blown her cool and she knew it. The questions just seemed so wrong under the circumstances.

"Mr. Poole, I know it's not your fault, and yes, the man lying on that gurney in the other room is my husband. But, I will spend nothing to have him buried, not after what he's done to me. I will spend absolutely nothing." She turned and hurriedly walked out the door.

He sat quietly for a moment. Keith was quite unaccustomed to receiving that strong of a response in the funeral business. He slowly started to gather up the documents which lay scattered about the desk. He knew that there were some monies to cover part of the cost for the indigent. He would have to begin that process. He felt convinced that he wouldn't get Mrs. Fugate to come to Carlisle again. He thought about her last statement. He remembered it word for word. *I will spend nothing to have him buried, not after what he's done to me. I will spend absolutely nothing.* Keith felt he had a better understanding. Mrs. Fugate had most likely been subjected to repeated abuse from her husband. That would explain the scarred lips and the bruising on her face.

Woozy sat in her car in the funeral home parking lot as she attempted to calm down. She felt she'd done so well for part of the meeting, anyway. She wished she could have told the Coroner the whole story, the whole damned terrible story. But, why should she subject him to that. He had a job to do. He was just doing it. She looked at her face in the mirror. She was a sight; her mascara had run and all her make-up was smeared. Great and I'm supposed to meet Tom in a few minutes. She pulled her cosmetic bag out and tried to repair the damage. She was sure that Tom wouldn't say anything, no matter what she came in looking like. That was just the kind of man he was. He was such a sweet, gentle man. She really wanted to look nice for him.

Wilson paced the floor angrily as he thought about the lab results. There were prints on the shells, and there was DNA on the cigarette butts, but, none of this helped him. It seemed that the procedure for submitting DNA evidence had changed. Now they required that things be submitted in paper bags, not plastic. Wilson wondered if this was one of those paper/plastic eco friendly things. The prints were not on file, so the shooter had no record. Padgett's prints would have been on file, because he was a former police officer, the Chief of the Mt. Sterling Police Department. Did this mean that Padgett wasn't the shooter? Not to Bill Wilson, it didn't. Did this change anything? No, it just slowed down the inevitable, but, as far as Wilson was concerned, only slightly.

If only he had that Mexican girl, things would be totally different. Wilson knew that the group of Mexicans was long gone. He also knew that they would never be found. The Mexicans would probably be back in old Tijuana by now. So, some stupid hunter had probably mistakenly shot the man who had been found dead in the Clay Reserve, not slippery old Padgett. But, Wilson was positive that Padgett was connected with Jimmy Fugate's death. He just had no way of proving it. It was another dead end. Dead ends were another thing that Wilson hated. He put his hat on, adjusted it while he looked in the mirror. Even though he felt stressed, he still looked good. He hiked up his trousers and headed out the door.

Tom was already at Garrett's. He was seated far from where the cops usually ate. Today, he wasn't interested in what was happening around Nicholas County. He was waiting for Woozy. Tom wasn't sure if this could officially be called a date or not, but he was still nervous. He thought back to the short-lived fling that he and Becky Adkins had had. He wondered if it might have gone somewhere. Probably not, it was just a lustful moment. It was probably just the alcohol that did most of the talking. He didn't feel the same way about Woozy. She was definitely more grounded than Becky had ever been. Woozy had just made some bad decisions in the men that she chose. Everyone makes mistakes. He hoped that she was holding up okay with Jimmy's identification.

The door opened and Woozy slowly walked in, looking for Tom. A waitress approached her and pointed in Tom's direction. Tom stood up as Woozy took her seat. They each said hello and then seemed at a loss for words. Tom had only spoken with Woozy when he'd been at O'Rourke's, when he'd been drinking. And, she'd only spoken with Tom when she was behind the bar serving drinks. This was definitely an awkward moment. They were like a pair of young kids on a first date. Both realizing this at the same time, they began to laugh. Tom thought Woozy looked so relieved. Woozy thought about how little they actually knew about each other. They both smiled.

Just then, Wilson sauntered through the door. He immediately noticed Padgett and nodded. Tom gave Wilson a slight nod in return. Wilson joined a couple of the cops that sat at a table near the door. They were all talking about something or other that was happening in town. Tom ignored them. He wanted to focus on Woozy.

"Woozy, do you have to work tonight?"

Woozy joked, "Yes, I still have to make a living. I'm too young to retire."

Tom smiled, "I was too young to retire, too, but that didn't stop me. Some things are out of our control. Woozy, how'd you do with identifying Jimmy's body? I bet it was difficult."

She thought for a moment, "When I first got to the funeral home I was ready; I was ready to be done with it. But answering all those questions, and being asked where I wanted to have the funeral. I kind of lost it. I'm afraid I acted sort of out of control."

Tom had been studying her face as she spoke. He could see that it was helping her to talk about it. She'd kept everything bottled up inside for years. Now she could finally say exactly what she thought.

"Woozy, that's not your fault. You're allowed to act like that, and you definitely earned the right to act like that. Jimmy was a monster. But now, that monster is gone."

They talked very little as they ate their meals. After they finished and their plates had been cleared, Tom asked, "Woozy, would you like some coffee?"

"No thank you. I guess I'd better be going. I think that they were supposed to be short-handed at work tonight, and I could definitely use the money. You know, the two weeks that I was off work, when I was home recovering, really put a dent in my bank account."

The door opened and Keith Poole ambled in. He nodded in Woozy's direction before he sat at a table near the front of Garrett's, alone. Wilson had finished eating and was enjoying coffee as he listened to the city cops complain about how difficult their jobs were. He wanted to suggest that he'd trade jobs anytime. He wanted to tell them how easy their jobs were compared to his, but then thought otherwise. He stood and moved over to sit for a bit with the Coroner.

Tom paid the tab, then he and Woozy made their way out the door. Wilson and Keith watched as they left. The waitress brought Keith's lunch. For the moment, he paid little attention to his food as he distractedly watched Tom and Woozy walk to their cars.

"Wilson, do you happen to know that guy?"

"Yeah, I know him. His name's Padgett. He's kind of new around here."

Keith chewed a bite of his hamburger before asking, "What's he do for a living, do you know?"

"Oh, he's supposedly retired, retired from the Mt. Sterling Police Department."

Keith took a long sip of his soda, "Policeman huh, that's interesting."

"Not only was he a policeman, but the Chief of Police of Mt. Sterling."

Keith cocked his head in thought, "That's really interesting. I wonder what his relationship is with the lady?"

Wilson was just about ready to leave, but suddenly his curiosity had been piqued. "Relationship with what lady? And, what's so damned interesting anyway?"

"That lady," Keith pointed out the window, "The one he just left with. That's Jimmy Fugate's widow."

Wilson nearly choked on his last gulp of coffee. "Well, I'll be. You're right, Keith. That's interesting, damned interesting."

CHAPTER 4

Thursday Morning

Shane Miller had done his share of dumb stuff in his lifetime. But for once, he was going to do what was right. His wife Joanne had been aware of his strange behavior all week. His actions had finally been too much; especially after he had refused to pull his truck out of the garage in order to get firewood. He suggested that they take her car and just stack the wood on some plastic sheeting in the trunk. That's what finally did it for Joanne.

She stared at him in disbelief, then accusingly asked, "What in the hell is wrong with you, Shane Miller? Why would we take my car to haul firewood? You've been acting weird for nearly a week now. Do you mind telling me why that is?"

Shane knew he couldn't continue to live like this. Somehow, he summoned some inner strength, "Joanne, remember last Saturday when I came home from hunting and parked my truck in the garage?"

"Of course I do. That was weird. You never park your truck in there, and you've been acting strange ever since."

"Well, there was a reason for me wanting to hide my truck. That day while I'd been hunting, I thought I shot myself a trophy buck. But, it wasn't a buck I'd shot, it was a man."

Joanne was shocked, "Shane, you've got to be shitting me? You shot a man just like that stupid cousin of yours did? You didn't kill the guy, did ya?"

"I'm pretty sure I killed him. I shot him twice. It was dark and I was so excited about getting a big buck."

His wife stared open mouthed, not believing what she'd just heard.

"Shane, are you telling me that you shot the man two times?"

"I thought it was a buck. I just got carried away."

"You didn't leave him in the woods, did you? Don't tell me you left him in the woods, left him there to die?"

"I was scared. I didn't know what else to do. I don't want to go to jail."

"Well, Shane, you should have thought about that, long before you pulled the damn trigger."

He stood up from his desk and stepped out onto the courthouse steps. Wilson needed some fresh air and he also needed to think. He had just gotten off the phone with some hot-shot attorney from Flemingsburg. The attorney claimed to represent a man that had something to do with the shooting that happened out at Clay WMA. The attorney and his client were coming to Carlisle to discuss the matter. Wilson scratched the stubble on his chin. Maybe, he was about to get a confession; that would be an unexpected bonus. Yes, that would be a super bonus. He walked across the street to Garrett's. He suddenly felt the urge for another coffee, but he still had some paperwork to get together. He had to collect his thoughts for the upcoming interview. He'd speak with the pair in his customary spot, over in the Carlisle Police station's interrogation room.

Wilson hummed a Lee Greenwood song, I'm Proud to be an American, as he carried his coffee back into the courthouse and entered his cramped little office. He set his cup on the desk and pulled the Clay WMA file from his shelf. There wasn't a great deal of material in the folder, but if he was lucky enough to get a confession, that wouldn't matter. He went over the evidence in his mind; the cigarette butts and the slug shells. Soon, he would have the actual fingerprints on file. He was a little sad about one development though, this would likely clear Padgett. He had to stay focused during the interrogation. He didn't want to blow such an opportunity. He needed to find out where the attorney's client had been the day that Jimmy Fugate was killed. He needed to learn if he had possibly shot both men.

It was another windy day, but at least it was warm. Tom enjoyed his beer while he stood on his front deck. He laughed as he looked down at it. It wasn't really a deck, it was only a wheelchair ramp, and it didn't even have room for chairs. Today, it was probably sixty degrees, being this warm in early December was fine by him. Even though they'd just hiked three miles in the woods, Bella was still out running around. She'd found some new energy. Tom wondered how long it'd last. Her appetite had spiked recently. He wasn't sure about that, either. She had some new ailments though. Now, she appeared to be getting moldy. Add this to Bella's ever-growing list of illnesses. Ticks, fleas, yeast infections, dry skin, allergies and now mold. The vet would be able to retire soon, especially if Tom continued to take Bella there for her ailments.

His phone rang. Tom stepped inside the trailer and out of the wind, to hopefully have reception. Cell reception inside the trailer could be spotty at times. Tom noticed the ID. It was his son.

"Hello, Andy, how are you doing?"

"I'm doing pretty well."

"This is a surprise to hear from you so soon. Is everything alright?"

"Yes, Dad. I just called to tell you the news. Nancy and I have changed our wedding plans. We're moving them up. We're getting married in a couple of weeks."

"Wow, that's kind of fast, son. Are you sure about this? It's a huge decision; not one to jump into."

"I know it's a big decision, Dad. We want to get married and don't want to wait."

"Ok, I'm happy for you. When's the date?"

"You should be getting your invitation soon. It's two weeks from Friday."

Wilson had just returned from the East End where he'd only had a snack for lunch. He wanted to get the unsolved hunting accident put to bed. When he walked into his office, the attorney from Flemingsburg and his client were already waiting for him in his office. They had arrived promptly at one o'clock.

The lawyer introduced himself, "I'm Darrell Walters, and this is my client, Shane Miller."

"Nice to meet you. I'm Sheriff Wilson. Will you follow me across the street over to the police station? They have more room there. We can talk privately and it'll be more comfortable."

Wilson immediately took a dislike for the lawyer, Mr. Walters. He was tall and incredibly thin, probably six foot six and Wilson doubted he weighed a hundred seventy pounds. Tall and skinny. Wilson didn't like anyone that was taller than him.

At the police station, Wilson attempted to get comfortable. As he got ready to deliver his prepared spiel, Walters interrupted, "Sheriff, let me explain some ground rules to you. First, my client is entitled to his day in court. I will not allow you to intimidate or badger my client, is that understood?"

Wilson was immediately irritated by Walters' attitude, but managed not to get angry.

"Mr. Walters, I have no intention of badgering your client. You are the one that contacted me, remember? I want to hear what your client has to say on his behalf."

"Fine, Sheriff, I will let my client speak with you. But, if I hear even a hint at heavy handedness, I'll shut you down in a heartbeat."

Tom got up from his spot on the sofa and grabbed another beer. So, his son was getting married in two weeks. Andy was marrying that same spoiled brat that he had introduced to Tom a while back. Tom figured he probably shouldn't worry about it. Andy was pretty spoiled himself. Andy was an adult; he should be able to make his own decisions. Maybe they'd complement one another's actions and manage to survive.

Why were they in such a rush to jump into marriage anyway? Tom thought back to their first meeting when Andy had brought Nancy to his trailer. How would Tom be able to tolerate the girl? He probably wouldn't have to. If Andy had any say in the matter, he'd be content to see his father once every couple of years. An occasional get together should be doable for them all.

He threw his empty into the recycle bin, and then got himself another beer. He hadn't planned on drinking more than a beer or two, but the latest father/son exchange made him change his mind. He shook his head at his thought, why would Andy jump into the fire blindly? Tom could imagine Darlene's relationship with Nancy. They probably really hit it off. That would help explain some things. He remembered reading articles about how boys usually married girls that were a lot like their mothers. He wasn't sure if Nancy was that similar to Darlene, but it was obvious that she was nothing like Tom. Another thing was certain, Nancy didn't like him. After their first meeting, he could safely say that he felt the same way about her.

He was satisfied with how things had turned out. Wilson had been able to ask the Miller boy his whereabouts when Fugate had been shot. He had a solid alibi. Shane claimed to have been hunting in Lewis County with two other guys. Wilson believed him. Maybe it was because he desperately wanted to keep his *Fugate killed by Padgett* theory open. Shane claimed that he had shot the man in the Clay WMA, while he struggled to free himself from a thicket. Obviously, Shane had taken the shot when it was still dark, before legal hunting hours. That was of no concern to Wilson. He'd be able to wrap up a case. He'd send Miller over to the Detention Center in Bourbon County and let his upcoming trial determine his fate.

He really didn't have much to go on regarding the Fugate case; that is, unless there were some connection between Mrs. Fugate and Padgett. Maybe she had hired Padgett to kill her husband. That seemed plausible. If she hadn't, how would they have known one another? Padgett doesn't seem to be that much of a lady's man. Surely, he wouldn't have multiple women in various counties all over Kentucky? Then again, maybe he would. Maybe Padgett was some kind of smooth talking charmer. The more Wilson thought about it, the more logical it seemed to him. He didn't like to admit it, but he could see where the ladies might be sucked in by his southern gentlemanly charm. If Wilson had his way, Padgett the charmer, was going to be spending time in a cell really soon.

Thank God it's Friday, Tom thought to himself. Why would he worry about that, anyway? He was retired; everyday is a Friday. He continued to walk toward his trailer. He had just gotten the mail. As Andy had promised, he had the invitation in hand. It was another warm day, so he sat on the step and opened the envelope. He thought of all the upcoming situations as he read the invitation. Unfortunately Darlene would be there, which meant he'd have to see her. He might even be asked to stand next to her in the reception line. He dreaded that. There would be a rehearsal dinner on Friday; the wedding was on Saturday afternoon, followed by the reception. Tom wrestled with whether or not he should even attend the rehearsal. If he went to the rehearsal, he'd have to meet Nancy's family. He wasn't sure if he cared to meet her family.

He tried to remember something about wedding traditions. Did the groom's family pay for the wedding, or for the rehearsal dinner? He had no idea; he'd have to search on-line to find out. No, damn it, he'd have to talk to Darlene. He dialed her number and was disappointed when she answered. He would have rather have left a message. Thankfully, the conversation was short. Tom found out what he needed to know, and it wasn't good. So, the groom's parents were supposed to pay for the rehearsal dinner. It sounded like the bride had a huge family. There were going to be no less than a hundred people at the dinner. A hundred people at $25 a pop; $2500 so a bunch of people Tom didn't know, and didn't care to know, could enjoy themselves.

Darlene had informed him all about her financial hardships. She cried in his ear about how hard it'd been, since the divorce. It seemed she was barely getting by on what she earned. She was totally strapped for cash. Hell, she received half his pension. So, what would that say about his financial state? $2500 on the dinner, plus more for some kind of wedding gift, and then a couple of nights stay in a hotel in Lexington; this was going to be expensive. Tom had almost forgotten about Bella. He would have to put her in the kennel. He was really dreading the entire event. Wasn't it supposed to be a joyous occasion?

Wilson was relieved. He almost had another week under the belt. The man that Shane Miller had shot had been identified. His name was Harold Stubbs. It appeared that Mr. Stubbs had come from Lexington to hunt at Clay WMA. Apparently, he had never been to Clay before, and Wilson joked to himself, *he'll never be back again either. Why would anyone even attempt to find a hunting spot in the dark? Especially if they'd never been to the area before? Not that this fact changes anything, but, it would have been the difference between life and death. Yeah, Shane Miller pulled the trigger. If Stubbs hadn't been lost out there thrashing around in some unfamiliar place that morning, he'd still be alive.*

Next week would be a pivotal time. If Wilson could prove that Padgett and the Fugate woman were connected, he would have something solid to pursue. That would be a great start to the week. But tonight, he wasn't going to worry about police business, he was heading home for some much needed relaxation. Yes, Wilson had been thinking about Jim Beam for half the afternoon, and he wasn't about to stop thinking about it now. He looked around the office once more, switched off the lights, pulled the door closed behind him and locked it. It had been a good week. He felt he deserved a drink. He felt that he had been handling his drinking problem well. He hadn't gotten out of control, not once. He smiled to himself. *It might even be a good night for some karaoke.*

Tom daydreamed as he drove along Abners Mill Road. That wasn't a good thing to do on that treacherous narrow road, yet he was. He was thinking about Woozy. He had to keep level headed. He didn't need another spur-of-the-moment relationship. Maybe he and Woozy could start dating the good old-fashioned way, slow and easy; not that high paced stuff so common today. He laughed at the thought of some of the latest fads, like speed dating and online dating services. All the dating services bragged about their success with the *so-called* match-making process. They offered things, such as personality profiles or compatibility screenings. Tom knew for a fact, that people rarely filled out questionnaires honestly, especially when it came to personal information.

When he turned into the Gyp Joint's lot, he noticed that Nick's car was already there. Tom hoped that Nick hadn't been there long. It'd be kind of nice to carry on a sober conversation, for a few minutes anyway. When he entered, he found Nick telling stories as usual, talking to anyone that would listen. Some things never change. Steve, the bartender, placed a Budweiser on the bar for him. Tom pulled a stool up, next to Nick and sat down. Nick kept talking. He hadn't acknowledged Tom yet. The story he was telling must have been too important for him to pause. Tom knew Nick would eventually need to take a breath and have a swallow of beer. He listened and tried to catch the gist of what Nick carried on about. He finally got it. It had to do with an event that happened in Walmart that day.

Nick finally finished the story and turned to Tom, "Hello, I was telling everyone about the comings and goings of Walmart." Tom wasn't about to hurt his friend's feelings by telling him that the group sitting at the bar could care less about what happened in Walmart. But he said nothing and just smiled.

Nick wasn't done, "I might get a job in store security. I'd have to wander the isles and try to prevent shoplifting."

"Good for you, Nick. Is it a promotion, and would you get a raise?"

"I'm not sure about that, but it'd be a more exciting job."

"I'd have to agree with you about that, just about anything would be more exciting than being a store greeter at the Mart."

"I haven't seen much of you lately, what have you been doing?"

Tom told Nick about the upcoming wedding and complained about the cost of the rehearsal dinner. "You know, I don't think this is right for me to have to pay for a hundred peoples' meals, especially since I don't know any of them. No, I take that back, I do know two of them, my son and my ex-wife. But, I'm a pensioner for god's sake."

"I agree with you a hundred-percent. Maybe you'll get to know them, and become good friends?"

"Ever the optimist, my friend, ever the optimist. I seriously doubt that I'll get to know any of them. Hell, I barely know my own son. And that fiancé of his is definitely no bargain. How he can blindly jump into that fire, is beyond me." Tom motioned for another round. "It seems my son and his fiancé have even made arrangements for lodging; for her family, and for Darlene. Of course, I have to fend for myself. Does any of this sound right to you?"

"No, that seems kind of shitty to me. You know if it were me, I'd make sure and get pretty damn drunk at the reception dinner. That should help with livening things up."

Tom laughed at the thought, "You're right, Nick, that sounds like a great idea. That is definitely a good idea. It might be the only way to keep me from smacking somebody over the course of the evening. You know the really sad thing though? I believe the only reason I'm even being invited to the damned wedding, is to

42

pick up the tab for the rehearsal dinner. It feels more like a family reunion dinner to me."

Wilson was home and had changed into some comfortable clothes. He couldn't believe how warm it was, especially for December. He carried his drink outside and stood on his back porch. He looked around the yard and noticed all kinds of things that needed to be done. Wilson had never been much of a handy man. He wasn't about to waste his weekend picking things up, just to store them away for the winter. All that junk could stay right where it was.

He pulled the cover off the grill; maybe a couple of steaks for dinner would be nice. Wilson could hear the neighbor's storm door open. She stepped onto her back porch and stared over at him. He stared back at her. He wondered how their relationship had gotten this way, he couldn't remember if they'd ever even had a conversation.

Back inside, he pulled two sirloin steaks from the freezer. They were frozen solid. He threw them in the microwave and set the timer for five minutes, on high. Wilson poured a healthy glass of whiskey and grabbed two potatoes, to complete the menu for a hungry meat and potatoes kind of guy. He hit the pause button. Then Wilson put the potatoes on top of the steak and hit resume. After the timer went off, he pulled his nuked food from the micro. They were damn near on fire. The steaks looked well cooked on the outside. Wilson thought they would finish nicely on the grill. He wrapped foil around the potatoes, walked into the living room, and cranked up the stereo. *Yeah steak, whiskey, and loud as hell music, this is what life is all about.*

Wilson opened the windows over the kitchen sink, and then stepped back out onto the porch. In one hand, he balanced his plate of steak and potatoes. In the other hand was his whiskey. If he dropped anything, he'd make sure it wasn't the Jim Beam. Priorities, Wilson knew all about priorities. The music sounded just right, it was almost loud enough to drown out his damned neighbor. Wilson placed the steaks on the grill and they immediately flared up. He then moved the meat above and put the potatoes on the lower burner. He sat and watched them cook and sipped his drink. *Yes, this is the life, steak and whiskey on a warm December night.*

He needed a refill, so he stepped back inside the kitchen. *Might as well use the toilet, while I'm here.* Wilson returned to the kitchen, took a generous drink from his whiskey, and then tried to remember what he'd been doing. He heard some screaming from the back yard and wondered what could be going on. That was when remembered what he'd been doing. Smoke rolled around the grill as he struggled to shut off the gas. His steak was done, no doubt about that. His neighbor stood at the fence glaring at him. He knew she had something to say, as he attempted to get the burned food onto a plate.

"Hey Wilson, I hope you enjoy your dinner. It sure does smell good."

CHAPTER 5

Tom and Bella were on their way out of the woods. It was a comfortable day, because over the weekend it had cooled considerably. They were nearly to the trailer when Tom heard sirens. The constant screeching noise didn't make Bella happy. It sounded as if emergency vehicles were coming to his trailer. Tom picked up his pace and began to run. He smelled smoke and slowed down when he had a better idea where it was coming from. Fortunately, the fire was farther away than Tom had originally thought. As he stood on the trailer's porch, Tom could see the smoke rise from across the river. Might be worth going to have a look, "What do you think girl?" He opened the door of the F-150 and Bella jumped in.

"Let's go see what all the excitement is about Bella?"

Tom had a fairly good idea where the fire was located. He pulled onto Abners Mill and headed towards Route 68. The fire was near the river, probably less than a mile from his trailer. Bella stuck her head out of the window with her nose in the air as they rolled along. Tom turned southwest toward Lexington, and then turned left after he crossed the bridge over the Licking River. Stoney Creek Road, he remembered it well. The previous spring, he'd looked at property there. He slowed the Ford as he approached. There was plenty of manpower futilely fighting the blaze. It was a large barn and it was full of tobacco. The fire roared. Tom stopped and watched the blaze. The volunteer fire department battled in vain. If the tobacco hadn't been dry, it might not have burned so quickly.

Wilson was just settling in when his phone rang. A

45

moment later, he ended the call. He didn't need that distraction, not today. He had too damn much to do. He carefully placed his hat on his head, and then walked out the door. The call he'd received was about a fire in progress on Stoney Creek Road, and the caller said it looked suspicious. Wilson wasn't in the mood to do the fire department's job. Why couldn't they handle things? He threw the transmission in gear and flipped on his lights and siren and accelerated away from the courthouse. The corner people, as Wilson called the local druggies, stood in their usual spots and blankly stared in his direction. Wilson felt his emergency response gave the people first-hand knowledge of their elected officials at work. And Bill Wilson was one of those officials.

His indicator flashed as he slowed to make the turn. Wilson had seen the smoke. It could be seen for miles. He could have found his way even without an address. Wilson assumed it was a large barn. He approached slowly and watched the fire department personnel running around in obvious confusion. It would be different if Wilson was in charge; if he were running things. That group would have been organized. He would have seen to that. But, then again, he thought about his department and his deputy. Maybe things wouldn't be as organized as he believed. He passed a truck parked on the side of the road and smiled. Wilson came to a stop. He looked in his rear view mirror and saw Padgett in his truck, watching the fire.

Tom saw the Sheriff's truck slowly roll by. He wished his curiosity hadn't got the better of him and led him here. It was too late for that. He watched Wilson climb from his truck. He laughed as he watched Wilson perform his ritual; first his hat, and it had to perfectly positioned. Tom couldn't remember, did Wilson usually put his hat on first? It didn't matter. Next, Wilson hiked up his pants and adjusted his gun belt. Talk about a creature of habit. Tom decided to get out and greet the man. He knew Wilson would be curious why he was there. Tom watched as he got into his well-practiced swagger, as Wilson made his way toward him.

"Padgett, I'm surprised to find you here. You don't usually hang around the scene of the crime. Why are you here this morning? It's just not like you."

"Wilson, I thought I'd come over to the barn burning just to hang around. Since I'm here, it should give you something new to suspect me of."

Wilson smirked, "Yeah, I was working on something really interesting when this call came in. I'm not sure if you're an arsonist, but if I find a meth lab inside, I'll definitely reconsider."

"You never quit. Isn't there anyone else in the county you can hate? Why am I the object of your obsession?"

"I know you think you're a slick bastard. But, one of these days, you're going to screw up. When you do, I'm going to be there. I'm going to bust your ass."

Tom stared at Wilson, shook his head and climbed into his truck. Wilson's lips continued moving as Tom started the Ford. He did a u-turn and glanced in the rear view mirror. Wilson's mouth continued to work. Tom headed back toward 68. He ventured another glance in the mirror. Wilson still stood there watching him. Tom thought it impossible for Wilson to become more of a pain, but it seemed he was. Wilson seemed more anxious than ever to blame crimes on him. How much more of Wilson's harassment could he take? Thinking about it, gave Tom a strange sensation. It was as if part of him enjoyed screwing with Wilson. Could it be because Wilson was so easy to mess with?

Back at home, Tom made a late breakfast. He'd gotten hungry after the hike and then the ordeal with Wilson. Sausage and eggs might hit the spot. Bella loved it when Tom made sausage. She knew when he did that a special treat usually came her way, the leftover grease on her food. When breakfast was over, Tom needed to find a room in Lexington. Andy had reserved rooms for himself and his fiancé, plus her family. They were all staying at the Griffin Gate Marriott. Andy also reserved a room for his mother, but he hadn't bothered with one for Tom. That didn't surprise him. Deep down in his heart, Tom knew that Andy was a mama's boy. Besides, the Marriott was too pricey for his blood anyway, especially considering the cost of the rehearsal dinner.

Tom decided to take Bella with him. He didn't want to leave her in some nasty kennel. He found a Ramada which was reasonable and pet friendly. He made the reservation and then went to the on-line registry for the wedding gifts. He picked some items he felt were practical, and also inexpensive. He really hated this kind of thing. It could qualify as one of his least favorite things. Making the reservations and getting through the registry had been time consuming. Finally, he finished. It was after eleven; time for a beer. He'd already had an overly eventful day. Bella was glad when Tom got up from his perch in front of the computer. She'd been trying to get his attention for some time. She wanted to go outside.

It was determined that the fire had been deliberately set. Wilson wasn't surprised. He'd have to figure out who did it. It would cut into the time he planned to devote to Padgett. Maybe he could wrap the arson activity up quickly. Wilson phoned Leland, and told him to meet at the burned barn, for some on-the-job training. At the scene, there were remnants of broken bottles that had previously contained used motor oil. The bottles had been stuffed with rags, which served as wicks. Wilson thought about oil lamps. The bottles had been placed strategically around the barn and the rags were lit. Wilson and his deputy had asked around, and no one had heard or seen anything. No suspicious vehicles or persons. Wilson had a hard time believing this. Luckily, he managed to get the name of the property owner. The man didn't live in the county full time. He lived in Lexington.

At the courthouse, Wilson left the Clerk of Courts with the owner of record for the property where the arson occurred in hand. A few minutes later, he hung up the phone. The owner was Charles Jackson. He hadn't heard that his barn had burned. As far as Wilson was concerned, Jackson didn't seem bothered about it either. This struck Wilson as odd. Jackson stated that he had no insurance on the structure. He said the tobacco that was hanging in the barn belonged to a neighbor. It took Jackson a moment, but he eventually remembered the neighbor's name, Mark Settles. Jackson claimed he leased the farm to him. Mr. Jackson said that he planned to build on the property in a few years. After he retired, he planned to tear the barn down.

Wilson got Settles on the phone. Mr. Settles was not a

happy man. Yes, he had heard about the barn fire. No, he didn't have insurance on the tobacco. This was obviously a huge loss to a small-time farmer. He was already having a difficult time making ends meet. Wilson was about to hang up when Settles asked about the investigation.

"Sheriff, are there any suspects?"

"No, there aren't. But, we are early into the investigation."

"Surely someone had to have seen or heard something out of the ordinary?"

"No, sir, so far we've come up with nothing. We're continuing to check. With the information we have now, finding the person responsible will be difficult, maybe even impossible."

"How the hell, am I supposed to make my payments? I was counting on that crop."

Wilson didn't have an answer, so he hung up.

He hadn't walked Bella while on a lead for some time. Tom thought it wise to see how she behaved. Soon, they were going to Andy's wedding. Tom would need to keep Bella under control, while in the city. He figured she would throw a fit when he put the lead on her. She had grown quite accustomed to her freedom. Tom checked the Weather Channel and learned that rain was expected later in the week. Once it started raining, they might be stuck inside for a while. He had hoped to explore Blue Licks State Park for some time. Today seemed like a good time.

At Blue Licks, they walked along Heritage Trail. It had a pedestrian bridge that crossed over Route 68. Heritage Trail was a couple of miles in length, much of which bordered the Licking River. There was an old fort in the valley, which was near the river. Tom was sure it was in the flood plain. Most of the trail was out in the open, and was treeless meadow. Tom preferred hiking the woods near his trailer to this. But, Bella was enjoying herself. She was the main reason they were here. Tom unhooked her leash after they'd crossed Route 68, and Bella ran free. She had behaved well the short time she'd been on the lead. Tom was confident she'd be no problem while they were in Lexington.

He sat at his desk, thinking. Wilson was considering the farmer's attitude. Sure, Settles had good reason to be upset. The barn that held his crop had burned to the ground. That didn't give him justification to get mad at Wilson. *Hell, I didn't advise the guy not to buy insurance.* Wilson thought of the circumstances that surrounded the barn fire. *Maybe Settles couldn't buy crop insurance? If the owner didn't have insurance on the structure, that might have made the crop uninsurable. Why would someone want to burn the barn down? It was located in a really remote area. Who would go in there to do something like that?* Wilson was turning these thoughts around, when his phone rang.

"This is Wilson."

"Sheriff Wilson, this is Detective Sparks with the Maysville Police. I understand you wished to speak with me."

"Yes I do, Detective. I have some questions about Jimmy Fugate, and more specifically, about his wife Woozy."

Detective Sparks paused, "I have information about Jimmy Fugate, but that's all. I understand you have a dead man on your hands. To us, Fugate was a fugitive that died in your county; end of story."

"Why do you think he ended up down here?"

"Sheriff, I can only assume that he was hiding out there. He recently spent thirty days in the Maysville Detention Center for abusing his wife. It wasn't long after his release that he again put her in the hospital. He was going back to jail, so he ran."

"Detective, do you know a man named Tom Padgett?"

"The name doesn't ring any bells. Is there a reason it should?"

"I'm not sure. I have a feeling Padgett and Mrs. Fugate might have had something to do with her husband's death."

"I don't know what to tell you, Sheriff. As far as Mrs. Fugate's concerned, she is recently widowed and happens to reside in Maysville, which isn't against the law. If there's anything I can help you with regarding your investigation, I will. As far as Jimmy Fugate is concerned, we've closed the book on him."

Wilson thanked the Detective and ended the call.

Tom was at Garrett's eating lunch when Wilson walked in. Tom nodded in his direction and returned to the article he'd been reading. The story of the barn fire on Stoney Creek was on the Carlisle Courier's front page. Tom was tempted to say something about it, but decided not to. It had been a while since Wilson had accused him of anything, maybe he'd let sleeping dogs lie. The story said that the fire appeared suspicious, and so far, no suspects had been identified. Tom recalled how Wilson had threatened him the morning of the fire. He said if evidence was found that indicated the possibility of a meth lab, then he'd consider Tom a candidate for arson. Wilson was original. He had to give him that.

Tom folded the paper and pushed his plate aside. He was about to leave, when he saw Wilson slide back from the table. He would wait; this might be entertaining. Tom watched as Wilson stood and placed his hat on his head, and adjusted it, so it was perfect. He spun on his heel and looked in Tom's direction, hiked up his pants and adjusted his gun belt. Wilson began to walk toward Padgett with his familiar swagger. Tom wished he had left five minutes ago.

Wilson's phone rang. "Wilson." He stood still, no more than five feet from Tom.

"Uh huh, Route 68, near Old Maysville Road. I'm leaving Carlisle now. I'll be there in ten."

Wilson glanced at Padgett, then reversed direction and left Garrett's.

51

Deputy Leland was who had called the Sheriff. Leland wasn't usually the first on the scene, and he was enjoying this. He stood to the side as the fire department worked the blaze. It was a mobile home fire, located off Route 68. Fortunately, the trailer wasn't occupied, so there was little urgency to put it out. Leland knew the trailer was in bad shape, anyway. It didn't have electricity to it. So, how could a fire have started? *Maybe it's arson,* he thought. *Maybe an arsonist is running wild in Nicholas County?* He heard sirens. Leland watched as the Sheriff's truck rolled to a stop.

The Sheriff climbed from his truck and ambled over to Leland.

"Deputy, has the fire department said anything about a cause yet?"

"Not to me, Sheriff. I believe the trailer was abandoned, anyway."

"What makes you think that, Deputy?"

"I drive past it every day; I can't help but notice it. It's all bent and crooked. It doesn't have electricity run to it. It looks like it hasn't been lived in for years."

Wilson considered what his Deputy had said. "That's good, Leland, you're learning. That's using your head while demonstrating skills of observation. That's a major step toward becoming an effective investigator."

"Thank you, Sheriff."

Tom slowed as he passed the burning trailer. He noticed that the Sheriff's truck was there. That's the reason Wilson left in such a hurry. Tom considered the trailer that was burning. Something about it had caught his attention earlier today. Why would it be burning? It wasn't being lived in. It was an old, abandoned trailer. It didn't have power to it. Wilson was going to be busy; that was good. If Wilson was busy solving crimes, he wouldn't have time to worry about him. Tom accelerated back onto the highway. He was anxious to get home. A light rain started as he turned onto Abners Mill. By the time he pulled into his driveway, it was raining steadily.

Bella wagged her tail wildly as she jumped in the air and spun around. She was behaving like Tom had been gone for days. "Bella I was only gone a little while, calm down." He wasn't really up for a walk. That didn't matter, because Bella was. It was supposed to rain for the next four to five days. He might as well drag out the rain gear. Obviously, he needed to take his little baby for a walk. Usually Bella didn't care if she got wet, but she could act prissy. Sometimes she worried about getting her paws wet. Today wasn't one of her dainty days. Tom pulled up his hood and put on his vest and then snapped Bella's vest around her. Now, they were wrapped in blaze orange. They were protected, just in case hunters were about.

CHAPTER 6

Lonnie Eldridge was a thief. He had just turned twenty-two. Lonnie had been a useless person for most of his twenty-two years. He had been stealing for as long as he could remember. He wasn't a big thief or a bank robber, nothing like that. He guessed he was what would be considered a petty thief. But, after years of petty thieving, he'd managed to do harm to a great number of people. Lonnie considered some of his virtues. That was difficult, because he had only a few. He was tall and skinny. He assumed this to be a plus. He hadn't been successful with the ladies, but he didn't care much about them, anyway. After another moment's consideration, he determined that his chosen profession of thievery might be fitting.

Lonnie moved away from home last year and hadn't adjusted to living on his own. His parents had always been alright people. They tried to help Lonnie to do right. But, Lonnie had been impossible to control. Now he rented a trailer, out on Goose Creek Pike. It wasn't much, but the rent was cheap. It wasn't like Lonnie didn't have opportunities. He didn't care. He was content with doing just enough to get by. It was amazing that he'd even finished high school. Lonnie owned an old Chevy S-10, long-bed. The truck also had a camper shell. If the S-10 was empty, it could hold a bunch of stuff.

Lonnie had an unusual hobby. He liked to drive around, to scope things out. He looked at things that lay about in yards, to see what was to be had. Then, after dark, he'd circle back around and whatever he'd seen earlier, he'd take and load in the back of his truck. He usually did this on Friday or Saturday nights. Then, he would go pawn his score on Monday. He didn't get a great deal of money. Sometimes, on good weekends, he could earn two or three hundred bucks. It didn't bother him that he was stealing a five year olds first bike, or another kid's birthday football. To Lonnie, this was cash, just his for the taking.

Sometimes he'd break into houses, but not often. He had to be absolutely certain that no one would surprise him and come home. Lonnie wasn't a big risk taker. But, since he'd started drinking after he'd turned eighteen, he had gotten more careless. Lonnie was beginning to tire of his small-time theft adventures, anyway. He longed for bigger paydays. He knew there would be more risk involved, but the rewards would be worth it. Lonnie would still employ some of his neighborhood casing techniques, but now, as he did his exploratory casing, he focused more on the actual houses. He was interested in signs that indicated people weren't home. He paid attention to things like old newspapers lying in the drive for more than a day or two, or one car in the drive, where there were usually two.

Mike Underwood backed his truck through the mud; he needed to get closer to the remains of the burned barn. He climbed from the comfort of his cab, out into the cold rain and quickly began to load the metal roofing. A few minutes into the task, he realized he'd need to make several trips. They paid good money for scrap metal these days. There was a scrap yard down in Winchester. That was where Mike was headed. He had heard that they paid cash, no questions asked. After he loaded his truck, he looked at the pile that remained. Mike mentally calculated that there were two, maybe even three loads still lying on the ground. He could easily do two loads a day. He'd be finished by the weekend. This was going to be easy money. He pulled out onto Stoney Creek Road in the direction of Carlisle.

Wilson sat at his desk, thinking. *Another day, another fire. Yesterday, it was an old abandoned trailer. Who would do something like that? Both fires had been deliberately set. Who ended up getting hurt? Settles had, he'd lost his entire tobacco crop. But, the old derelict trailer was one of many eyesores on Route 68. Could scrap metal really be that valuable? Could it be so valuable that people would go to these lengths to steal it?* Wilson had had plenty of complaints about copper pipes and wire being stolen. *But old sheet metal?* He stepped outside onto the courthouse steps. He breathed in the moist morning air. It was raining, coming down hard. It was beginning to look like a good day to go home and take a nap. He watched as a blue Chevrolet pickup loaded with burned metal roofing drove past the courthouse. The truck was heading east, toward Moorefield. *Could it be the metal from that barn over on Stoney Creek?*

Wilson sat back down at his desk. He wondered about the truck he'd just seen. He convinced himself that the metal couldn't possibly have been from the same barn. *Even extremely stupid thieves wouldn't drive a truck loaded with stolen goods right through town. Right through the middle of town, in plain sight of the Sheriff's Department.* Wilson decided against a nap, maybe he would visit Padgett. *Yeah, a social visit, as Padgett likes to call them. This might be a perfect day for that.* He stood, stretched, and cracked his neck. He was kind of excited, just at the thought of surprising Padgett. One of these days, Wilson was positive; Padgett's luck was going to run out. He was going to make a fatal mistake. Maybe that day was today.

It was raining hard as Bella and Tom reached the halfway point of their morning trek. He regretted the fact that he had allowed Bella to pester him into a long walk this morning, especially in the cold December rain. She was sniffing about as if the woods were teeming with all sorts of scents. He wasn't sure about the scents. In Tom's mind, the smell factor had to be greatly reduced in the nearly freezing downpour. He remembered something he'd read about dogs' sense of smell. Supposedly dogs' sense of smell was ten-thousand times better than humans. Tom had a hard time believing some of those statistics. They were nearly to the gap in the fence that served as their gate. Tom was looking forward to another cup of coffee. But first, he needed to get Bella inside and toweled off before she shook all over the place. He didn't feel like cleaning up after her.

They entered the back door into the kitchen and Tom

quickly grabbed a towel and gave Bella a vigorous toweling. She loved getting toweled dry. Especially, if you covered her head and pretended you couldn't see her. "Where's Bella, where's Bella?" She'd stand perfectly still. She actually believed she was invisible under the towel. Bella was dry, now she could stretch out and have her rest over by the heater.

Tom had a bad feeling and then glanced out the front window. Damn, Wilson was out front. Obviously, he had been waiting for them. Should he let Wilson know he was home? Finally against his better judgment, he stuck his head out the door and yelled.

"Want coffee, Wilson?" Tom added water and coffee to the percolator as Wilson entered and wiped his feet.

"Yeah, wet out isn't it?"

Tom looked at Wilson. Why doesn't he ever get to the point? Tom wanted to know what the hell he wanted. But, he knew getting angry wouldn't change anything. He might as well play the small talk game that Wilson seemed to enjoy.

"Yeah, you're right, it is wet. As a matter a fact, it's miserable out. What brings you out in all this misery today?"

Bella hadn't bothered to get up as Wilson entered. Tom approvingly glanced her way. Maybe she's learning how to tell friend from foe.

"Were you out walking, Padgett? I didn't see you return. I've been sitting in my truck for the past twenty minutes."

"What's so important that you'd wait twenty minutes in this freezing rain to talk to me? Is there something I need to know?"

Tom handed Wilson a cup of coffee and they both sat down. Tom waited. He had watched Wilson do this gather-his-thoughts scenario on numerous occasions.

"I was driving by and thought I'd stop in and talk with you about some things. I've got a few things I'd liked to clear up."

Tom wasn't in the mood to finish the man's thoughts for him. He would wait.

"Yesterday, at Garrett's, I was coming over to talk with you. Unfortunately, I was interrupted with a call about another fire."

"I saw that fire, as I was on my way home. Do you have any suspects?"

"No, not yet. But that's not what I wanted to talk to you about. The other day when I saw you at Garrett's, you were with a woman. I understand that she's Jimmy Fugate's widow."

"Her name is Woozy. You're right, she was Fugate's wife."

"So, my question is, how did you come to know Mrs. Fugate?"

"I'll try and keep this simple, Wilson. Yes, I know Woozy. She tends bar in Maysville. I go there on occasion. You can check the bar, it's called O'Rourke's."

"Do you have any information about Mr. Fugate? About how Mr. Fugate ended up down here in Nicholas County, only two miles or so from your trailer?"

"I told you about Mrs. Fugate and how we met, and as for why Jimmy Fugate ended up where he did, you'll need to ask him."

Tom stood and refilled their cups. Wilson ignored the remark about Jimmy. He needed to remain calm and not left Padgett frustrate him.

"So, Padgett, did you ever meet the deceased?"

"Yes I did. I met him once."

Wilson liked what he heard. "You say you met the man. So, you must have talked with him?"

"I talked with him briefly. To be perfectly honest with you, Wilson, I didn't like him very much. I'm not a big fan of wife beaters."

"What did you happen to talk about, Padgett?" Wilson's phone rang. He picked up and stepped closer to the door. "Wilson. Huh, is that right? I'll be there in a few minutes. Good work, Leland."

Wilson clicked off and then turned to face Tom.

"I've got other business to attend to. But, I look forward to continuing our conversation."

Tom watched as Wilson climbed back into his truck. Yes, he looked forward to that next conversation, also, but Tom wasn't going to tell Wilson about any conversation he had with Jimmy. That was between him and Fugate, and it was going to stay that way. Tom continued to watch as Wilson sped away; he turned right and was heading towards Route 68. The rain hadn't slowed. Tom walked to the sink and poured out his coffee. He opened the fridge and grabbed a beer.

Wilson pulled slowly onto the partially gravel, muddy track and stopped. He recognized the blue Chevrolet pickup. It was the same one he'd seen earlier today hauling metal through Carlisle. Leland was talking with the driver as they stood in the rain. Both of them were soaking wet. Luckily for Wilson, he had rain gear. He wore it as he stepped out into the rain. Wilson was happy to continue the interrogation out in the elements. That should help to keep the damn thief off guard.

"Who do we have here, Leland?"

"Sheriff, this is Mike Underwood. He told me he's been asked to clean up the metal."

"You don't say, huh? And who asked you to clean up the metal?"

"The owner did, Charles Jackson."

"Oh, so you know the owner? You didn't happen to start the fire did you?"

"No sir, I was just picking up the metal like the owner wanted me to do."

Damn, this sounds convincing. I'll have to try another tactic. "So, Mike, can I call you Mike?"

"Yes, sir."

"Mike, do you know anything about the trailer fire over on 68? The trailer fire, it happened yesterday?"

"No, sir. I don't know nothin' about no trailer being burned. I'm just cleaning up this here metal."

"So, you already hauled a load earlier today. Where did you take it?"

"I took it down Winchester way. They pay cash."

"You were going to split the money with Mr. Jackson? Or did he tell you to keep it?"

"I'm 'sposed to keep it for my trouble."

"Leland, I'm going to make a phone call. You wait here with Mr. Underwood. I'll only be a minute."

Wilson climbed back into the warmth of his truck. His phone registered one bar, hopefully he'd have service. He checked his contacts and dialed Charles Jackson's number. Jackson answered after several rings.

"Mr. Jackson, this is Sheriff Wilson. I'm at your farm and there's a man here that's removing the metal from your burned barn."

"Great, great that's wonderful news."

Wilson wasn't sure how to proceed. "Mr. Jackson, did you ask someone to come clean up the remains from the fire?"

"No, Sheriff, but I'm glad that it's getting taken care of. That's one less thing that I have to worry about when I retire."

"Do you happen to know a man named, Mike Underwood?"

"No, Sheriff, I've never heard of him."

"You didn't ask a Mr. Underwood to come haul off the metal?"

"No, Sheriff, I already told you, I don't know the guy. But, as long as he's cleaning up the mess, it's fine by me."

"Mr. Jackson, you may be happy that he's removing the mess, but I have a strong suspicion that he might also be the one that started the fire."

"Sheriff, are you suggesting that he might have started the fire and is now stealing the metal? He's not some scrapper that scours the countryside looking for scrap metal, is he?"

"No, sir, this isn't a scrapper. This man claims to know you. He probably knows you don't live here full-time. He's made Mr. Settles' life miserable by destroying his tobacco crop."

"Sheriff, what do you want me to do?"

Wilson climbed back out from the comfort of his truck back into the elements. He thought about his best course of action. A plan suddenly materialized. He smiled.

"Mr. Underwood, you say the owner asked you to clean up the metal. When did you speak with Mr. Jackson?"

"Oh, I'm not real sure, maybe sometime last week."

"Was the barn still standing? Or was that after it'd burned down?"

"It must have been after it burned down. Otherwise why

61

Sterling Young

would he want the metal hauled off?"

"OK, Mike, let's cut to the chase and quit wasting each others' time. I just got off the phone with Mr. Jackson. He said he's never heard of you. Doesn't that seem odd? Do you think he forgot about your arrangements?"

"I didn't actually talk to Mr. Jackson. Someone else told me to clean up the metal."

"You just told me that…oh, never mind. And who might this someone else be?"

"I don't know if I should tell you. He'll get in trouble if I tell you, won't he?"

Wilson watched as the rain streamed down Mike Underwood's face. He liked seeing lowlife suffer. This was exactly the kind of treatment guys like him deserved.

Wilson had come up with more scare tactics, "Mike, let me explain a couple of things to you. One, if you know who burned this barn down, its best that you tell me. Otherwise, I have no choice, but to suspect you. Two, even if the person you're trying to protect didn't set the fire, without a name I have no other suspects. Do you see where I'm heading?"

Mike wasn't the sharpest blade in the block, but he got the gist of what the Sheriff was saying. "Yes, Sheriff, I understand."

"Good, now let's have a name. So we can all get out of this nasty rain?"

"The guy that told me to come clean up this metal is named Lonnie. He lives around here someplace."

"That's it, huh, you don't happen to know Lonnie's last name?"

"I'm sorry, Sheriff, that's all I know. I just know him from Ladobee's. We have drinks over there sometimes."

"OK, Mr. Underwood. I'm going to let you off for now. But, don't be hauling any more of this metal, not until we get to the bottom of this investigation. And don't think about leaving town, is that understood?"

"Yes, Sheriff."

CHAPTER 7

Friday Morning

The big day had finally come; the day Tom had been dreading for the past two weeks. He sat unmoving at the kitchen table and stared at the clock on the wall. He had taken Bella on a hike, he'd read the paper, he'd surfed the internet, and he'd packed his suitcase. He must be ready, but still he sat, motionless. He didn't want to go to the rehearsal dinner. He could care less about meeting Andy's fiancés' family. He didn't care to see Darlene. He wasn't looking forward to spending the night in a hotel. There was nothing about this afternoon/evening that he could get excited about. *What was there to rehearse anyway?* He sat there and looked up at the clock. He was already dressed for dinner. Hopefully, it wasn't formal. He had a suit for the wedding, tomorrow night, although he wasn't sure if it still fit.

He looked at the clock for what must have been the fiftieth time. He thought about tonight's agenda. Check-in was after two o'clock. So, he needed to leave in an hour. The dress rehearsal started at five. Afterward there would be photos taken. The dinner started at seven o'clock, and would probably last until ten or eleven. How late the rehearsal dinner lasted, didn't matter to Tom. He planned to leave early and return to the hotel. There he could watch TV with Bella. It'd been some time since he'd had a good session of channel surfing. He was sure that he would be good and ready to call it a night, early; especially being in that crowd, hanging out with a group of people that he didn't know. Tomorrow evening after the wedding, he planned to take Nick's advice. He was going to let his hair down at the wedding party. That might make the event tolerable.

Wilson hung up the phone and smiled. Leland had done some checking around and had succeeded in coming up with not only a name, but also an address for Mike Underwood's drinking buddy. His name was Lonnie Eldridge and he lived in a rural part of the county, out on Goose Creek Pike. Wilson and his deputy were going to pay Mr. Eldridge a visit after lunch. It wasn't very often that you get leads handed to you, especially for a crime like arson. Arsonists don't usually go around talking about their work. If Eldridge ended up being the arsonist, Wilson would definitely celebrate tonight. Yes, if he could solve both fire cases, he would be one happy man. Then, he could refocus on the main objective, Padgett.

Wilson and Leland pulled into the drive where Eldridge lived. There was a Chevy S-10 in the driveway. Wilson knocked three times and the door opened. A skinny guy wearing sweat pants and a UK tee-shirt stared blankly at them. Lonnie blinked a couple of times, as if trying to comprehend why they were standing outside his front door.

He was unsuccessful, so he asked, "Yeah, what do you want?"

Wilson did not appreciate any lack of respect, so he immediately took a dislike to Eldridge.

Wilson cleared his throat, "Mr. Eldridge, we'd like to ask you some questions."

"What about? I'm kind of busy right now."

Wilson could feel the blood rising up his neck, but he stayed calm. "Could we come inside, so we don't have to stand outside in this weather? It shouldn't take long."

Lonnie said nothing. He undid the screen latch and opened the door. Wilson stepped inside, his deputy followed. Wilson studied the interior of the trailer, looking the place over. He was examining it to see if anything suspicious caught his eye. Leland found a spot to his liking on the couch and plopped down.

"Mr. Eldridge, we'd like to ask you some questions about

65

the barn fire, which happened over on Stoney Creek Road. I assume you've heard about it?"

"Oh, yeah. I read about it in the paper. What would you like to know?"

Wilson did not like this guy's smart ass attitude. He forced a smile, as he thought about his next question.

"So you read about it in the paper, huh? You mean to tell me you know nothing about the fire, and how it got started?"

Lonnie's eyes darted between the Sheriff and Deputy. He understood what the Sheriff was insinuating.

"Wait a damned minute, Sheriff! I had nothing to do with that fire. I'm no arsonist."   Wilson smiled at his next thought. He had the guy right where he wanted him.

"Mr. Eldridge, if you're not an arsonist. Then what are you?"

"What the hell are you talking about Sheriff? I was sitting here, trying to watch some TV. In you come, and start harassing me with a bunch of silly ass accusations."

Wilson considered him for a moment longer before speaking. "Lonnie, we have received information that you told someone about the burned out barn. You also told that same person, that it'd be alright to go there and take the metal. You told that same person that the property owner gave permission for doing this, when in fact, he did not." Wilson paused and smiled. He was satisfied with his last statement.

A light seemed to go on in Lonnie Eldridge's head. He realized exactly what had happened. He started to laugh out loud. Wilson clearly did not like this, and his face turned bright red. Lonnie continued to laugh, but now he held his hands up, attempting to let Wilson know that soon he'd be back under control.

Wilson waited. *If that skinny ass doesn't quit laughing, I'm going to knock the shit outta him.*

Lonnie finally regained his composure, but occasional burst of laughter continued to escape, "Sheriff, this person you keep referring to, is Mike Underwood. Yeah, I told him about the barn and the metal that was there for the taking. Regardless of what you think, Mr. Jackson indicated to me, that he wanted the metal gone. He told me a couple of years ago, that if something ever happened to the barn, you know something like a fire, now that would be great. He planned on tearing the barn down anyway, when he retired. If that's not giving permission, I'm not sure what is."

Wilson suddenly felt that the wind had been knocked from his sails. He'd been so confident, so sure. Now he had nothing.

He asked meekly, "Would you have any information, about who may have started the fire? Have you heard any rumors, anything at all?"

"No Sheriff, like I said, I read about it in the paper. That same evening, I was over at Ladobee's having a few beers. Underwood happened to be there. He asked me if I knew how he could make some extra cash. I remembered what I'd read in the paper. I told him about the barn fire, and what the owner told me. I also told him where he could take the metal to sell it for cash."

Wilson started for the door, and handed Lonnie a business card.

"If you hear anything about the fire, anything at all, give me a call, will you?"

"Sure thing, Sheriff."

Tom checked into the Ramada. Bella was happy with the accommodations. It had wall-to-wall carpet, a big comfy bed, even a heating system that worked. It had everything a dog loved. Tom realized the next two nights might feel like being on vacation, especially compared to living in his trailer on Abners Mill. He told Bella he'd be back, as he pulled the door closed. Bella probably wasn't worried if Tom came back or not.

When he got to the church for dress rehearsal, he was surprised by how few cars there were. That was good as far as Tom was concerned. Could that mean that the dinner that followed will also have few guests? Tom would love to escape the evening, without spending two or three thousand dollars.

He walked into the church and was greeted by Andy and his bride to be, Nancy, sweet little Nancy. Everyone was casually dressed; this pleased Tom. Andy introduced Tom to his soon to be in-laws, and some of the groomsmen. Pleasantries were exchanged, and the preacher or minister or whatever, entered. The preacher began to go over the arrangements for the wedding ceremony.

Tom saw Darlene, his ex-wife. She was there, in all her glory. She must have sprung for some visits to the tanning salon. If he hadn't known her for the past twenty-five years, he would have sworn she was Jamaican. One hour later, the dress rehearsal was over. Tom said his goodbyes and exited. He had picked up a twelve pack of Budweiser. It was waiting in the hotel's fridge, and he could use one.

Wilson drove to Carlisle in silence. He chose to ignore all the Deputy's incessant questions. Unfortunately, Lonnie Eldridge hadn't started the fire. He'd read about it in the paper and passed the information along, to that ignorant metal-stealing friend of his. *Guess its back to the drawing board. Damn, I felt so confident that I had a slam dunk.* He thought about Mike Underwood and his ability to make up stories on the fly. *Was he a pathological liar?* Wilson decided to let the owner of the barn be the one to communicate with Underwood about cleaning up the metal. He was finished dealing with Jackson.

Pathological liar, that's an interesting condition. Could Padgett be one? Probably not. Padgett might be a liar, but he doesn't fabricate stories on the fly. He thinks long and hard about his lies. Wilson was upset about not being able to solve the arson case. But, a new window into Padgett's past may have opened.

Maybe there's some information to be gleaned from this? He could do some digging into Padgett's history with the Mt. Sterling Police Department. Wilson suddenly felt better. Maybe it will be a good night for a Jim Beam or two, after all. The arsonist was still out there, but Padgett was getting sloppy. Padgett was going down.

Lonnie Eldridge turned off the television and lay back on the couch. The Sheriff and his sidekick Deputy had just left. He laughed about the Sheriff thinking that he was an arsonist. He wasn't an arsonist. Up 'till now, he'd been a petty thief, but things were going to change. Lonnie had decided that he was going to move up to bigger ticket items. He would find out how good the Sheriff and his sidekick Deputy really were. He had some places in mind that he'd been casing across the Licking River. He was going to hit them this weekend.

He might lay low tonight, but tomorrow night, he'd be busy. He had definitely been rattled when the Sheriff showed up. But, the joker was just following leads. They were trying to find an arsonist. They didn't have anything on him. If things went well this weekend, he should have one of his best scores. There was one place in particular that he was anxious to hit. It didn't look like much from the outside. He felt positive that the guy living there had money. Some of those people living down on the river would surprise you. And, the Sheriff probably paid little attention to the area.

Tom drank a beer and petted Bella. She was happy with her temporary digs at the Ramada. He was ok with them too, but would rather be home. Tonight, he wasn't really in the mood to rub elbows with Andy's in-laws, or chat with his ex-wife. But Tom decided that he might as well go find out what the hell he was paying for. Andy's soon to be mother-in-law had made all the arrangements for the rehearsal dinner. She had picked the entire evening's menu. Tom felt that was awfully nice of her. Was she going to insist that everyone in attendance drink red or white wine, stating that beer wasn't allowed? He could drink a snooty glass or two of wine, if he was forced too.

Luckily, Tom had been wrong about the drink options. At dinner, they did have Budweiser and Bud-Lite in addition to red and white wine. That was great by him. He learned that he had been forced to share a table with a few of the other outcasts. They were all grouped together at the same corner table; Tom and the others that nobody wanted anything to do with. The conversation at the outcast table had been non-existent. That was okay by Tom, as long as they kept the beer coming. Dinner was served in one of the Griffin Gate Marriott's banquet rooms. It wasn't time to eat yet, so Tom scanned the room. He hadn't seen Darlene yet. Maybe she wasn't coming. That would be alright. There appeared to be over a hundred people in the room already. Shit, this was getting worse by the minute.

Tom noticed as Andy got up from the table that he shared with his new parents to greet his mother as she entered. Well, I'll be damned. Darlene held hands with Bud Blankenship; old Bud, the Mayor of Mt. Sterling. That wasn't a welcome sight to Tom. *If that bastard thinks I'm paying for his meal, he's got another thing coming.* Tom continued to watch as Andy led his mother and the Mayor to the table of honor. *They're sitting with the bride-to-be and her family. Isn't that sweet? Talk about being odd man out.* Looks like Andy planned to continue his ambitious attempt to ignore his father. Tom drank the last of his beer and motioned for another.

Wilson couldn't shake his newest suspicion that he had about Padgett. *Maybe there is some deep, dark secret buried down in Montgomery County.* Who could he talk to? The Chief of the Mt. Sterling Police Department didn't appear to be helpful. He was probably an old buddy of Padgett's. There had to be someone with an ax to grind; there always was. He might have to take the day off on Monday. Maybe he'd run down to Mt. Sterling in an unofficial capacity, to snoop around a bit. *That sounds like a great idea.* Wilson sipped the Jim Beam and felt the warmth of it. He felt a great deal of satisfaction knowing that he had a new thread to follow on Padgett. This was exactly what he needed.

Who would give Padgett up? Who had something to gain? A fellow officer or someone Padgett had busted that was currently in prison? Finding dirt on ex-officers can be difficult. There's that camaraderie thing that exists within the force. There has to be someone willing to talk. He took another sip. Boy, the Jim Beam tasted good. *Wait a minute. Didn't Padgett recently get divorced? Wasn't that part of the reason he'd moved here? An ex-wife. They usually didn't have any allegiance to their ex-husbands. If I could track her down, maybe she would be willing to talk about some of Padgett's darker moments.*

Tom was asked if he preferred steak or chicken? *Steak, of course, and, another beer would be great.* This was going to be expensive. He was getting more worked up by the minute. He was trying to calculate the cost of this boring shindig. Andy was off introducing his mother and the Mayor to various people. No introductions necessary for his dad. Besides, Andy had a new father, anyway. Tom was sulking, and he knew it. The beer probably didn't help. *But, aren't I part of the equation? Aren't I the dad, regardless if our relationship is strong or not? Doesn't that count for something?*

Dinner was finally over, and Tom was ready to get out of there. Just then, Andy's new father-in-law approached, a pudgy little man with a smug look. He had his hand out. Was it something about settling the tab?

"Twenty-nine hundred dollars, not so bad," he let Tom know. He told Tom that Darlene had chipped in. Surprisingly, she had contributed five-hundred dollars toward the meal.

"Well, bless her heart," was all Tom said.

He handed the father of the bride a check and made his way out the door. Before leaving, Tom glanced over at the wedding party table. He watched fat old Bud Blankenship wolf down another piece of dessert. He might just have something to talk to *Little Napoleon* about tomorrow night.

Wilson refilled his glass. He'd need to slow it down if he wanted to think clearly. Padgett's ex-wife might hold the key. *Did she keep Padgett's last name and still live in Mt. Sterling?* He took a pull from the Jim Beam as he thought. *She probably does. That's most likely the reason Padgett lives in that run-down, poor boy trailer, out in the boonies. She probably took his ass to the cleaners. Padgett's ex might be the missing piece to the Tom Padgett puzzle.* Wilson took another swallow. *Yeah, and while I'm at it, I might as well try and talk to that widow, Woozy. Regardless, of what that Maysville cop said, it's a free country. If I wanted, I could visit that bar where she works; the place where Padgett claimed to have met her. What's it called? O'Rourke's?*

When Tom returned to the hotel, he found Bella stretched out on the bed. "What's up big girl, I hope you're comfortable." He let her out to go to the bathroom, then went to the mini-fridge and grabbed a Budweiser. He was stewing, mostly about the mayor being at the rehearsal dinner. *Darlene had managed to come up with five-hundred dollars toward the dinner. No matter how you look at it, I paid for dinner. She did get half of my pension. Does she have a part-time job?* Tom doubted it. He drank from his beer and thought some more. *Andy, Nancy, Darlene, and Bud; one big happy family.* He had been effectively ostracized. *We'll see how the family reunion goes tomorrow evening.*

CHAPTER 8

Saturday Morning

The big day had arrived. Today, his son was getting married. Tom wore his only suit. He hadn't had it on in years. Tom painfully recalled the memory. He hadn't worn the suit since Cole Bishop's funeral. Cole had been Tom's partner while he was on the Mt. Sterling Police force. He had been shot to death in a failed robbery attempt, over twenty years ago. Tom let the thought go; he didn't need to start getting depressed. Tom located Saint Paul's Catholic Church, in downtown Lexington. There were plenty of available parking spaces. It didn't matter, on Saturday, parking was free. One of the groomsmen led Tom to his place. He was seated in the same row as Darlene and Bud. There were a few people seated behind them. Tom had two sisters, but neither of them was here. His family struggled with closeness issues. Tom looked across the aisle. He recognized many of them. Most of them were part of the hungry group that he fed last night. He hoped the ceremony was short and sweet. He knew better, Catholic weddings were never short and sweet.

Lonnie Eldridge had slept in. If things went as planned, tonight he would be busy. He needed to be well rested. He had a list of places he planned to visit. Some of the spots on his list were working farms that farmers only visited during the day. A couple of the others were actual residences. He had learned that two of the homeowners were going to be out of town. One night, at the Gyp Joint, he had overheard two men talking about an upcoming wedding. It was this weekend, and he knew where the guy attending the wedding lived. He had seen his truck parked at his trailer before. The barns might not yield much, but the trailers he planned on hitting might. He would visit the barns first. He planned to visit the residences last, just in case someone came home early.

The ceremony was long, as Tom had expected. Luckily, it was over now. There was an open bar at the reception, which was good. Tom asked for a beer, and then found a spot in the room that wasn't crowded. He was content to stand apart from the others and let them mingle. Tom realized he was brooding again. He needed to get over it. But, he couldn't forget about the past. His son had ignored him for the past two years. The only reason he was even invited to the wedding was to pay for the rehearsal dinner. Tom drained his beer and got another. He was going to take Nick's advice, drink and make the most of the evening.

Tom was on his third beer when Andy wandered over and thanked him for coming. *Is he kidding? Thanks for coming? I'm his father, for Christ sakes.* This was just great. Andy was off again. He worked the room, talking with more of his newly adopted relatives. Nancy kept well away from Tom. That was probably a wise thing. It was time to form the reception line. *That should be one hell of a lot of fun.* Tom glanced up the line; first there was Nancy and Andy, and then Andy's mother in-law and father-in-law. Darlene was next, and finally Tom, last of course, sucking hind tit again. The relatives walked by. They stared coldly at Tom and then offered the most limp-wristed, impersonal handshake possible. They move up the line, enthusiastically greeted Darlene, along with the rest of the family.

Lonnie Eldridge killed the S-10's engine and listened. It was quiet where he was parked, surrounded by trees. It was getting dark. He was anxious to start the evening's thefts. He moved behind the barn and slid the door open. He saw pieces of farm equipment. They were no good, too big. He kept looking. He spied his first score, a Craftsman tool box, and it was heavy. There were some garden tools. Lonnie decided against them. They wouldn't bring much. Next, he saw an electric fence charger and it was still in the box. That had to be worth something. He didn't need to get greedy. He had several places to visit tonight. He gathered his score and loaded it in the truck. He checked his watch that had only taken fifteen minutes.

Lonnie felt emboldened. He pulled into the next lane and parked directly behind the barn. The tool box that he stole was so heavy it nearly hurt his back. Luckily, this barn didn't even have a back door. That didn't mean there was nothing to steal. It was dark now, and Lonnie turned on his penlight. First thing he saw was a garden tractor. *Damn, if I only had a trailer.* There was a five gallon gas can, and it was full. He put it in the truck. A Homelite string trimmer, which should bring a few bucks. Next, he saw some roofing nails, too heavy. He was ready to leave, when the beam from his light reflected off of something, Lonnie whistled. A thousand-foot spool of 12-2 copper wire.

Tom was happy when the reception charade ended. Once again, he was at the bar. He wasn't going to stray far from it. He glanced to his left and watched as Darlene and pudgy little Bud wandered in. Bud looked his way and nodded. Tom didn't return the nod. The Mayor was an asshole. If it hadn't been for Bud, Tom might still be on the force. *Hell, if it hadn't been for Bud, I might still be married. Who knows?* Tom asked for another beer. It was beginning to take hold. Tom was beginning to slur his words, maybe he should slow down. *To hell with slowing down. It's my son's wedding. It's a joyous occasion, a time for drinking and merriment.*

Tom could tell someone was staring at him. He turned and noticed that Darlene was glaring at him. She looked totally disgusted. Tom lifted his beer, and then smiled at her. "Congratulations on the marriage of your son," Tom slurred. She turned and left. In her wake was Bud. Tom looked over his shoulder, and realized that people were moving toward the dining area. *Looks like dinner is served.* He found his way to a table with his name on it. He found that he was once again grouped with the outcasts; the crowd from the previous evening. The same damned people, the people that either nobody knew or wanted anything to do with.

Lonnie had finished the barns on his shopping list. He did surprisingly well. It wasn't Christmas yet, but it was starting to feel like it. There was quite a cache of things in the back of his truck. The evening was going better than he would have imagined. He was excited about the next stop. So far, the barns had proven to be treasure troves. He hoped that the trend would continue. The next trailer he was going to stop at was situated close to the road. There weren't many places to park. Luckily, Abners Mill Road wasn't busy this time of night. He pulled into the drive and parked next to the trailer. This partly hid his S-10 from view.

He tried the back door. It was locked. Was it dead bolted? Not to worry, he had his flat crowbar in hand. He would make short work of the lock. He pushed the breaker bar under the jamb. The door popped open; *no sweat*. He shined his light around the kitchen and dining area and saw nothing of interest. He opened the closet; again nothing. *Wait a minute, a shoe box.* He pulled the box down. It contained cash. Not a great deal, but that was alright. He walked down the hallway to the bedroom. He rooted through the dresser drawers. He smiled when he found a handgun. That was a pleasant surprise. It looked like a 38. It should bring quite a bit of change. *Damn headlights.* Lonnie killed the penlight, and waited in the dark while the car sped past.

Dinner wasn't much. Tom's table-mates had nothing to say. Andy's best man, whom Tom had never met, got up to say a few words. Very few, probably only ten, and for that, the genius had to reference a piece of paper. Nancy danced with her father and Andy danced with his mother. The newlyweds danced with each other. Festivities over, it was time for mingling. Tom stood around while he drank a beer; he watched some drunken bridesmaids try to dance. It was mildly entertaining. Andy approached and said that he needed to speak to him, in private. This took Tom by surprise, "What do you want to talk about, Andy?"

Andy asked Tom to follow. They needed a more private

area. Tom had no idea what this might be about. His son wanted to have a private conversation. After years of no conversations, this seemed odd. Tom was getting full, but managed to follow along. Andy stopped when they were alone. He seemed to have lost his confidence.

Tom slurred, "Andy, congratulations on your wedding. You have my undivided attention. What's on your mind?"

"Dad, you remember how you advised me about getting married too soon?"

"Vaguely, I guess so."

"The reason we were anxious to get married, was that we had to get married."

Tom was feeling his oats, but he caught the crux of what Andy said. "Don't tell me, Nancy's pregnant?"

"Yes, Dad, but only a few months."

"Well, Andy, I guess more congratulations are in order. When is the baby due?"   "In July, but we're not announcing it yet."

"What do you mean, not announcing it?"

"Dad, you're the only one that knows Nancy's pregnant, besides Nancy and me."

"Why am I the only one you have elected to share this secret with? You usually don't confide with your father, especially, with things of this magnitude."

"I'd like you to tell Mom. Could you break it to her? Not tonight, though. Maybe sometime next week, when Nancy and I are away on our honeymoon."

Tom wasn't sure why, but he started to laugh. "You want me to tell your mother that the reason you got married is because Nancy is pregnant?"

"We intended to get married; we just moved the date up by about a year."

"What about Nancy's parents? You expect me to tell them, too?"

"No, we were hoping, that you could suggest to Mom, that she tell them. That way, when we return in two weeks, hopefully, all the dust will have settled."

Tom chuckled and then swallowed the rest of his beer. "Andy, I am glad that you finally confided in me after all this time. I wish that it could have been under different circumstances, though. I'm going to get a beer, would you like one?"

"No thanks, Dad."

Lonnie was glad that the car didn't slow. But, he was ready to leave. He had one last stop tonight. It was further down Abners Mill Road. After the last job, he was going to call it a night. He drove slowly as he made his way to the last place. He checked his cell phone. It was ten-thirty. That was perfect. He pulled across the ditch and into the driveway. The trailer had a bright security light on one corner. He would park opposite. There was also a light on inside, which would be helpful. He knew no one was home, because he had heard the guy talking about going to a wedding. Besides, his truck wasn't there.

He walked to the back door. It was dark in the shadows. *Wait a second, why are there wheelchair ramps? The guy that lives here doesn't need them. I sure as hell hope there isn't an invalid waiting inside.* He listened for sounds coming from inside the trailer. He heard none. He pulled out his crow bar. The door offered little resistance. He was inside in no time. He walked down the hallway. He needed to make sure the place was empty. Satisfied, now Lonnie could see what there was to steal. He was excited, especially after he saw the laptop on the table. That might be the icing on the cake.

After Andy left to join his bride, Tom returned to the dance floor. Several people were dancing. He saw Darlene shaking her stuff with the Mayor. Tom had to laugh, he had no idea the squatty little guy could move like that. *Maybe Bud had some surprising moves in the bedroom, too. Maybe that's how he won Darlene's heart.* Hell, there was one of the drunken bridesmaids, and she was staggering in Tom's direction.

The bridesmaid was really out of it, "Mr. Padgett, could I have this dance?"

"Sure, let's show the rest of this group what dancing is really like." She seemed to like that comment. *So, let the dancing begin.* She wasn't very steady on her feet, but neither was Tom. However, they still managed to spin from place to place. Tom was having a lot of fun, in some drunken way.

"Mr. Padgett, you're a good dancer."

"Are you kidding? The last time I danced, you weren't even born yet."

"That doesn't matter. I watch *Dancing with the Stars* and most of those people have nothing on you."

"Why thank you, and you're pretty good yourself." Tom looked over and noticed that Darlene and Bud had stopped dancing. Not only had they stopped, Darlene had her hands on her hips and glared at Tom and his partner. Tom smiled as he and his drunken bridesmaid partner whirled past. Darlene grabbed Bud's hand, and together they stomped from the dance floor.

Lonnie Eldridge couldn't believe his good fortune. The laptop wasn't brand new, but it should still fetch a good price. He opened the fridge and noticed a twelve pack of Budweiser. He grabbed a beer and pulled the tab. He was going to take his time. He had nothing to fear. He rifled through the drawers in the kitchen and didn't find anything. He opened the closet and whistled. A brand new compound bow, plus a set of arrows. He made a trip out to the truck, carrying the bow and the laptop. He tossed the empty beer can in the yard, and then stepped back inside. He pulled another beer from the fridge, and popped it open as he strolled down the hallway.

A shotgun hung over the bed, an old Remington 870, but it appeared to be in excellent condition. Lonnie looked down at the electric heater that clicked away at his feet. It was of little value. He pulled open the dresser drawers and found some cash, about a hundred dollars or so. He was really enjoying this. He opened the closet and found a nice pair of binoculars. He looked under the bed and saw an orange plastic case, and dragged it out. The case contained a new Husqvarna chainsaw. Lonnie thought he should get ready to leave, but he was having too much fun. He carried the latest items outside and put them in the back of his truck. The S-10 was nearly full.

He tossed another empty can in the grass. That beer was an added bonus. *Why not? I'll have another, while I take one last look.* He popped the top on the beer and returned to the bedroom. He rooted around on the top shelf of the closet, but found nothing more. He looked under the bed again; there was nothing else there. He sat on the bed and sipped from the beer. *This has been one great night.* He dug through the drawers some more and pulled something out. *What's this?* It was a badge. *Mt. Sterling Police Department. Shit, the guys a cop.* He jumped from the bed, ran from the room, and as he did, he tripped on the heater. He glanced over his shoulder and saw the heater turn over. *It will turn itself off.* He slammed the trailer door, then started his truck and left.

Tom sat down on a stool. *What the hell, one more for the road. What would it hurt?* Darlene and Bud must have shared that sentiment. They sat at the opposite end of the bar. They both stared Tom's way. Finally, Darlene couldn't take it anymore. She had something that she needed to say. She walked over and stood directly behind Tom. He didn't move. He had nothing he needed to say to her.

Darlene blurted out, "You outta be ashamed of yourself." Tom slowly turned and faced her. "I said, you outta be ashamed of yourself, Tom Padgett." Tom smiled at her. He enjoyed it when she called him by his full name. It was her way of stressing a point.

Tom was curious, "What am I supposed to be ashamed of, Darlene?"

She paused and thought about what she wanted to say. "You should be ashamed for dirty dancing with that underage drunken whore."

Tom laughed loudly, "You're kidding, aren't you? You're in no position to be calling any woman, young or old, a whore."

Darlene acted hurt. She couldn't believe what Tom had said. "What in the hell are you implying?"

"I'm not implying anything. I've always heard that if the shoe fits, wear it."

Darlene looked aghast, and then turned in Bud's direction. Bud got up from his bar stool and ambled toward them.

Bud asked, "Is everything alright, Darlene?"

"Hell no, everything is not alright. Tom just insulted me. He called me a whore." Bud's pudgy face was already red from too much drink. Now it turned scarlet.

He glared at Tom. "Padgett, you worthless bastard. I've wanted to have a go at you ever since the first time I met you. Now it looks like you've given me a reason."

Tom chuckled, "Bud, I don't know what your problem is. Maybe you should think about your chivalrous actions." Tom turned and motioned for another beer.

"Padgett, I'm talking to you."

Tom didn't pay any attention to him, which made Bud even madder.

"Damn it, Padgett! I said I'm talking to you."

"Bud, what's your problem?"

"Get up, Padgett. I'm going to teach you a lesson you won't soon forget."

Tom sipped his beer and smiled. Darlene leaned against the bar to watch.

Bud yelled, "I said get up, damn it."

Padgett didn't like taking orders from anyone, especially from pudgy drunk Bud. He slowly stood and stepped away from the bar. He turned to face Bud.

"Ok, Bud, I'm up. Now what?"

Bud reared back. He was obviously preparing to wallop Tom with a tremendous haymaker. Tom laughed to himself as he watched the slow motion punch develop. Bud swung with everything he had. As he did, Tom took a step backward. The slight move caused Bud's wailing haymaker to miss. Bud spun around in a circle, crashed headfirst into the bar and then crumpled to the floor. Darlene went to him.

Tom looked at Bud as he lay on the floor, "Hey, anytime you want to have another go at me, just give me a call." Tom left the bar. He'd had enough wedding festivities for one night.

CHAPTER 9

Wilson was awoken by his ringing phone. *Damn, it's 12:45.* "Wilson,…uh huh, uh huh,…Abners Mill huh? I'll be there in half an hour." *Another damned fire, another trailer out in the county on fire.* He got dressed and was out the door in ten minutes. He glanced at his neighbor's house as he backed out of the driveway. *For once that nosy bitch isn't staring at me. Maybe she does sleep.* Wilson waited until he was out of town before he turned on his siren. *That was uncharacteristic of me. Maybe I'm getting soft.*

He turned east off of Route 68 onto old Maysville Road, and then took a right at the Abners Mill turnoff and drove down the hill. He glanced over at the Licking. It was high. The moon was full, he could see it clearly. Up ahead he saw lights. The firemen were at the trailer, doing what they could. As it turned out, not much. Padgett's truck wasn't here. *Had he said something about his son's wedding?* The fire was nearly out.

The Chief greeted Wilson. "It might be premature, but I'm thinking it looks like an accident."

"How so, Chief?"

"I don't see any evidence of arson, but I'll have a better idea in the morning."

Wilson walked around the trailer and surveyed the damage. *Padgett won't be able to salvage any of this.* For once, Wilson felt something that could almost be considered sympathy for Padgett. He actually felt bad. He knew how much this would change the man's life.

He dialed the number. Padgett answered after several rings.

"Hey Padgett, you don't sound so good.... No, this isn't a social call. Padgett, I'm afraid I've got some bad news. I'm at your trailer, it burned down.... We're not sure about that yet. We'll have a better idea in the morning. So, you might as well sober up and get some sleep. I'll see you later this morning."

Tom disconnected the phone. Was he really awake, or was it another dream? *My trailer was on fire? How can that be?* There wasn't a damned thing he could do about that now, he needed sleep. The way he felt, he needed a lot of sleep. He had been tossing and turning since he had returned to the hotel. Fortunately, Bella was sound asleep. He listened as she snored. He wondered if the Mayor had recovered from his mishap. Tom wished he had a camera when Bud took that swing at him. It would have been great to capture Darlene's reaction, too. *Damn, my trailer burned down.* Tom rolled on his side and pulled the pillow over his head.

The following morning, Darlene woke early. Bud was still asleep. She couldn't believe how he had embarrassed her. If he had really wanted to get Tom, then he should have gotten his ass up off the floor, and tried again. Tom had insulted her and Bud's response was one of weakness. He was absolutely useless. Darlene looked at herself in the mirror. She had dark circles under her eyes. She applied some eye makeup. She was going to the lobby for breakfast. If and when Bud woke up, he could join her. She recalled how Tom had insulted her. She had done nothing to deserve that. Somehow, she would get even with him for that.

Bella jumped on the bed. She obviously needed to go out. Tom glanced at the clock, "Bella, its 4:30." He opened the door and then led her outside. "Hurry up Bella. I'd like to get some more sleep." He crawled back into bed. His head was pounding. He lay there, unable to sleep until 6:00. His head was pounding; there was no way he could get back to sleep. The hotel offered a free continental breakfast, but that wasn't until 7:00. He could take a long shower, have a cup of coffee, and then watch the news. He needed something in his stomach before he drove home, home to what? He would find out soon enough.

Wilson was there when Tom arrived. Tom stared at the trailer's remains, as he climbed out of his truck.

Wilson approached, "Morning, Padgett. Sorry about your loss."

Tom said nothing, he wasn't functioning very well. He still had a pounding headache. "Any idea about how it started?"

"The inspector thinks it was an accident. He believes a portable electric heater turned over. That was what caught the bedding on fire, and then it spread from there. Sorry about your dog, Padgett." Tom opened the truck door and Bella jumped out.

Wilson was shocked, "You mean you took your dog with you?"

"Of course I did. I've been gone all weekend."

"Oh, I didn't know that."

Tom walked the perimeter of the trailer as Wilson followed.

"Wilson, you told me that the inspector believed the heater started the fire? He said it was turned over. Does he have an idea how the heater turned itself over?"

Wilson considered that. "I don't know about that, Padgett. Did do you have anything in there that was worth stealing?" Tom realized Wilson meant nothing by the insensitive remark. He said nothing.

Wilson's phone rang, "Yeah, uh huh, you don't say. I'm down the road. I'll be there in a few minutes." He disconnected, "You might be in luck, Padgett. There's another trailer up the road a bit. Last night, it was burglarized."

Lonnie Eldridge slept well. He had had a successful night. He had three-hundred bucks in his pocket from his little thieving spree. He could easily get rid of the things he had stolen. However, the guns might be difficult. He emptied the contents of the stolen gas can into his truck. *That's an added bonus, go on a thieving spree and even get gas for your trouble.* First thing Monday morning he planned to drive down to Morehead. There was a pawn shop there that treated him alright. He would hang on to the guns for a bit, just in case. Guns got the attention of law enforcement. He would bide his time.

Tom followed Wilson at a distance until he saw him pull from the road and stop. Tom now knew the location of the other robbery, so he turned around. Back home, he pulled into his driveway. He would do his own investigation. Wilson had no intention of pursuing Tom's accidental fire any further. Tom would have to do the investigating himself. Tom remembered something from his childhood, something his father always said. *If you want something done right, do it yourself.* As Tom looked at his ruined home, he knew that his father had been right.

Wilson studied the back door of the trailer. It had been jimmied. *Looks like a crow bar was used.* Leland took notes as Wilson wandered around the trailer. The owner had claimed that a hand gun and a couple hundred in cash had been stolen. Wilson glanced about the trailer again. He seriously doubted there had been two-hundred dollars in a shoe box. People always inflate the amount of money taken in robberies. The handgun though, a thirty-eight, now that was a hot item. Wilson was sure the gun would turn up at a pawn shop; maybe not right away, but eventually, it would turn up.

He checked what remained of the back door frame. Tom could see that it had been pried open. Inside the charred trailer

86

remains, he saw no trace of his shotgun. His bow and his chainsaw were also missing. He was sure that the thief would have taken his cash and binoculars. There was no melted plastic, where the table frame lay, so his laptop was gone. He examined the charred space heater. It laid face down a few feet from where he remembered it being. Tom figured the thief must have gotten spooked. He must have left in a hurry and tripped on the heater as he hurried out.

What could have made a robber panic, scare him enough to trip over the heater? Tom bent down; he found the remains of something. *Son of a bitch*, he exclaimed, as he studied what remained of his ruined badge. That was the driving force which caused the thief's quick exit. Tom stuck his head into the gutted bathroom. The cracked mirror was there, and surprisingly it hadn't sustained any additional damage. It appeared to be the only thing in the trailer that wasn't ruined. That old cracked mirror had been left when he moved in. He might have to keep it. Maybe it'd bring good luck.

Wilson finished his investigation and was ready to return to Carlisle. The owner had no other information about the handgun; no serial number, no record of ownership. It seemed the gun had been given to him by his father years ago. Wilson was frustrated. *So what, I have some knowledge, a thirty-eight caliber Colt single action revolver had been stolen. How many of those damned guns were in the county, anyway?* He climbed into his cab and turned back the way he'd come. He slowed as he passed Padgett's driveway. He almost came to a stop. *Hell, maybe Padgett was robbed, too?* He reconsidered. *So what? Padgett probably deserved it.* Wilson accelerated quickly, away from Padgett's place.

Tom was in the back yard. There were empty beer cans lying on the ground. *Looks like the son of a bitch helped himself to my beer.* Tom could feel that he was getting angry. He was going to find the thieving loser. He checked the ground where he believed the thief may have parked. Sure enough, there were tire tracks. One tire had decent tread, the other was nearly bald. Tom was positive the tracks were from the thief's vehicle. The fire department would never have trucks with bald tires. The thief pulled way up here, next to the trailer. That allowed him to remain hidden from the security light.

Tom called Nick and told him about his situation. Nick was more than happy to put him up for a while. *How would it be to live with Nick for an extended period? Staying over one night was fine, but this could easily turn into weeks, perhaps months.* Tom looked back at the ruined trailer. It hadn't dawned on him yet, the severity of what had happened. He was surprised as he realized that both wheelchair ramps were unscathed. He looked around the yard. At least the thief hadn't taken his firewood. Tom tried to remember the amount of insurance he had taken out on the place.

Nick smiled as he disconnected the phone. That was an unexpected surprise. Nick was truly sorry for Tom's loss, but the fact that Tom would be staying with him for a while was good. Nick walked into the guest bedroom to see if anything needed attention. Tom had spent the night on one previous occasion. That night, like many, was because they'd both drunk too much. This time, it was going to be different. It would be like they were actually roommates. Maybe this would end up being a blessing in disguise. Nick was pleased. He thought the room looked good. He walked to the kitchen. He needed to do a few days worth of dishes.

Tom rapped on the trailer door and it opened quickly. A man of perhaps thirty-five stared at him. He asked what Tom wanted. Tom introduced himself, and then explained their shared interest. Tom told him that he had also been robbed, and he believed that they were robbed by the same person. The man said his name was Bill. Tom asked if he could take a look at the door where the thief had entered. Bill hesitantly agreed and then led Tom around back. Tom looked at the door's frame. He noticed that the pry marks were the same as those at his house. Tom moved to the driveway and found tire tracks. One of the tracks had decent tread while the other didn't. Tom removed a tape measure from his pocket and measured the distance between the tire tracks.

Bill watched as Tom took the measurements. "The Sheriff was just here. He didn't do any of that measuring stuff."

"Bill, the Sheriff is new, he's still trying to learn how to do his job. I was in law enforcement for thirty years. Let's assume that I have more experience. Do you mind if I ask you what was stolen?"

"He took some money and a gun my dad gave me."

"He took money from me, too, plus a bunch of other stuff. But what I'm pissed about is that the asshole knocked over a space heater, which caused a fire. My trailer was destroyed, along with almost everything I owned."

"I'm really sorry to hear that."

Wilson was glad to be home. He never had liked to work on weekends. He had worked Saturday night and Sunday morning helping Padgett. That wasn't something he cared to do, anyway. He opened the door of the liquor cabinet. He smiled as he pulled out the bottle of Jim Beam. He was glad he was taking tomorrow off. He hoped his search would turn out to be worthwhile. He poured a generous amount of whiskey into a glass, and then carried it out onto the back porch. He thought about Padgett's bad luck, and it was so damned close to Christmas. Wilson grinned. *Merry Christmas, Padgett.*

Nick opened the door; naturally, he was smiling. "Come on in, Tom, and you too, Bella. You know where the bedroom is. Go ahead and make yourself at home."

Tom thought he had had his fill of beer the previous evening, but he was ready for one. "You wouldn't happen to have a cold beer in the fridge, would you?"

Nick was way ahead of him. He handed Tom a Bud Lite. "I'm sorry about your loss, Tom. Do you have any idea what happened?"

"I've got a pretty good idea. I was robbed, and I believe for some reason, the thief panicked and knocked over a portable heater. That is what started the fire."

"Does the Sheriff think he'll be able to come up with anything?"

"The Sheriff is not going to waste his time. Wilson is going to pretend the fire was accidental."

"What makes you believe it wasn't accidental?"

"The crow bar marks on the door, and the things that were stolen. It's pretty hard to deny, but Wilson isn't interested in helping me. It wouldn't surprise me if he didn't try to somehow, lay the blame on me."

"Why would he want to do that?"

"I don't know. Actually I have no idea."

Wilson planned to enjoy the rest of his afternoon. It was nearly 50 degrees and the sun was shining. Wilson thought about something his father used to say. Whenever it was warm in the winter, he would say something about an Indian summer. He watched as his nosy neighbor stepped out onto her porch and then turned her head in his direction. She saw the whiskey bottle on the table and the glass in Wilson's hand. But for once, she said nothing. Wilson had nothing to say to her, either. He sipped from his glass and he enjoyed the afternoon. He had big plans for the week ahead. He was anxious to get out of Carlisle. It would be nice to leave Nicholas County for the day, also. He hoped that nothing happened in his absence.

CHAPTER 10

Monday Morning

It was only 4:30 when Tom woke up. He might as well stay in bed. Bella was sleeping soundly. He listened to her steady snoring. He had yet to consider all the implications of what had happened, and what in his life had changed. Lying in the guest bedroom at Nick's gave him time to do just that. He had lost everything; not that he had a great number of possessions. Still, they had taken him a lifetime to accumulate. It dawned on him that he had lost all his photos. All those memories from his childhood were gone. Darlene had a digital camera, but he hadn't taken any photos for years. That shoebox that burned held a lifetime of pictures, mostly from his childhood.

Tom had not seen his sisters in years. Before he got married, he and his siblings used to get together often, but that was years ago. Their parents died in a car accident twenty-five years ago. The accident happened near Stanford, Kentucky, soon after he and Darlene were married. Fortunately, his sisters managed to make time for their parents' funeral. However, since that day, neither of his sisters wanted anything to do with him. Could Darlene have been part of the problem that caused his family to drift apart? Probably not; Tom hadn't received a return phone call from either of his sisters in over a year, so he had nearly given up calling them.

Today, Tom was going to meet with Farm Bureau Insurance to get that process started. He realized he had almost nothing; no clothes, no dog food. He was lucky to have an extra toothbrush. He had plenty to do. He was going to meet the insurance adjuster first thing this morning. While the adjuster did what he needed to do, Tom could poke around inside the trailer to see if anything could be salvaged. He disgustedly remembered the deer meat that he had stored in the freezer. It was for his neighbors, the Burnetts. They definitely could have used it. Realizing they wouldn't get the venison he had promised them made him even angrier. Tom was going to find who did this.

Wilson enjoyed a cup of coffee. It felt good to know that he wasn't going to the office today. Maybe he'd get an early start for his trip to Mt. Sterling. He might as well wait and eat breakfast down there. Wilson showered and got dressed. He was going to be casual today. That would feel good. No uniform, no gun, no hat. On second thought, maybe he'd wear his ball cap, the one that was embroidered with Sheriff. He stepped out of the front door and out of habit glanced over at the nosy neighbor's. Damn, there she was, glaring at him. One day, he hoped to learn what her problem was.

Lonnie was on his way to the pawn shop in Morehead. He had stored the stolen guns. They were hidden in the old milk house in his parents' barn. His dad didn't have cows anymore, so he had no reason to go in there. He didn't want to have the guns in his possession, just in case the Sheriff came to snoop around. He whistled a tune as he drove down Route 32. He was happy to be in and out of the pawn shop in less than an hour. He'd done well on many of the items, and less so on some of the others. But, that was the nature of dealing at pawn shops. Besides, he had little to complain about; none of the shit was his anyway.

Tom searched through the remains of what had been his home. There was little to salvage. The fire had been effective. If the fire department had been closer, the end result would probably have been the same. Tom recalled that he had wrestled with the idea about whether or not to buy insurance. He was glad that he made the right choice. The bedroom where the heater was located was the most gutted room in the trailer. He stepped into the bathroom and pulled the cracked mirror from the wall. He studied the mirror. *Had it been in a fire before?* Tom heard a car pull in.

The insurance agent got out of his car and introduced himself. "Mr. Padgett, I'm Denny Earlywine."

"Nice to meet you, Denny."

"Wow, looks like you've lost about everything, I'm sure sorry about that."

"Yeah, that makes two of us."

"Mr. Padgett, I'm sure you have plenty to do. I wanted to let you know that it's not necessary for you to hang around, unless you really want to."

"I'll look around a bit more to see if there's anything else I might be able to save."   "Sure thing, but, just to put you at ease, Mr. Padgett, we'll process this claim quickly. By the way, do you need temporary accommodations?"

"No, I'm staying with a friend. I'd really appreciate that fast settlement though. I've got rebuilding to do."

Wilson saw a McDonald's and decided an Egg McMuffin or two might hit the spot. As he turned into the lot, the sight of three police cruisers at Jerry's caused Wilson to change his mind. Some of the city's finest were having breakfast. He entered Jerry's and found three officers from the Mt. Sterling Police Department there, having coffee. Wilson sat at a table nearby and ordered. He could tell, based on their conversation that they were getting ready to leave. Wilson didn't want to miss this opportunity.

He stood up, "Excuse me, gentlemen. I'm Sheriff Bill Wilson from Nicholas County. I wonder if I could impose on you all for a moment."

The officers stared at Wilson, so he continued. "I'm looking for some information on a former officer in your department. He is retired now, and he now lives in Nicholas County. His name is, Padgett. Are you familiar with Tom Padgett?"

They nodded in unison. One officer answered for the group, "Yes, of course we are. What would you like to know?"

Naturally, Wilson liked the sound of this. Cooperation, yes that was what was needed. He had had far too little of that lately, especially within the law enforcement community. "I'm trying to learn about his time on the force. Most importantly, I'm trying to find out why he left the force? And, why he elected to tell folks in Nicholas County that he was only a retired cop. He failed to mention anything about his position as Chief."

Now the officers looked uncomfortable. The spokesman volunteered, "It might be best if you speak with the Chief, John Stamper. Talk with him and see if he's willing to answer your questions."

Wilson said thanks and the officers headed for the door.

Tom rolled up Route 68. He needed to get supplies at Walmart. He toyed with an idea as he made a left turn. He had driven past the metal sales operation on several occasions. Finally, he had a reason to stop. The shop was apparently Amish- owned and sold metal roofing. Tom was curious. *Do they build barns?* He entered and found two men inside, talking. Tom nodded and stepped to the counter.

The men stopped their conversation, and one of them asked, "Can I help you?"

Tom thought that was an understatement, but kept it to himself. "Yes sir, I believe you can. My name is Tom Padgett and I need help, a lot of it."

The owner of the establishment was August Schmidt. He listened to Tom as he explained his situation. When Tom finished, August repeated what he wanted. "You want a four-horse metal pole barn, with a workshop in the middle, and two of the stalls you'd like to be framed out, so they can be converted into living quarters. Also, you want a concrete pad poured. Does that sound about right?"

"That's what I have in mind, and the size I'm thinking, is twenty-four by forty-eight feet. Oh, I nearly forgot. I'd also like to have a loft above the workshop."

"A loft above the workshop, that changes it a bit. It requires a different roof structure, which is no problem."

"Will it be possible to get it built before winter sets in?"

"Winter, yes. Its coming, sometimes it's mild, sometimes it's not. Luckily, this year has been mild. The ground isn't frozen yet. We could start right away if you want, Mr. Padgett."

"August, I haven't received my insurance settlement yet. You might need to wait a few days."

"Mr. Padgett, you look like a man of his word. The longer we wait, the more difficult the weather becomes. And, you need a place to live now, isn't that so?"

Wilson watched out the window, as two of the cruisers pulled onto the main drag. He chewed on an egg. *Damn, if only they'd had something to offer.* As he dabbed some egg yolk onto his bread, he heard someone clear his throat.

"Excuse me, Sheriff." One of the patrolmen moved next to the table.

"What is it, Officer?"

"Sheriff, I didn't want to say anything in the company of my fellow officers. You know how those things are?" Wilson didn't really, but he feigned understanding.

"Sheriff, I don't know about Padgett's past, except for the rumors. My suggestion would be to talk with his ex-wife."

"I intend to do that, but finding her might prove difficult."

The officer offered a grin, "Sheriff, it may not be as difficult as you imagine."

95

"Why is that?"

"My girlfriend works downtown at a tanning shop called, *All Seasons Tanning Salon.*"

"So, what's that got to do with finding Padgett's ex?"

Again the officer grinned, "From what I gather, Ms. Padgett comes into the tanning salon almost every day, like clockwork."

Now Wilson smiled, "Do you happen to know what time?"

Darlene slept in late on Monday. She still hadn't gotten over being angry. She was furious at both Tom and Bud. She was absolutely disgusted with Tom; the way he'd been dancing with that slutty little drunk girl. That was so embarrassing. And then he made those accusations about her, openly calling her a whore. Making matters worse, Bud further embarrassed her by failing to stand up for her, he was pitiful. Yesterday, she had allowed Bud to sleep in while she ate breakfast alone, at the hotel. They'd argued on the trip home, the entire way, from Lexington to Mt. Sterling. Today, she had no intention of returning Bud's calls.

Bud left for work early. Darlene pretended that she was sleeping as he dressed. They had lived together for three months. Sometimes, she wondered if it was worth it. *Yes, he takes care of many of my bills. But sometimes, he's such a disappointment. Tom made them both look like fools.* She felt depressed. She should be happy because Andy was married. She finally had a daughter. But, Darlene wasn't happy. Things hadn't turned out like she'd planned. She needed something - a boost to lift her spirits and to help get her out of her funk. A trip to the tanning salon should help. She hadn't been there in three days.

Walking the aisles of Walmart could nearly make Tom crazy. Finally, he was finished. He met Nick for coffee in the cafeteria. Nick asked him if he wanted to go to O'Rourke's or to the

Gyp. Tom had to decline. There were too many things that needed to be finished. Tom had to get the trailer remains hauled off, and he needed to locate the electric, plumbing and septic lines. He had much to do.

Nick looked confused. "Tom, you don't have to kill yourself by trying to get everything finished. You can stay with me as long as you need."

"Believe me; I won't be moving anytime soon. By the time I move, you'll be tired of Bella and me."

"Oh, I don't know about that. I've lived alone for eleven or twelve years. Visitors are always welcome. Not that I'm lonely or anything like that."

"Nick, I've got to run, I'll see you later."

Wilson stood at the counter of the tanning salon. It was 10:30. He glanced around at the women in the place wondering which one was Mrs. Padgett.

A young girl approached, "Are you interested in tanning, sir?"

Wilson displayed a practiced smile, "No, young lady. Actually, I'm looking for someone. I understand that a lady named Mrs. Padgett comes in to use your tanning beds quite often. Could you tell me, is she here now?"

"No, she's not, but she usually comes in about this time."

"Would you mind if I wait here in the lobby? And, when she comes in, if you would you be kind enough to point her out to me."

"I guess that would be alright."

Wilson sat down and perused an issue of *Cosmopolitan*. He hadn't seen one of these magazines in a while. *Man, these women are skinnier than the ones back in Carlisle.*

Wilson was closely examining a picture of a rather busty model when the receptionist interrupted, "Sir, that's Mrs. Padgett, she's getting out of her car."

Wilson looked over his shoulder and then laid the magazine on the table and stepped to the door. "Thank you, young lady."

Darlene locked her car door and turned toward the salon.

"Mrs. Padgett, could I have a few words with you?"

Darlene looked at Wilson. She was puzzled. "Do I know you?"

"No, ma'am. I'm Sheriff Bill Wilson from Nicholas County. I'd like to ask you some questions about your ex-husband."

"Sheriff Wilson, what questions could you possibly have for me? Is Tom alright?"

"Yes, ma'am, he's fine. I was hoping to get a better understanding of the man. I have some unanswered questions that keep nagging at me. I'd be willing to buy you lunch."

"I'm late for my appointment." Darlene paused for a moment, "Actually, now that you mention it, I am sort of hungry, and thirsty. If you can wait for me, my tanning session won't take long."

Tom could have kicked himself. He forgot about the trailer shell and the wheelchair ramps that needed to be removed. He was sure that he'd find no phone number for August. Tom remembered reading that the Amish only had communal phones, which were only used for emergencies.

He entered the shop and found August. He was busy unloading some roofing. "August, I'm sorry to bother you. There's something I forgot to mention. The remains of the trailer and a pair of wheelchair ramps also need to be removed."

"Mr. Padgett, if you'd like, I'll see to all these things. I'll do everything necessary to get your property ready to build on. I have many, many connections. Even in the Amish community, I can be very resourceful."

Tom appreciated this. He turned and was about to leave, when August called, "Mr. Padgett, if you like, I can act as your general contractor."

"Yes, that would be great. Thanks, August."

A few minutes after eleven, Darlene exited the All Seasons Tanning Salon. To Wilson, she looked at least one shade darker. *Why does she need to be any darker? Right now, she could rival a coal miner after a day in the hole.* Wilson asked if there was any place in particular that she liked to eat?

"There is, follow me. I have a soft spot for Applebee's." After arriving, Wilson opened the door, and Darlene made her way inside. The hostess asked if they needed a table for two.

Darlene didn't wait for Wilson's response, "Yes, in the bar, please."

Wilson was going to enjoy this. He'd buy her a couple of drinks to loosen her up, and in no time he would have the goods on Padgett. Darlene ordered a margarita, Wilson decided on a draft beer. He didn't want to get into trouble, not in Montgomery County.

Darlene took an enormous swallow and immediately released a satisfied sigh. "So, Sheriff Wilson, what is it you hope to learn about my ex-husband? Tom hasn't done anything wrong has he?"

Wilson imagined, *if she was ten years younger...* He snapped to attention after hearing her question. "I need to clear up some things about your husband's past, back when he was working at the Police Department."

"Ex-husband. Let's try to keep that straight."

"Yes ma'am, I'll remember that." Wilson hoped that the chastising wasn't about to begin. It seemed as if most women had been chastising him lately.

"Let's start over again, what do you want to know about Tom?"

"I'm curious, why would he retire from the department as Chief, and then tell people in Nicholas County he'd only been a policeman? Why not mention he'd been Chief?"

"There's plenty of mystery that surrounds Tom Padgett." She lifted her glass for the bartender to see. "Anyway, why Tom would want to live a lie, I have no idea. But, I know some much more interesting things about his past, secrets that only I and his friend John Stamper have knowledge of. I assume you know Chief Stamper?"

Wilson nodded. He loved where this was heading and held his glass up for the bartender to see. "Do you care for something to eat?"

"Not just yet, Sheriff. Having a drink and talking about dirt feels quite satisfying. Oh, how much time do you have? This could take a while."

Tom quickly drove to Flemingsburg. He wanted to get his groceries in the fridge. He and Bella were going out to the trailer, to have one last look around. Bella was glad to be out of Nick's back yard. The fenced in yard must have reminded her of her confinement period, when they lived in Mt. Sterling. That was a painful period for both of them. Bella was in the back of the crew cab. She had her paws on the armrest and her head hung out the window as they rolled along. Tom pulled into his lot and stopped. He studied the remains. He was surprised his little garden shed hadn't been damaged. He pulled a lawn chair from the shed and sat

100

down, facing the remains.

He needed to get a mental picture of exactly how he wanted the house to be situated. Bella began to wander. She sniffed contentedly near the edge of the woods. Back to the barn, Tom's plans called for two exterior barn doors. It was going to be a drive-through. He only wanted one door that entered the living quarters and another that exited it, out into the workshop. The two horse stalls would have rolling doors, which allowed entrance from the workshop only. Presently, he didn't have plans for horses, but why not be prepared? His live-in barn would definitely be an improvement over the trailer. Tom hoped his insurance settlement would be enough. He didn't want to dig into his savings. He was still feeling the effects from the rehearsal dinner.

Tom's phone vibrated. "Hello,...hey how you doing?... Is that right?... Red huh? And they were sure it was a Chevrolet S-10?... Well, thanks for calling, Bill. I'll keep you posted. Wait a second, you guys haven't had any more trouble have you?... That's good. Have you heard anything back from the Sheriff?... Uh huh, that's sounds about right. I'll see what I can find out, and I'll give you a call."

Tom hung up. One of Bill's neighbors had noticed a truck parked in Bill's drive the night he'd been robbed. The neighbor was positive it was an older Chevy S-10. The width of the tire tracks that Tom had measured would verify that. An old S-10 with a red camper shell; that should make it easier to find.

CHAPTER 11

Wilson intently listened as Darlene prattled on. She seemed almost desperate to create some sort of hardship for her ex. The information was better than Wilson expected. He learned how Padgett's partner, Cole, had been killed, all those years ago. He also heard about the lengthy investigation into the shooting. Personally, he couldn't blame Padgett for his reaction. He thought that under the circumstances, Padgett's actions were perfectly legitimate. If he were in Padgett's shoes, he would have done the same thing. Was Padgett's ex holding something back? Was there something she was afraid to get into?

"Mrs. Padgett, all that happened so long ago. That can't be the reason he left the force. There has to be something else."

"Of course there was, Sheriff. He left because of the Mayor, Bud Blankenship. He was the man that forced Tom out. He made his job situation unbearable. Tom couldn't stand the desk job he was forced to take, so he resigned."

"How would the Mayor know what it would take to force Padgett out?"

Darlene sneered, "Sheriff, Bud and I were having an affair. Bud was sleeping with the Chief's wife. He knew many things about Tom Padgett."

"So you advised the Mayor about which buttons to push?"

"Exactly, it was truly one of my finest moments."

Tom hesitantly, passed the Gyp Joint. Unfortunately, he

102

didn't have time to stop. He turned left on Route 32 and headed to Nick's. As he and Bella entered the kitchen, they found Nick at the table, nursing a beer.

Tom yelled, "Honey, I'm home." Naturally, that got a grin out of Nick. Tom grabbed a beer and sat opposite his friend. "How was good old Walmart today?"

"It was kind of slow, actually. Not many shoplifters. It was almost boring."

"Nick, I have a hard time picturing you as a store detective. How's it going?"

"It's ok. I don't believe I'm detective material, either, but I did get a thirty-cent raise."

"Great, let's see, thirty-cents at sixteen hours, that's nearly five bucks a week."

"No, it's better than that. I picked up another day, so that's twenty-four hours, which comes in at seven bucks and change."

"Hell that calls for a celebration. I'll get a couple beers."

"Did you hear anything on the fire, anything from the Sheriff?"

"Nothing from Wilson, but, it's what I expected. I did get a call from a neighbor up the road. We were both robbed the same night. He gave me a lead on a truck that was seen parked in his drive the night he was robbed."

"Did he notify the Sheriff?"

"I'm not sure if he did or not."

"Are you going to call the Sheriff and report what you learned?"

"No, I know if I told Wilson anything, it would be a waste of time. I'm going to check around and ask some questions. I should be able to find the truck and its owner."

"Are you sure you should get involved, Tom? You're not a cop anymore."

"I know. Sometimes, you just have to take care of things yourself."

Darlene finished her third margarita as Wilson chugged the rest of his beer. He was afraid he might lose her, as she motioned for another round.

"Do you really believe that putting Padgett in a desk job he didn't want would make him retire?"

"I asked Tom for a divorce at the same time. We double teamed the man. He was ready to get the hell out. Tom had no ties to Mt. Sterling. He had no reason to stay."

Wilson was beginning to feel the effects of the beer. "But, to move to Nicholas County and not tell anyone that he was the former Chief of Police, doesn't make sense. Why would he do that?"

"Like I told you, Sheriff. Why Tom Padgett does some of the things he does was always a mystery. Why he wanted to be anonymous in your county is anyone's guess. There's one other thing." Darlene closed her eyes as she considered something.

After several seconds, Wilson was worried that she might be falling asleep. "What's that, Mrs. Padgett?"

"The investigation, maybe. Tom didn't want any dirt dug up about the investigation. Yes, that could be the reason."

"You've lost me. Internal investigations are never fun. Why wouldn't he want to forget it? He did nothing wrong, it's just procedural bullshit, looking into shootings."

"No, you're wrong. There was an extended investigation into Tom. It was much more than just procedural. The psychological extent of the investigation was what was unusual."

"Mrs. Padgett, I have no actual experience in those proceedings. I believe that the psychological part of the evaluation is standard procedure after a shooting."

"Sheriff, the primary psychiatrist that analyzed Tom believed Tom suffered from MPD; that is multiple personality disorder. He believed Tom has more than one person inside his head."

Wilson's heart skipped several beats, "Would you happen to remember the doctor's name?"

"Of course I would, it's Dr. Sharma, and his practice is in Lexington. That was years ago though. He's probably retired; he might even be dead."

"Thank you, Mrs. Padgett. Are you sure you wouldn't like something to eat?"

"No, I feel great. Suddenly, I'm not the least bit hungry."

Lonnie Eldridge stopped by Ladobee's for a drink. The bar was opposite Lake Carnico on Route 68, probably four miles from Carlisle, and only ten minutes from his trailer, which was good. Lonnie was bellied up to the bar when Mike Underwood came in. Mike pulled up a stool and ordered a beer.

Lonnie turned, "Hey, Mike, have you been turning anybody else's ass into the Sheriff lately? Did you get a reward for turning my ass in?"

"What are you talking about, Lonnie? I didn't turn nobody's ass in."

"Then how the hell did the Sheriff and his Deputy know to come knocking on my door? Especially, since you were the only one I mentioned that burned barn to?"

"I went to get the metal you told me bout and the Deputy showed up, he 'musta called the Sheriff. The Sheriff asked me who said I could take the metal. I told him it was the owner. How was I 'sposed to know he'd call Jackson? Anyway, I only told him your first name, he 'musta found out from somebody else."

Lonnie let this sink in. "So, you didn't start blabbing that I was running around starting fires, huh?"

"No I 'didt say 'nuttin bout no fire."

Lonnie ordered a couple more beers. "Mike, it's no big deal. The Sheriff doesn't have shit on me. I didn't start any fires. I don't do shit like that."

Mike looked down at his beer, as if in deep thought. "Ya know, there's been a lot of fires lately. Don't that seem weird? I heard 'somethin bout one on Saturday night over off Abners Mill."

"Oh yeah? Whereabouts, on Abners Mill?"

"I dunno, maybe a mile or two past the water plant. It was another trailer."

Lonnie had nothing else to say. He considered the statement he'd just made, the one about not starting fires. He was thinking about one of the trailers he'd broken into, the one where he'd found the badge. He remembered knocking over the heater as he ran from the trailer.

Wilson was a happy man. He felt as if he had conquered the world. He was finally going to get Padgett and nail the bastard's ass to the cross. He knew Padgett was dirty. He knew that was the only reason he hung out in Nicholas County. Now, all Wilson had to do was prove it. So, Padgett did have something to hide. He had a huge something to hide. He had some kind of split personality. Padgett was a damned nut. Wilson had to correct his truck as his tire slipped over the shoulder. *Steady. Don't do anything stupid, especially when I'm so close to home, and so close to busting Padgett.*

As he neared Carlisle, Wilson relaxed. Nothing would

happen to him here, this was his county. He was the law in Nicholas County, and he was going to make sure justice was served. But not tonight, he had celebrating to do. He was beginning to sober up, he would fix that problem. No more sissy-ass beer for Bill Wilson, not this evening, the Jim Beam was coming out. He was even going to take another day off tomorrow. He would go to Lexington to find that shrink. Dr. Sharma, another damned foreigner.

For once, that didn't matter. If the shrink could help him bust Padgett and bring the man to his knees, that would be fine, no matter what country he was from.

Tom and Nick carried on until well into the evening. Nick was glad Tom was staying with him, and that it would be some time before Tom's house was finished. Bella lay stretched out beneath them on the floor as they talked. Tom was preoccupied while Nick rambled on about something that happened at Walmart. Tom thought about the vehicle's description he had received. Tomorrow, he would scour the area and find it. He knew the truck's tread pattern, one tire had tread and the other didn't. He could easily ID the truck.

Nick invaded his thoughts, "You're not seriously considering looking for the guy that robbed you?"

"Yes, I am. You remember what I said about taking care of things yourself? I don't believe Wilson's up to the task."

"But, he was elected to that position. What makes you think he's not capable?"

"Nick, elected officials initially may or may not be qualified to do their jobs. But, after enough time, they usually learn them, the gist of them anyway. Sometimes they learn the hard way. Wilson hasn't learned much since he's been Sheriff. He has spent too much time worrying about me and not enough time honing his skills as Sheriff."

"But, if you interfere with his investigation, how is he

supposed to learn?"

"I have no intention of interfering with Wilson's investigation. I don't know how to convince you of that. I'm sure Wilson is doing little investigating. I can almost guarantee you that he's concentrating on one thing, and that's me. I don't know why that is, but, that's the way the guy works."

"Maybe you two should sit down and talk. Maybe then, you would have a better understanding of one another."

Tom laughed and got two more beers. "Wishful thinking, wishful thinking."

After Lonnie left Ladobee's, he had every intention of going home, but halfway home, he had a change of plans. He took a right turn on Old Maysville Road and another on Abners Mill. Lonnie wanted to be sure. He needed to clear his conscious. It was dark that evening, the moon was barely visible. Lonnie couldn't see a thing as he stared through the darkness and up the drive. He slowly pulled into the driveway in an attempt to shine his headlights on the trailer. He had to pull in quite a way before his beams hit the structure. *Damn, I can't believe it. Underwood was right, the trailer is totally gutted. That's why the security light isn't working.*

He sat in his truck and looked at the remains, he needed to think. *I really should get the hell out of here. What if the cop comes home? Home to what? Why would he come here tonight? Why would he ever come here again?* Lonnie backed into the grass to turn his truck around. He slowly crossed the ditch and drove back the way he'd come. He tried to convince himself that he wasn't responsible for the fire. *I robbed the place, that's all. That heater couldn't have caused the fire. Maybe it was the arsonist. Who am I kidding? What are the chances of an arsonist setting fire to the trailer, the same night that I robbed it? Probably not much,* he realized.

Wilson stepped into the night air, it was comfortable out. Maybe he would move outside. He picked up the bottle and carried it with him to the back yard. He walked in the grass as he drank his Jim Beam. *Soon, it will be spring again. Spring, what a great time of year. Why do I think spring is just around the corner? It's December, winter has just begun.* Wilson's thoughts were jumbled. *Is it the whiskey, or the excitement of getting Padgett?* He didn't care. He was looking forward to tomorrow.

Suddenly, a thought came to him. *What if I did bust Padgett? Who would I have to pursue then?* The more he thought about it, the more he realized, *I enjoy dogging Padgett. If Padgett is found guilty and locked up, I'll have to find someone to replace him. Someone I hate the same way I hate Padgett, just to keep life interesting.* Wilson was sure that Padgett felt the same way about him, but things couldn't continue the way they were. *In life there are winners and losers.* Wilson sipped his whiskey and thought of winning. *It's inevitable. I'm going to win, and Padgett is going to lose.*

CHAPTER 12

The Following Morning

Tom went to his home site. He had some recommendations about the demolition for August. He pulled into the drive and climbed from his truck, parked away from the work area, and walked toward the remains. Bella was out running. This morning, she was wild. She behaved like she had been in captivity for years. Tom glanced down at his feet and noticed fresh tire tracks. They were the same ones that were here the night of the fire. He followed the tracks up the drive until they stopped. The vehicle turned around at this point. *Why would anyone in their right mind come back to visit the scene of the crime?*

He listened as trucks approached. Tom needed to verify a couple things before he turned the job over to August. Today, the crew would concentrate on the removal of the trailer and wheelchair ramps. They would need to locate the water, the electric, and the sewage lines. After Tom talked with August, he climbed back into his truck. *Why would the person most likely responsible for burning my trailer return? It doesn't make sense. Does he want to get caught? Was the guy emboldened because he felt the Sheriff was inept? Maybe, I know that's true.*

Lonnie had hardly slept, which was unusual. Normally, he had no problem sleeping. But, what he learned last night really bothered him; that he had destroyed a person's home. Especially, since that old trailer belonged to a lawman. He sat on the sofa as he munched on a bowl of cereal. He was trying to rationalize things. The Sheriff probably wouldn't do anything about the fire. It was in part of the county that he rarely visited. The cop, who lived there, wouldn't bother with him either, because the trailer was a total loss. There was probably little trace that he had been there.

Wilson felt alert this morning. He had behaved himself last night and not drunk too much whiskey, though he had good reason to. He rooted around in the hall closet until he found what he was looking for. It was an old Lexington phone book. He flipped through its pages and found the listing for Dr. Sharma. He figured it was a waste of time to phone ahead. He knew that the direct approach worked best. He made himself some toast and smothered it with butter, and enjoyed it with his morning coffee. Wilson was out the door by 7:30.

He felt good about today's prospects. He was excited about bringing serious issues to bear on Padgett. He hummed as he rolled through Millersburg. As he exited the town, he immediately became frustrated. *Damn, they're still working on Route 68.* The speed limit was forty-five, and a no-passing zone ran all the way to Paris. Of course, there was some slow-driving idiot in front of him, the sort of driver that was content to keep his speed ten miles under the limit. Wilson was no longer in his county, but that wouldn't stop him. He blew past the slow-driving asshole and accelerated back up to a reasonable speed of sixty-five.

Tom watched the crew work for a few minutes. Once he was satisfied, he pulled his truck out onto Abners Mill. He knew that it would difficult to find the truck without a license or a VIN. Fortunately, he had a description, an old Chevy S-10 with a large red camper shell. Today, he planned to follow Abners Mill Road to Route 32, and from there he would turn towards Carlisle. Then, he would work his way around the small roads that led to Route 68. He felt the guy must be a local, they usually were. Crimes like that were usually committed by hoods that were familiar with the area and the people that lived there.

This morning, Tom had already seen two Chevy S-10s. He was considering the possibility that the thief might have removed the camper shell. He immediately forgot the thought after he rounded the next bend. Tom pulled to the side of the road. Up ahead was an S-10 with a red camper shell, parked in front of a trailer. That surprised him. He hadn't expected to find the truck so quickly. He had possibly found his guy, but Tom wasn't sure how to proceed. As he considered his options, a tall skinny man stepped outside. He walked down the steps and then jumped into the truck. Tom quickly formulated a plan. It wasn't elaborate. He slowed to read the mailbox. He would follow him, he would follow Lonnie Eldridge.

Lonnie didn't treat himself to a meal out often. But, the cash that was in his pocket was itchin' to be spent. He paid no attention to the black Ford that was parked on the shoulder of the road. He was anxious to get to town. He was going to the East End. He hadn't eaten there in some time. He loved many of the specials they offered, kind of like Mom's cooking, but without the motherly intrusion. He hoped to run into someone that was interested in buying a shotgun. He couldn't advertise it, but he could ask around, discreetly. There was usually an unsavory character or two hanging about the East End, usually someone hanging out that was looking to make some extra cash.

Wilson had transitioned from humming. The farther away from Carlisle he got, the louder he sang. He was looking forward to talking with Dr. Sharma. He was very excited about what he might learn. He pulled into the parking lot and parked. He studied the sign in front of the office, *Doctor of Neuropsychiatry and General Psychiatry. That sounds impressive. I wish I had some special title or maybe a handle.* He reread the title before it dawned on him. *Wait a minute. The Doctor's name isn't the same. Wasn't Dr. Sharma the man in charge? Did he share space with other Doctors in his office? There's only one way to find out.*

He entered the office and removed his hat, which was unusual. It was something Wilson rarely did. He looked around at the intricate woodwork that covered the walls. *This is very impressive. The doctor must charge plenty.*

112

"May I help you?"

"Why yes, young lady, I surely hope you can. My name is Bill Wilson, and I'm Sheriff of Nicholas County. I hope to talk with a Dr. Sharma. Is he in?"

"I'm sorry; I'm not sure who you're looking for, Sheriff. Did you say Dr. Sharma?"

"Yes ma'am, that's right."

"One moment, I'll be right back."

Wilson looked around the office until she returned.

"Sheriff, I'm sorry, I'm new here and I didn't realize that Dr. Sharma worked here."

"Well, that's quite all right. We're all entitled to a mistake every now and then."

"Dr. Sharma did work here. He sold his practice when he retired five years ago."

Wilson offered a sincere smile, "Would you have a phone number or an address where I might find Dr. Sharma?"

"I'm sorry; I can't give you that information."

Tom was two cars back as he followed Lonnie Eldridge through town. Something occurred to him. *I hope Lonnie isn't going on a road trip.* Lonnie's turn signal blinked and he pulled into the East End parking lot. Tom slowed and watched him walk inside, then parked as he continued to watch. He saw Lonnie sit at a table. Tom was satisfied. It appeared that Lonnie was staying for lunch. Tom needed to be discreet as possible. This might prove difficult, the place was busy. He wandered over to where Lonnie had parked. Unfortunately, there were three men standing nearby, talking. Tom examined the driver side front tire, it had plenty of tread. He intentionally dropped his keys underneath the truck's front end and gave the passenger front tire a look.

Just as he thought, bald as hell. This was the truck. Tom was positive it was the one that was in his drive the night of the fire. Tom had a decision to make. *Am I going to settle the score with the hood, or let Wilson and the legal system deal with him? Where the hell is Wilson, anyway?* Lonnie had probably robbed the other places out on Abners Mill, also. He was undoubtedly responsible for Tom's trailer fire, *and here he sits, relaxing as he enjoys his lunch in the East End.* Tom couldn't imagine what Wilson, the so-called Sheriff of Nicholas County, was up to.

Tom figured it would be a waste of time, but he would stop by the city building to see if Wilson was in. He entered the courthouse at 11:45. The clerk was on the phone, so he waited.

After the clerk hung up she asked, "Can I help you?"

"Yes ma'am, is Sheriff Wilson around?"

"No, the Sheriff took the day off. He had business to attend to in Lexington."

"Will he be in tomorrow?"

"I hope so, but he was supposed to be here today. He called and said he had some sort of emergency, that couldn't wait. He's doing follow up on something that came out of that meeting he had yesterday. The one over in Mt. Sterling."

"Thank you ma'am."

Wilson didn't like to be told he couldn't do something. He didn't like being denied things when he asked for them. Yet, that receptionist had done just that. *No, she can't give me the information I'm seeking.* No reason for him to remain pleasant now. Wilson slammed the door as he left the office. That should let the receptionist know how angry he was. *That receptionist needs to understand that you don't mess with Bill Wilson, especially, when I'm in pursuit of a criminal.* He started his truck and left. He had one more place to go.

Wilson pulled into the lot at the Tates Creek Library and jumped from his truck. He was optimistic that he would be able to get some help here. As he entered, he glanced around the foyer, no phones here. Wilson remembered. *It hasn't been long ago that public phones were everywhere.*

He approached the desk and displayed another of his sincere smiles, "Hello, would you happen to have a Lexington phone book?"

The girl wore a blank look, "Oh, I don't know. I don't know if we have phone books anymore, I'll have to ask someone."

"Thank you."

Wilson looked around the library, there were people everywhere and most of them were working on computers. He didn't have time for that luxury. He was too busy addressing crime in the county.

"Here you go, Sir. It's a couple of years old. I hope it will do."

"Why thank you, young lady."

Wilson flipped through the pages and found listings for three Dr. Sharmas. They were all MDs. *Is a Psychiatrist an MD?* Wilson wasn't sure. Maybe he could use one of the computers and do a search.

He returned the phone book to the librarian, "Could I use a computer, for a bit?"

"Yes, Sir, pick any terminal that's not being used."

Wilson settled in and began his search. Two of the Dr. Sharmas were apparently still practicing. They were both medical doctors. The third Dr. Sharma wasn't advertising. Wilson assumed he was the one. He closed the browser window and headed for the door.

Wilson nodded and smiled at the librarian, then left the building. He checked his watch; time to get something to eat.

Lonnie was in luck. He might have found a buyer for the shotgun he had stolen. It would be good to be rid of it. Especially, since he now knew the owner of the shotgun was a cop. He had the buyer's number and rang him. After he hung up, Lonnie smiled. He made arrangements to meet the guy later, in the Gyp Joint parking lot. The potential buyer seemed pleased with the price that Lonnie quoted. Lonnie was only asking two-hundred dollars. Why wouldn't he be pleased? The gun was worth at least that, maybe more. The Remington was quite a few years old, but it was in excellent shape. Lonnie was in no position to haggle over prices. He needed the damn gun gone.

Tom had a successful day and was on his way to Flemingsburg. Work was underway on the trailer cleanup and he had possibly found the thief that had robbed him. *Yes, I should be feeling good. But, why aren't I?* The last piece of information he had learned about Wilson's whereabouts bothered him. He knew Wilson probably had no business dealings outside Nicholas County, unless there was some county line issue. Nicholas and Montgomery County didn't share a common border, so the possibility of Wilson working with anybody in Montgomery County for any reason, was unlikely.

Tom shook his head. He was frustrated. He had no idea what Wilson was up to. He was damned tired of Wilson's continual harassment. He needed a way to make him stop. There had to be something, something that would force Wilson to focus elsewhere. Tom understood the difficulty with that. For Wilson, to focus on anything other than Tom Padgett was impossible. Wilson had a one-track mind; that was obvious to Tom. Wilson couldn't stop thinking about him. Tom needed to forget about it and stop worrying about Wilson. He rolled to a stop. He was at the intersection of Route 32 and Route 11. He turned left; he was almost home.

Wilson parked on the street and looked at the house. He had no idea there were houses like this in Lexington. It was huge. It had to be four or five times the size of his. He rang the doorbell. Wilson was surprised, the damned thing worked.

A moment later a sharply dressed man answered. "May I help you?"

Wilson wasn't sure, was he a butler? He was suddenly at a loss for words. "Yes, I would like to speak with Dr. Sharma. My name is Bill Wilson. I'm the Sheriff over in Nicholas County."

The man didn't move. He held his ground, and stared coldly at Wilson. "Sir, was Dr. Sharma expecting you?"

"No, I probably should have phoned ahead, but I decided to take a chance. I hoped that I could visit with the Doctor."

Another man came to the door.

"What is it, Alfred? Who is this man?"

"Sir, his name is Wilson, and he claims to be Sheriff of Nicholas County."

Dr. Sharma asked, "What might I be able to assist you with, Sheriff?"

"Dr. Sharma, I have some questions about a previous client or patient of yours."

"Sheriff, I've had thousands of patients over my thirty-plus-year career. How would you expect me to remember a particular patient? Besides, even if I did remember, I have an obligation to doctor-patient confidentiality."

"Maybe after you hear his name it will help. Help you decide whether or not to help me."

"I doubt that Sheriff, but if you insist, who is it?"

"Doctor, does the name Tom Padgett, ring any bells?"

Dr. Sharma was certain his expression betrayed him. He thought he would never hear that name again. He stepped aside, and opened the door.

"Come in, Sheriff."

Bella had been in the back yard all day. She was excited when Tom unlatched the gate and attached her lead. Living in Flemingsburg wasn't the same for Bella. She had to be on a leash. She hated being restrained. There was a field nearby; that's where they were headed. Tom undid her leash as they reached the field. Bella ran and ran. Tom slowly followed along as he watched her run. She was thoroughly enjoying herself. He had nearly forgotten the phone call he was supposed to make. He wasn't sure why he agreed to do his son's dirty work. He really dreaded calling Darlene.

She answered after several rings. She obviously knew it was him.

She snapped, "Yeah, what do you want?"

Tom paused. *How do I remain civil with that?* "Darlene, I called to give you a message. It's from your son."

"What message would Andy give you that he wouldn't have already given me?"

"That's a good point; normally none. But believe it or not, he has given me one to give to you. It's not sweet, so I'll keep it short. Nancy is pregnant."

For a moment, Darlene was silent, "They just got married. She can't be pregnant."

"I'm just the messenger. But, before I hang up, I have another request from your son and new daughter-in-law. They would like you to inform Nancy's parents about the situation.

118

They're afraid to tell them. They passed that responsibility to me, now I'm handing it over to you. They're hoping to have all that drama behind them, when they return from their honeymoon. Talk to you later."

"Wait a second, Tom? Before you go, there's something you might like to know, I assume you know Sheriff Wilson?"

Tom sure as hell didn't like the sound of this, "Yeah, what about him?"

"He visited Mt. Sterling yesterday, and he was asking a lot of questions about you. Naturally, I tried to be helpful, you know, co-operating with law enforcement. He was anxious to learn about your past and curious about your relationship with Dr. Sharma. I hope, I didn't say anything I shouldn't have." She hung up.

Tom continued to hold the silent phone. Finally, he snapped from his motionless state. *Who do I hate more, Darlene or Wilson?*

The Doctor had a call to make. He claimed he would only be a minute. Wilson waited in the library of the grand house and stared at the shelves that were lined with medical books. For the first time in years, Wilson felt inferior. He thought back to a time in grade school. He was in the principal's office. *I was there because I'd gotten into a fight on the playground.* He again glanced at all the books on the shelves and wished the Doctor would return.

When Dr. Sharma returned, he spoke quickly, "Sheriff, what I'm about to share with you is strictly off the record. If anyone asks me about this, I will deny everything about this meeting and our conversation, do you understand?"

"Yes, Sir. Why are you worried about Tom Padgett, after all these years?"

"It's not Tom Padgett I'm worried about. It's the doctor-patient relationship. Surely, you can understand that?"

"Yes, Sir."

"Good, obviously you have prior knowledge about Tom Padgett's condition, so some of what I'm about to tell you shouldn't surprise you. Where did you learn about my dealings with Mr. Padgett?"

"From his ex-wife. She told me about his condition, the MPD."

"Sheriff, under normal circumstances, I would never speak to you about a prior patient. But, Mr. Padgett was not a normal patient. In my entire career, I never had a client discourage me so. While being interrogated, he discouraged me to the point of quitting. At times, it was almost as if he was the doctor and I, the patient. What has happened that has caused you to come see me? What has Padgett done?"

"He is a new resident in my county. But, since he moved in, mysterious deaths and unsolved crimes have happened. I suspect he is involved, but, I've been unable to prove anything. He was in the area when many of the crimes occurred, but his hands always come up clean. Many of the crimes are almost, like revenge?"

The Doctor scratched his chin as he contemplated. "I see, that's interesting. The condition I diagnosed Tom Padgett as having twenty years ago should have regressed by now. However, there are extremely rare cases where the condition actually worsens with age. I fear this might be the case with Mr. Padgett."

"What am I supposed to do about him? How can he be held responsible, if he has no knowledge of the crimes?"

"There is only one way to get a person with MPD to expose his other self or selves. It's usually a very traumatic event. There are no guarantees, Sheriff. The understanding of patients with MPD is still relatively limited."

Wilson thanked the Doctor for his help. Wilson knew he really needed to get back to Carlisle. He couldn't spare another day off, not with Padgett running around loose in the county and Padgett free to do whatever he damned well pleased. Wilson was going to put an end to that. He didn't give a damn which Padgett he busted. He had another thought. *Maybe I should drive to Maysville, to that bar. O'Rourke's? My luck has been good this week, maybe it will continue. Maybe I'll run into Woozy this afternoon.*

CHAPTER 13

Tom and Bella had finished their walk and had played for an hour. He needed to get out of the house. He and Nick decided to go to the Gyp for a couple. Nick drove while Tom talked. He told Nick he had possibly found who had broken into his trailer.

"Did you let the Sheriff know?"

"No, not yet, I'm still not sure I trust Wilson. I know I don't trust him enough for him to bring the guy to justice."

"But it's his job, Tom. Remember, you're not a policeman anymore."

"I know, Nick. But for some reason, I might have to deal with this in my own way. I have zero confidence in Wilson."

"Maybe you could work with Wilson, and then together, you could solve the case and bury that hatchet at the same time."

"Yes, Wilson would love that, especially that part about burying the hatchet. He'd love to bury it, in my head."

As they entered the Gyp, they were surprised at how busy it was. Their stools were the only two seats available.

Steve slid beer in front of them. "Hey, Tom. It's been a while since you've been in here. Is it true what I heard, about your trailer burning?"

"Yeah, but if everything works out with the insurance, I should be alright."

"That's good to hear. If you need anything just let me

know."

"Thanks, Steve; that's nice of you."

Nick wasn't finished with his questions. "Tom, you can't take the law into your own hands. You'll end up a criminal, just like the guy you suspect."

"It's a tough decision, but trust me, I know Wilson. I know he's not even slightly concerned about helping me. Even if I handed the guy to Wilson on a silver platter, he'd still try to turn the thing around on me."

Nick considered this and for the moment seemed satisfied. That was good for Tom, because tonight, he didn't feel like being interrogated, especially about Wilson. Tom motioned, "Two more, Steve."

Lonnie pulled into the lot at the Gyp Joint and waited. A few minutes passed, before a man knocked on his window. Lonnie opened his door and climbed out.

"You the guy that has that Remington 870 for sale?"

"Yeah, you got the money?"

"Yeah, I got the money. You said two-hundred bucks, right?"

"Yeah that's right. The gun is in the back of my truck."

Lonnie opened the camper shell and pulled out the gun. He could immediately tell, based on the guy's expression, that he was excited. He knew he should have asked more. The guy ran the gun through its movements and seemed satisfied. He reached into his back pocket and drew out a wad of cash.

"Two-hundred bucks; here you are, man."

Lonnie watched as the guy trotted across the parking lot. He continued to watch as the guy put the gun into his truck and tucked it behind the seat. Lonnie thought about a cold beer. No, he couldn't take a chance on being seen inside the Gyp. Lonnie started his truck and turned for home.

Tony Griffin was pleased with the gun he'd gotten. He reclaimed his stool at the bar and began to brag loudly about the score. "Two-hundred bucks for an old 870, and it's in perfect condition," he said as he chugged the rest of his beer.

Tom couldn't help overhearing him. The guy was shouting. He said that he'd just bought a shotgun, out in the parking lot, an old 870. He wondered if the guy would mind showing it to him.

Tom turned his stool toward him and asked, "I couldn't help overhearing what you just said. Sounds like you got a good deal on an 870. Would you be interested in selling it, for a quick profit?"

Woozy was scheduled to work two hours earlier than normal. One of the other girls had something to do and had to leave early. That was fine by her. She could always use the money. With Jimmy and her daughter both gone, it was easier to get by. But, she knew it was just a matter of time before her daughter Charlene would come back home to live with her. Woozy thought that it would be nice if Charlene could somehow manage a long term relationship. But Woozy knew her daughter, and she was sure that she'd be absolute hell to live with.

Woozy always walked to the bar. Today, she was relieved that it wasn't busy. She didn't mind working hard, but this afternoon she was tired. A guy at the bar motioned for another drink. She'd never seen him in O'Rourke's before. Something about the man was familiar. She placed a beer in front of him and noticed the hat he wore, Sheriff. Suddenly, she had an uneasy feeling. It was as if he wanted to talk to her. She turned to serve another person down the bar.

Wilson spoke. "Woozy Fugate, I remember you. I remember seeing you over at Garrett's in Carlisle. You were there eating lunch with Tom Padgett."

Now she remembered him, he was the Sheriff of Nicholas County. What was he doing here?

Tony Griffin didn't like it if people listened in on his conversations. Especially if the conversation was supposed to be private. The fact that he was shouting really shouldn't matter. He liked to know who was listening to him. But one word had caught Tony's attention, profit. Yes, that was like music to his ears. He slowly pivoted on the stool to face Tom.

He looked Tom up and down, as if noticing him for the first time, "What makes a person interested in a gun that they haven't even seen?"

"It was hard not to hear your description. You claimed it was a nice older 870 for two-hundred bucks?"

"I said that's what I paid for it. As a matter of fact, I'm already kind of attached to it. So what kind of profit are we talking about?"

"I'm not sure. I'd like to have a look at it first."

Tom followed Tony outside and over to his truck. Tony unlocked the cab and pulled the gun from behind the seat. Tom was impressed with how clean the gun was, and the guy was right about it being an older 870. Tom knew exactly how old the gun was, he'd bought it when it was new, which was thirty-five years ago.

Tom whistled softly, "Yeah, you're right about this being a good gun. And the fact that's its older, I can attest to that. Was the guy you bought this from driving a Chevy S-10, and did it have a red camper shell?"

Tony stared at him for a second, "What the hell are you talking about? What's that have to do with anything? You want the gun or not?"

"Yeah, I want the gun, and like you, I'm kind of attached to

125

it. I've been attached to it for a very long time, thirty-five years to be exact."

"What are you talking about? Are you saying this is your gun?"

"That gun was stolen from me. It was stolen the night that bastard you bought it from, burned my home to the ground. I'm not going to ask you again. Was the truck an S-10 with a red camper shell? And, was the driver tall and skinny?"

Woozy considered Wilson's question, and she suddenly wished that O'Rourke's was busier. She maintained her composure and turned back toward him. "Yes, I was at Garrett's. And yes, I was having lunch with Tom Padgett. There's nothing wrong with that. I assume from your hat, that you're the Sheriff?"

Wilson grinned. He loved it when he succeeded to get under peoples' skin. "Mrs. Fugate, I realize you're working, but since you're not very busy, I was hoping to be able to ask you a few questions. Would that be alright?"

"I don't see why not, Sheriff. As you mentioned, I'm not very busy. What can I help you with?"

"Woozy, is it alright if I call you that?"

"That's what everybody calls me Sheriff. I don't see why not."

"Woozy, how long have you and Padgett been seeing each other?"

"Wait a second, Sheriff. Who says I'm seeing Tom Padgett? Tom is a customer here at the bar. We met here a few months ago. That's the extent of the relationship. Anything else, Sheriff?"

"If you're not seeing Padgett, how is it that you were having lunch with him in Carlisle?"

"We're friends, Sheriff. Having lunch together doesn't have to mean that we're dating."

Wilson smiled, so Woozy was going to be a feisty one. "Let me rephrase the question. Why did you meet Padgett that day? It was the same day you identified the body of your late husband. Do you and Padgett share secrets, secrets about Jimmy's death?"

Woozy slammed her fist down on the bar. "How dare you, Sheriff. How dare you come in here with accusations about my husband's death? I suggest you leave now, before I call the police."

Wilson chuckled, but continued to sit motionless, then drained the rest of his beer. "Woozy, I'll be in touch. I believe Padgett was involved in your husband's death. I'm not ready to eliminate you as a suspect either in my search for the murderer of Jimmy Fugate."

Tom borrowed Nick's keys and locked the shotgun in his trunk. He thought it odd that he'd paid $250 for his own gun. But, it was a good gun and it was worth the investment. Tom had to decide. Did he plan on using the gun on Lonnie Eldridge or not? He sat down next to Nick as Steve gave him another Budweiser.

Nick stuffed the keys back into his pocket, "So, you bought the gun?"

"Yeah. You know, now that I think about it, it's strange, buying my own gun."

"How can you be so sure it's your gun, Tom?"

"Nick, you are something else. Why do you doubt everything? I've owned that gun for thirty-five years. I recognize it. Don't you think you'd recognize your car if it was parked in a lot full of similar cars? Don't you believe there would be something that would enable you to differentiate your car from the rest of them?"

"I guess so. But, you always seem so sure of things; like how you feel about Wilson, and how you believe he has it in for you. How can you be so confident about things like that?"

Tom knew it was hopeless. Nick would never get it. He wanted to drop the whole damned thing. "Let's forget about it, Nick. Would you like another beer?"

"That would be great. There's only one thing that I enjoy more than talking, and that's drinking beer."

Tom looked over at his friend. He wanted to say something, but then thought better of it. He already knew Nick preferred drinking beer to talking. Mentioning this fact would have only raised another slew of questions.

Wilson was pleased with the progress he'd made today. He had some additional leverage to use against Padgett. Woozy was protecting Padgett's ass. He was sure of it. Tomorrow, it was time to get back to the old grind. He was sad to think about it. He had enjoyed his detective mission of the last two days, but Wilson had a county to look after. He had neglected his duty with his desire to get Padgett. That quest was soon coming to a conclusion. Yes, Bill Wilson was finally in a position to bring Padgett to justice. There was nothing that was going to save Padgett this time.

Woozy served drinks as the early evening crowd began to file in. She thought about the accusations that Wilson had made. Could Tom really have had something to do with Jimmy's death? It wasn't as if Jimmy didn't get what he deserved, but could Tom really have been there? Had she been wrong in her assessment of him? She thought that Tom was such a kind and gentle man. Granted, he had roughed Jimmy up that one night. But, he only did what needed to be done. Woozy was deep in thought. She didn't hear when someone asked for a beer. She quickly served it and then returned to her thoughts. Could Tom have shot Jimmy?

Tom couldn't sleep. The bed he was lying in was uncomfortable, but that wasn't the reason he lay awake and stared up at the ceiling. He considered his options regarding Lonnie Eldridge. He had not only robbed him, he'd burned up everything he owned. The guy had no regard for other human beings or their property. Wilson would be able to solve some of the recent robberies with the information Tom had. But, Tom didn't really care to help Wilson solve cases. He'd tried that in the past and Wilson always managed to screw something up. Tom was convinced that taking the law into his own hands might be his only option.

CHAPTER 14

The Following Morning

Since he'd been unable to sleep, Tom found himself at the job site early. August and crew had made excellent progress. Tom believed they'd be finished in another week; then, he'd take over. Tom planned to do his own electrical and plumbing. He was going to insulate and drywall the living quarters, maybe even the workshop area. He wasn't sure yet, it depended on his finances. He was leaving the stall area unfinished for the time being. He'd finish it after he determined what he wanted to use it for. That morning, August had given Tom an idea about the completion date. If all went well, he should be able to begin the finishing work the following weekend.

Tom decided to buy a wood stove. That would help keep his electric bills low. The living area wasn't huge, but he and Bella didn't need much room. He calculated what the finishing expenses would cost. He'd be economical in his material selections. He had to be, because the insurance settlement hadn't been as much as he'd hoped. He was lucky he didn't have a woman living with him. It didn't matter, if he was married or just living with a woman, it would have made the decorating more expensive. Tom's plans were simple. He'd be happy with a very basic home, as long as it was livable. He climbed up into the F-150. Bella wasn't with him this morning. Once again, she was home all alone and he could imagine her pouting. He made a right turn out onto Abners Mill. Tom had one other place to stop.

Wilson was in the office early. He browsed through a file which contained information about the recent arsons. There had been little headway made, and so far, there were no suspects. Wilson's thoughts inevitably strayed back to Padgett, but, he needed to catch up on unfinished business. Wilson had several phone calls to make, after that he had little to do. Maybe he should take more time off. His thoughts drifted back to what Dr. Sharma had alluded to. *How could I push Padgett? Push him so damned hard that his inner self would wake and come out of hiding?* Wilson had spent hours planning ways to make this happen. Wilson's daydreams were suddenly interrupted.

"Morning, Boss. Are you here for the whole day, or do you have some more unfinished business to take care of?"

Wilson disgustingly glared at his Deputy. "Deputy Leland, if I have unfinished business to attend to, that's my concern. And damn it, what have I told you about calling me Boss?"

"Sorry, Sheriff. I've been having quite a bit of fun while you were away, that's all. Since you're back, do we have anything new and exciting to pursue?"

Wilson stared at his Deputy for a moment. He thought that Leland had the mental capacity of a thirteen year old.

"Yes, Deputy, we do have new and exciting things to attend to. For starters, why don't you run over to Garrett's and get me a coffee?"

Tom was parked in the driveway. His eyes locked on the trailer. He'd been parked there for at least ten minutes. He needed to focus on the matter at hand, and at the same time, keep his wits about him. He didn't need to over-react. Tom stepped from the truck and opened the door of the crew cab. He grabbed the 870 and loaded it, and then he climbed the steps which led to the trailer's front door. He opened the screen and banged the butt of the gun against the door. He listened for sounds coming from the inside. He heard none. He was sure Lonnie was home because the S-10 was in the drive.

Tom noticed the curtains were moving. He again banged

the gun on the door; nothing but silence from inside the trailer. Tom tried the knob, it was locked. He pounded on the door with his fist and yelled. "Lonnie, I know you're in there. Open the damned door. We've got things to talk about."

A voice yelled back from behind the door, "I don't know you, man. Why would we have anything to talk about?"

"You know me, alright. I suggest you open the door. I don't want to have to break it down."

Tom could hear a chain being slid into place. Lonnie wasn't about to open the door. That was okay with Tom. He gave the door a kick and it flew open.

Lonnie stood directly in front of him, shaking like a leaf. Lonnie only had on boxer shorts and a wife beater tee-shirt. Tom pointed the shotgun at him and motioned him toward the sofa. Tom sat opposite on the recliner, rested the 870 across his lap, and he looked directly at Lonnie. Lonnie refused to make eye contact.

"Do you recognize me now, Lonnie? It's much easier to see me when you're not hiding behind the curtains. Don't you remember me, Lonnie?"

"No, Sir. I've never seen you before in my life."

Tom laughed, "You've never seen me before, huh? You haven't seen me once, in your whole miserable life? Why is that Lonnie? Is your memory failing?"

"Mister, I don't remember ever seeing you. If I had, I would have remembered."

"Your memory is sharp, is it? Let me help you remember. When you were hiding behind the curtains did you happen to notice my truck?"

"No, Sir. I didn't see nothing but you."

"My name is Tom Padgett and my truck is a black Ford F150. Does that help you remember me?"

Recognition began to register on Lonnie's face.

"I thought that little piece of information would help you and that sharp memory of yours. Since you remember my truck, I'm sure you remember this?"

Tom patted the 870. "It's a hell of a good gun. It's accurate, too. I've never missed from this range. You know what makes me really angry? I had to pay some guy $250 for my own gun. That doesn't seem right. Lonnie, does that seem right to you?"

Lonnie was extremely quiet, quieter than he'd ever been. All he could hear was the beating of his heart.

Wilson returned the calls he'd missed during his absence. Leland was trying to drive him crazy, so he sent him off on a mission. With Leland finally out of his hair, he would be able to concentrate. He tried to prioritize the things that he needed to get done. Wilson had never been one for prioritizing, but, he was going to try. He had the murder of Jimmy Fugate, which was unsolved. Thankfully, the shooting that had occurred out in Clay WMA, had been put to bed. Drug violations were down. Drug activity was down everywhere. It didn't matter whether it was pills or marijuana. *Could that be related to the time of year?*

The arsonist was still out there, but whoever started the blazes, seemed to have taken a break. It would be alright as far as Wilson was concerned if the arsonist lay low and never started another fire. He felt that if the arsonist did that, it'd be like letting bygones be bygones. Robberies that were unsolved weren't a big deal. The stuff that had been stolen from the trailer on Abners Mill was minimal. However, there had been a couple of new robberies reported that had also occurred on Abners Mill. Wilson planned to visit those places, this afternoon. Actually, things were looking pretty good in Nicholas County. The only troublesome area seemed to be out around Abners Mill. This naturally brought Wilson back around to his number one priority, Padgett, who just happened to live on Abners Mill Road.

Even though it was early, Tom helped himself to a beer out of Lonnie's fridge. Beer in hand, he sat down and faced Lonnie. Tom noticed Lonnie's feet. They were fidgeting.

"Do you need to use the bathroom?" Lonnie shook his head. "Go ahead, but don't try anything stupid, like climbing out the window or something. I'm not finished talking to you yet." By the time Lonnie returned, Tom had popped open a second beer. Lonnie was getting pissed, that was his beer, not this old man's. He would get the bastard.

Tom could tell that his latest tactic made Lonnie mad. That was exactly what he wanted to do. "So, you don't like it when an uninvited guest helps himself to your beer? Isn't that what you did, when you visited my home? You even threw the empties in the yard, didn't you? I've always been particular about my yard. Even if I was a rookie cop like Wilson, I would have wondered about the empty beer cans lying in the grass. Wilson isn't observant Lonnie, but I am. I already know the answer, but I'll ask anyway. Do you own this trailer?"

"No, I rent it."

"Too bad." Tom replied as he looked around the trailer. "From the looks of things, you don't have much of value in this place, anyway. What do you do with all the stuff you steal?"

"I pawn it, man. What do you think I do with it?"

"I'm not sure. A smart guy like you, no telling what sort of stupid thing you'd do with your winnings. So you pawned all the stuff you stole from me? Did you make much money? Let's see, there was some cash, a laptop, a chainsaw, a new compound bow with arrows, and some binoculars. Let's not forget the shotgun. Fortunately, I was lucky enough to buy that back. So, Lonnie, how much did you make from your little score?"

"I can't remember. What do you expect me to do about it anyway? The money's all gone."

"The money's all gone? Even the two-hundred dollars you got from the sale of the shotgun? I seriously doubt you spent that last night, especially in sleepy Nicholas County."

Lonnie's phone rang and he started to reach for it. Tom pointed the gun at the phone. Lonnie quickly pulled his hand away.

"So, what did you get from your little robbing spree, Lonnie? What was it, four, five-hundred bucks? Is that kind of money worth ruining a person's life over? You obviously hold a very low opinion of other people. You know what, Lonnie? If you had just robbed me, that would have been bad enough, but to burn my trailer and everything I own, that was an incredibly shitty thing to do."

"I didn't mean to burn your trailer. I didn't think that heater would keep running. I thought it would shut off. They're supposed to."

Tom was getting angry as he heard Lonnie admit that he'd known about the heater. He stayed calm. He had a solution to Lonnie's problem.

"Lonnie, don't your parents live nearby?"

"Yeah, but they haven't done anything."

"I know they haven't. I'm just trying to make a point; something you might be able to comprehend. What if they went away for the weekend, and then came home to nothing? They came home and all their possessions were gone. How would they feel?"

"How the hell am I supposed to know how they'd feel?"

Tom gave Lonnie a long look and shook his head. "Lonnie, the way I see it, there's no way you'll ever be able to repay me. There's nothing you can do to right the wrongs you've done to me. There are only a couple of ways to make things square. One, if I shoot you and then call it even. Two, I turn you over to the Sheriff. With all the information I have on you, even bumbling Wilson should be able to get a serious amount of jail time handed down. I wish there was some other way, Lonnie. But you've made your bed, now you'll have to sleep in it."

Lonnie relaxed somewhat as Tom talked. It seemed that a kind of turning point had been established. He watched as Tom stood, and then turned for the door.

At the door Tom paused, "Lonnie, I'll give you my decision soon. Right now, I'll leave you alone with your thoughts. You've got some serious thinking to do."

Tom left the trailer, got into his truck and drove away.

Lonnie ran to the bathroom. He suddenly didn't feel very well. He had some thinking to do, that's what the old man had suggested. He totally agreed with him. He had a lot of thinking to do. He threw on a pair of jeans and a denim jacket. Two minutes later he rolled along in his truck, en route to his parent's house. He was glad that he hadn't sold the handgun that he'd stolen. It would definitely come in handy right about now. As Lonnie walked away from the milk house, he stuffed the gun into his pocket. He was just about to his truck when he heard his mom yell. She stood on the front porch. He waved and said he'd call later. Lonnie started the truck and backed out of the drive.

Wilson pulled into Padgett's drive. He wandered around the place, watching as August's crew worked. After a few minutes, August noticed him.

August approached Wilson. "Is there anything I might be able to help you with, Sheriff?"

"No, no, I'm just seeing how you guys are progressing on Padgett's new home."

"Are you now? So, should I let Mr. Padgett know that you were here, checking on the progress? He stops by every morning."

"You say Padgett comes by every morning?"

"That's what he's been doing. I don't reckon he's going to

change. He's usually here by seven-thirty."

Wilson considered August for a moment. "I don't recognize you or any of your crew. Are you from around here?"

"We're from over in Fleming County. It's only fifteen minutes from here. If there's nothing else, Sheriff, I need to get to work. I've got a schedule to meet."

Wilson nodded, and then walked back to his truck. He watched for a few minutes more. He was trying to figure out whether the guys were Amish or Mennonite. He couldn't tell. Wilson had little knowledge of either group and he was content keeping it that way. He started his truck and pulled back onto Abners Mill.

Tom called Nick and asked if he wanted to meet later, at O'Rourke's. Naturally, Nick was game. When Nick entered O'Rourke's, he found Tom and Woozy engaged in a serious conversation. Woozy didn't even acknowledge Nick. She placed a beer on the counter in front of him, and continued talking with Tom.

"You're right, Tom, it doesn't matter who killed Jimmy. But I was just sort of hoping it wasn't you."

Tom glanced at Nick before responding. "Woozy, you can't listen to half of what Wilson says. The guy has a personal grudge against me. As far as he's concerned, I'm behind almost every crime that has happened in Nicholas County."

Woozy threw her towel on the counter and walked down the bar to serve some other people. Nick stared at Tom. *What's all this talk of Jimmy about?*

Tom turned and looked at Nick, "Don't you start on me, too. All I wanted to do was have a beer. I didn't drive all the way up to Maysville to hear crap about that bastard Wilson."

Nick saw that Tom was upset. He ordered a couple more

beers. Tom needed to relax. Nick was dying to learn what this was about, though. He loved to hear gossip, especially if mischief was involved.

Tom looked down at the beer in his hand, "What's it matter how Jimmy died, anyway? He was raping a young girl, for Christ's sake. She was only fifteen years old, damn it."

Tom swallowed the rest of his beer and got up to go to the bathroom. Nick sat silently on his stool, which was quite unusual. Woozy came back with another round.

"Nick, I don't know how much you know about Sheriff Wilson. But, for the Sheriff to come in here with accusations about Tom's involvement in Jimmy's murder, that kind of shook me up. He even made reference to me being involved. He even said that I'm possibly a suspect."

Nick remained silent when Tom returned.

CHAPTER 15

Tom sat on the edge of the bed. It was the middle of the night. It hadn't been a good night. He had awakened over an hour ago. He'd had another nightmare. They continued to get more bizarre. In the dream, *Wilson was the brother of Jimmy Fugate. Wilson was extremely pissed at Tom. He believed Tom had killed his brother. What made Wilson even madder was that he'd been unable to implicate Padgett.* But, what woke Tom with a start was the ending of the dream. *Jimmy wasn't dead, he was still alive. Now, both he and his brother, Wilson, were actively hunting Tom. Together, they were hunting him like a dog. They each carried incredibly sophisticated compound bows. They were both decked out in full camo gear. Tom was trying to hide in enormous woods. He had no weapon. He was wearing a bright white jump suit. All the trees were mature oaks and maples. None of them had branches low enough for him to reach.* But, the worst scenario was that *Jimmy and Wilson were both riding ATVs as they chased Tom and they were gaining on him. They were quickly getting closer.*

Tom wandered into Nick's kitchen and started the coffee. It was only five o'clock. Bella stretched as Tom opened the back door. He was thinking about Woozy and how upset she'd been after Wilson's questioning. He couldn't tell Woozy the truth about Jimmy. That would make her an accessory after the fact. He couldn't tell Nick either. Tom was sure that Nick would soon begin asking questions again, after he felt enough time had passed. Nick had tremendous curiosity. Maybe he'd been a cat in a prior lifetime.

Tom still hadn't decided which route to take with Lonnie. Granted, the guy had broken into his home and robbed it. He was responsible that it had burned to the ground. But, he hadn't deliberately set it ablaze. *Should that be a reason to let him off the*

139

hook, to turn the information over to Wilson? To let the system do what it's supposed to do? Tom sipped his coffee as these thoughts churned away in his head. Did he have a third option? Could he forgive and forget? Wilson would never be able to solve the robbery issue without Tom's help. He knew that Wilson would continue to try to tie all Nicholas County crimes back to him. That was just how Wilson operated.

Tom rationalized the situation for another hour. He'd considered every option multiple times. He'd showered and dressed and was making breakfast as Nick lumbered in. Nick seemed to have put on ten pounds just since Tom had been staying with him. Tom looked down at the sizzling bacon and realized that this wasn't going to help Nick's weight problem.

"Morning, Nick. How'd you sleep?"

"I slept like a log. I could easily have stayed in bed another hour or more."

"I know the feeling. You know what? If we plan on going to the Gyp or O'Rourke's anytime soon, let's try and keep the conversation light. No more heavy, heavy topics, alright? I didn't sleep at all last night."

"That's good by me, Tom."

Tom put the food on the table and then let Bella in. This morning she was getting a treat, her dog food soaked in bacon grease. She quickly gobbled it down, and then she returned to the kitchen. She was hoping that something would fall on the floor. This continued to be one of her favorite games. After breakfast Tom and Bella jumped into the truck; time to go check on the job site.

Wilson stepped from the shower and examined himself in the mirror. He was impressed with what he saw. His love handles were smaller than they'd been in months. He turned sideways and admired his naked profile. His gut even seemed smaller. This put him in a good mood. It was Friday and he planned to reward himself later tonight. He was going to pull the Jim Beam out of storage. Wilson was going to once again let his hair down. He quickly finished dressing and then swallowed the rest of his coffee. He had one more item of police business to attend to before he could officially start to plan his weekend celebration.

Wilson instinctively glanced at the neighbor's house as he backed out the drive. It had been quite a while since he'd seen the nosy bitch. He hoped she hadn't died. He whistled as he drove along Route 68. When he pulled into Padgett's driveway, Wilson smiled. Padgett was talking to August. He also saw his dog. What was her name? Bella? Wilson didn't care much for dogs. He got out of his truck and hiked up his pants as he tucked in his shirt. He put on his hat and checked his reflection in the truck's mirror. He looked very professional, but why wouldn't he? He was the Sheriff of Nicholas County, wasn't he?

Tom heard Wilson's truck as it pulled into the drive. He and August were talking about the day's building plans. He groaned and then excused himself. Tom turned and watched as Wilson approached. This morning, Wilson had an unusually loose swagger. If Wilson had been a woman, Tom would have sworn that he was intentionally shaking his hips. Unfortunately for Tom, Wilson was not a woman. He was just Wilson, which was quite simply, a huge pain in the ass.

"Morning, Padgett. Looks like they're moving along nicely on your new home. When do you expect to be able to move in?"

Tom rubbed his forehead and thought about how to play this exchange. "Wilson, it'll be a while before I can move in. I have to do all the interior finish work. That won't happen overnight. But, I know that's not what you're here to talk about, is it?"

Wilson let out a chuckle, "No, it isn't Padgett. You seem to have a good idea about what makes me tick. This could be another one of those social visits that you always refer to." Tom waited for Wilson to continue. Wilson looked around as some of the men lifted a truss into position. "Looks like this is going to be a big improvement over that trailer you had. Did your insurance cover everything?"

"Not that it's any of your business, Wilson. But no, the insurance didn't cover everything. A lot of this is coming directly out of my savings. What's on your mind?"

"I wanted to let you know about my week. It was quite eventful. I talked with your ex-wife, Darlene. I also talked with that shrink of yours down in Lexington. What is his name, Dr. Sharma? And, I had a nice conversation with your latest girlfriend, Woozy. All in all, it was a very good week. Now, all I need to do is put all the pieces together in order to solve the puzzle."

Tom waited a beat before replying. "Wilson, I'm glad you had such a good week. I'm dying to know, what puzzle are you trying to solve? Could it be the puzzle of me, the puzzle of Tom Padgett? That difficulty I always seem to threaten you with?"

"You're quite perceptive, Padgett. Dr. Sharma said as much. I'm working on some things; things that are going to help bring conclusions to old problems."

"Good for you, Wilson. Have you had any success at catching the thief that robbed half the places around here? The Abners Mill robber, is that one of your old problems?"

"No Padgett, I haven't solved the robbery issues yet. But, that is relatively new business. I'm getting ready to take care of some old business."

Tom turned and started to walk away. He had been way too congenial this morning. He could hear Wilson clear his throat.

"Padgett, I'll be in touch. And by the way, have a nice weekend."

It wasn't any of his business, the meeting between Tom and the Sheriff. But August was suspected that Wilson was not an entirely honest man. He had no such illusions about Tom Padgett. He glanced at Padgett after the Sheriff had left. He could see the man was changed somehow, something about him had darkened. Mr. Padgett's eyes followed the Sheriff's truck, as it moved slowly along Abners Mill Road. His eyes were not the same. Those eyes weren't the ones that greeted him and his crew each and every morning. They were different. But, Tom Padgett paid him and his crew to work on his house, and nothing more. He returned to the task at hand, they needed to finish a week from today.

Wilson felt exhilarated as he pulled onto the road. He had definitely gotten Padgett's attention. It felt as if he'd almost made him crack. The Doctor had told him about this possibility. Doc had mentioned that all that he needed to do was hit the right buttons. Wilson could see that Padgett was angry. He could tell he might even be furious, even though he managed to keep it in check. Yes, so the good Doctor had been correct. If he could find that magic combination and have Padgett come unhinged, then he'd have his ass. He was going to work at finding the right combination. He would devote the rest of the day to the task. Once again, Padgett was his number one priority. Wilson smiled at the thought.

Tom was angry. He was angrier at himself than Wilson. He knew that Wilson was constantly trying to rattle him. But, a couple of the things he'd said today had nearly done it. What if Wilson did manage to make him lose it, what then? Was Wilson prepared to deal with the consequences? Was Wilson prepared to dive into the unknown? Dr. Sharma had tried long and hard to get inside his head. In the end, he had even given up. It seemed Tom had little choice but to revert back to some of his proven techniques of deception, those same deceptive techniques he had used so effectively, all those years ago.

Wilson was back in his office and wrote down some of his thoughts on a pad of paper. He thought to himself that the task was his form of 'Wilson brainstorming'. He really wished he had a secretary, especially, if she was good looking. He would love dictating to some hot young lady. His thoughts were interrupted as Leland wandered in.

"Hey, Boss, what are you doing?"

"Damn it, Leland. How many times do I have to tell you not to call me Boss?"

"Sorry, Sheriff, I'm just surprised to find you in the office."

"Why is it so damned surprising to find me in the office? Where should I be?"

"I don't know, Sheriff. I just thought you might be out roaming around the county looking for bad guys."

"Deputy, is that your idea of a joke? What are you doing here, anyway? I thought you didn't come in until later this afternoon?"

"I was just bored sitting around the house, so I decided to come in early."

Wilson stared at Leland for a bit. He was getting more convinced, each and every day, that Leland wasn't Deputy material. But unfortunately, he was all he had.

"Since you're here, why don't you run get me a coffee?"

"Sure thing, Boss."

Tom was in Maysville again, shopping at Lowe's. He pushed a trolley up and down the aisles. He was here to get electrical and plumbing supplies. He shuddered at the price of copper wire. It was outrageous. He paused from his material search for a moment and thought about Lonnie Eldridge. This morning, he'd been prepared to turn all the info he had on Lonnie over to Wilson. But, after Wilson's surprise visit this morning, he wasn't sure if he really wanted to help the guy. Shooting Lonnie was obviously out of the question. He couldn't bring himself to do that. But, letting the guy walk didn't seem to be an appropriate response either.

Wilson had just finished a thought in his private brainstorming session. He leaned back in his chair and silently read what he'd written down. So far, he had a fairly good start on his list of ideas, ideas on how to make Padgett break. He thought that he might even take the list home with him. He could surely come up with some good ideas this evening. Yes, in two more hours the Jim Beam was coming out. It would definitely help him think more clearly. He'd be able to think outside the box, especially with a little bit of whiskey floating around in his veins. He looked at the clock, three-fifteen, another hour and forty-five minutes.

His phone rang; Wilson smiled, he recognized the number.

"This is Wilson. What might I help you with, Padgett?... Uh huh, so you think you might have uncovered the Abners Mill robber? And how, might I ask, did you make this determination?... You did, huh? You bought your own shotgun from a guy at the Gyp Joint and that led you to Lonnie Eldridge's door?... Well, Padgett, I'll definitely look into it. I'll see to it first thing Monday morning. You should realize that it's late in the day and I've got plenty of things to do.... So, you think it's important that I get out there this afternoon? I appreciate the advice, Padgett, but I'm the law around here, not you. Thanks for the tip Padgett. Now you remember what I said and have a nice weekend."

Wilson smiled broadly as he hung up the phone. He had Padgett right where he wanted him. He was running scared. He was even trying to help him solve his cases.

Padgett closed his phone. He sat in his truck in the Lowe's parking lot. He had gotten most of the things he needed. He was going to start doing his electrical and plumbing next week. He tossed his cell phone onto the dashboard. He wasn't crazy about giving information to Wilson, but justice needed to be served, and Wilson was the law around here. Regrettably, Wilson might screw around and let Lonnie Eldridge skip town. He had proven how good he was at that, on more than one occasion. Lonnie Eldridge's fate was out of his hands now. It was in the capable hands of

Sheriff Bill Wilson. Tom laughed at that thought. Wilson, what an imbecile.

Lonnie leaned back in his recliner, wrapped in thought. He took another swallow of beer as visions of Padgett flitted through his head. How long did the guy need to consider what punishment was due? He was leaving him hanging, letting him sweat things out. Padgett had suggested that he think about things. Lonnie was doing just that, and he returned to the recliner with another beer in hand. *That bastard had helped himself to my beer. That should help make us even.* Lonnie was getting madder by the minute. He only had two more beers, thanks to that thieving lawman.

Maybe I could lay in wait and shoot the bastard when and if he comes back. But what if Padgett had told the Sheriff everything? Padgett had been right about one thing; even Wilson wouldn't screw up this case. It was a slam dunk. His phone rang, it was his mother. He told her he'd call her later. Lonnie didn't have many options. He could just sit here. Sit here and wait for what? Either to get shot or to go to prison. Neither possibility held a lot of promise. He staggered to the refrigerator and grabbed another beer, he only had one left. He wrestled with what to do. Suddenly, a great idea popped into his head. He picked up his pen and began to write.

Wilson was on his back porch enjoying his first whiskey of the evening. He laughed at an idea. *Imagine that, Padgett trying to tell me how to do my job. If the bastard was so damned smart, how did he get forced into early retirement?* This was one of the hot buttons that he intended to use to provoke Padgett. *Boy, this whiskey is good. Another warm night, fantastic for the end of December.* Wilson listened as the neighbor's back door slowly opened. He had mellowed considerably as he sipped on his whiskey. The old woman stepped onto her porch and turned to apprise Wilson. Wilson lifted his whiskey glass and offered a toast to the busy body. The old biddy just stared back at him. The expression she wore could only be described as one of sorrow. She

146

slowly turned and walked back inside.

Wilson tracked her movements while refilling his glass. *Old bitch, what gives her the right to pass judgment on me?* He took a healthy swallow of Jim Beam and quickly forgot the old lady. Back to his main concern, burying Padgett's ass in a shallow grave. That would be most satisfying. Wilson picked up the pad of paper. He silently read from the list of items he planned to throw at Padgett. There were some good ones. He took another swallow. As he did, another idea floated into his consciousness. It would undoubtedly unhinge Padgett. This was one hell of a good idea. His one-man brainstorming session on the back porch was brilliant, all accomplished while he enjoyed the mind-stimulating whiskey.

Tom was so tired of Wilson. He thought about tonight's activities. He and Nick planned to go out, either the Gyp or O'Rourke's. But, he was already in Maysville. He rang Nick.

"Hey, Tom, what's going on?

"I'm over at Lowe's. I just finished shopping. Since I'm in Maysville, it seems silly not to visit O'Rourke's."

"I couldn't agree more. I'll be there in a half hour."

Tom disconnected and started his truck. He knew that Woozy would be working tonight. He might not get to talk to her much, since Friday nights were usually busy. He hoped she didn't want to rehash his possible involvement in Jimmy's death again. It might be nice if they actually went out to dinner sometime. He smiled. That would be nice. Maybe he'd ask her out.

Lonnie reread what he'd written down. He felt satisfied. It should produce the desired results. He contemplated whether or not to get more beer. He'd already drunk plenty. But, Ladobee's was just a few minute's drive. He picked up the handgun, just to get comfortable with the feel of it, while considering his next move. The gun felt good in his hand. He though back to the threats that

Padgett had made. *Who does that old man think he is? What makes him think I'd just sit here and wait for his sorry ass to return? Sit here and wait for him to return and shoot me?* Lonnie picked up his car keys and walked out the trailer door. He turned around and glanced down at the busted door frame. This pissed him off.

Wilson woke up and noticed he'd once again slept in the recliner. He immediately glanced around the living room. He was looking for any sign that he might have gotten out of control. He saw the bottle of Jim Beam. It was half empty and sat on the kitchen table. He let out a thankful sigh. Over the years, Wilson had learned a thing or two about alcohol. If he could keep himself in check and keep his consumption to half a bottle, he was usually ok and shouldn't have done anything stupid. But, half a bottle of whiskey was the limit. Beyond that point, Wilson blacked out. He didn't pass out, no Wilson never passed out. Things went totally blank. He'd have no recollection of anything, even though he might carry on for hours; Wilson would remember none of it.

He ambled into the kitchen and put some coffee on. He noticed the pad that he'd been writing on last night. *Oh yeah*, he vaguely remembered; *my list of ideas to get to Padgett, my one-man brainstorming session.* He read the first items on the list and thought they sounded viable. But, the further down the list he read, the more ridiculous the ideas seemed to become. Some of the ideas were downright stupid. *Had Leland been here last night?* He reread the last item on the list. *How infantile. Did I really believe that was a good idea?* Wilson looked at the bottle of Jim Beam again. *Maybe there's another empty lying about somewhere?*

It was still dark out when he woke. He could hear soft snoring close by. He was disoriented. He'd slept very little last night. Tom finally put two and two together and realized that the snoring was only Bella. He and Nick had actually been quite tame at O'Rourke's. They were home early, before nine o'clock. Nick had to work today. Tom planned to go over to the home site. He lay still a while longer and listened to Bella snore. *What would it be like to have Woozy lying next to me? I wonder whether or not Woozy snores? Not that it would matter. It would be nice to find out.* Last night the bar had been quite busy and Woozy hadn't been able to talk much. Tom was pleased that he had managed to get her phone number. Now, all he had to do was work up the courage to give her a call. Even though he had been to bed with Becky on a couple of occasions, he still wasn't comfortable with the idea of dating. The fact that he'd been married for twenty-five years still bothered him. He still felt awkward when he talked to women. But, if there was any woman that he wouldn't feel that way around, it was Woozy. They shared some common bonds. They had secrets. One of them, even Woozy, might never learn.

Saturday used to be Wilson's favorite day of the week. But, if he drank the evening before, Saturdays were usually long and painful. Luckily, today he had a plan. He was going to work on his list. He needed to weed out some of the drunken ideas he'd come up with. After he'd eliminated many of them, the list was again short. He poured himself another cup of coffee and retrieved the pad. There were still two or three potential things that might work. He mulled over one of the remaining possibilities, before he scratched a line through it. Now, he had only two approaches left that offered hope. That didn't seem very promising. He needed more ammunition if he was going to force Padgett to break.

He tried to remember everything he'd learned from Padgett's ex-wife. That day, he had written a couple of things down, but that was before he'd gotten distracted. Wilson could never concentrate after being distracted by a woman's breasts. That was the main thing he remembered from the meeting with Darlene at Applebee's, her boobs. Wilson needed to focus, he needed to think. Maybe a cold shower would do the trick. Wilson needed a woman, but he didn't have time for a woman right now. He was in the middle of a career-changing endeavor. He recalled what the Mayor of Mt. Sterling had done to Padgett. Then he got flustered. Breasts were suddenly consuming his thoughts. He saw them everywhere. Wilson couldn't stop thinking about boobs, big luscious boobs. He walked down the hallway. It was time for that shower.

He was taking a different route to the job site this morning. Tom wanted to do a drive past Lonnie Eldridge's place. He wanted to see if the guy was home. Tom had no intention of stopping in, although that might be enjoyable. He slowed his truck as he rolled past the trailer. Everything looked like it had on the prior visit. Although, there was something in the air. Tom felt that something wasn't right. He was about to turn around and go back, but then thought better of it. He'd already given Lonnie quite the scare. The ball was in Wilson's court now.

Thinking about the ball being in Wilson's court seemed ironic. Wilson totally disregarded Tom's recommendation about Eldridge. Tom knew that Wilson was going to do things the way he always did, Wilson's way. Tom slowed to a stop when he got to Route 68. He turned right and was at his property ten minutes later. He wandered around in the unfinished structure, trying to get a sense of the job ahead. Tom wasn't an electrician or a plumber. But, he knew that if a person read about it, and followed the local codes, a homeowner could do most of his own work and save a lot of money. Saving money was always a priority for Tom, especially now. Especially since he'd ended up on the short end of the insurance settlement stick.

CHAPTER 16

Monday Morning

Wilson was more anxious than usual. He was excited about the new prospects that he felt would nail Padgett. Over the evening, he'd managed to come up with a few more ideas some that would actually put Padgett over the edge. Something to put a chink in that damned armor of Padgett's. He had arranged for Leland to meet him in the office at eight-thirty. He wasn't interested in pursuing what Padgett had suggested, but he decided what could it hurt? The way Wilson figured, he and Leland could run out to Lonnie's, pay him a quick visit, and still be back in Carlisle early enough to fine tune his latest scheme. He hoped that Leland wasn't in one of his talkative moods today. Sometimes his Deputy just didn't know when to shut up.

As Wilson walked into the courthouse, he noticed that the door to his office was ajar. It was quite unusual for the County Clerk to unlock the door before her scheduled shift, and that was eight o'clock. It surprised Wilson that she was already here. She was ten minutes early. As soon as he walked into the office, he understood why the door stood open. The clerk wasn't in the office ten minutes early, Leland was.

"Morning, Boss."

"Leland, how many damned times do I have to tell you, not to call me Boss? How hard is that for you to remember?"

"I don't know, Sheriff. I thought you'd like to be called Boss. I know that if I was Sheriff, I would like being called Boss."

Wilson regarded his deputy and pondered Leland's latest

151

explanation. "Leland, you are not Sheriff. I'm the Sheriff, and you're my Deputy. Are you having problems remembering this?"

"No, Sheriff. How 'bout I call you Boss Man? I saw that on a prison movie last night. The inmates called the head guard Boss Man, you know, kind of out of respect."

Wilson was beginning to wish it was Friday night, all over again. He wished he had a nice glass of Jim Beam Black in his hand. But it wasn't Friday, it was Monday, and Leland was going to accompany him to Eldridge's. He needed to stay calm.

"Deputy, I don't want to be called Boss Man and I don't want to be called Boss. I want to be addressed as Sheriff. Can you understand that?"

Leland nodded in acknowledgment. He could tell the Boss Man was getting angry. He'd better knock it off.

Wilson informed Leland of the morning's plans. They planned to drive out to Eldridge's, and then they'd question Lonnie about his whereabouts on the night of the robberies. Wilson drove as Leland looked out the window. Wilson thought this was wonderful. His deputy was riding along quietly, and for once his mouth was shut. No sooner had the thought entered Wilson's head, when Leland had more questions.

"Sheriff, what if Eldridge denies being anywhere near Abners Mill Road that night? What are you going to do then?"

Wilson had been considering the same thing, but he wasn't about to let Leland know that. "Deputy, let's cross that bridge when we get to it."

This week, the barn project would be complete, and Tom was looking forward to starting on the finish work. So far, the weather had held for August and his crew, Tom was hopeful it would continue to cooperate. But, he wasn't optimistic. It was nearly January. The first thing he planned to do was install the wood stove. He considered the best place for the stove; in the living area, or in the work shop? The living quarters should be economical to heat and only require a small space heater. As Tom wandered around inside the house, August and his crew arrived.

Tom listened as August gave the crew the day's instructions. When finished, August turned to Tom. "Mr. Padgett, we're going to try and get finished early. I've just learned a major change in the weather is coming, I'd like for us to finish, so we can get out of your way."

"I appreciate that, August, but don't rush on my account. If the weather goes south, I'll just have to deal with it. Can I ask your advice about something?"

"Sure, Mr. Padgett, what is it?"

"I was considering putting a wood stove out in the shop and just a small heater in the living area. Don't you think the apartment should be economical to heat?"

"Yes it should be, especially if you use enough insulation. If it was me, I would do exactly what you're planning. I spend most of my waking hours in either my shop or outdoors. I have a feeling you're the same. Besides, you can add another wood stove later."

"That's a good idea. I hadn't thought about that."

"Mr. Padgett, you know how we Amish are about electricity. We think about things like wood stoves all the time."

Wilson turned into Lonnie's driveway. He turned off the ignition and silently studied the trailer. Lonnie's truck was parked in the drive, so he should be home.

Wilson glanced over at his deputy, "Leland, remember what I said, you listen and write down everything that's said. You good with that?"

"Yes, Sheriff."

Wilson and Leland both stepped up onto the deck. Wilson rapped on the door. As he did, it squeaked and moved slightly inward. It was then that Wilson noticed that the door's frame was splintered and broken. There wasn't any noise from inside the trailer. Wilson motioned for Leland to get behind him, and then drew his weapon. Wilson carefully pushed the door all the way open, using his left foot, before he slowly moved inside. The place was a mess. There were beer cans scattered everywhere. It smelled terrible, almost as if someone had puked and shit all over the place. Wilson moved into the living room. It was then that he realized what had happened.

Lonnie Eldridge was on the recliner. He seemed to be asleep. However, much of his face and nearly half his head were missing. Wilson needed air. He didn't want to throw up.

Wilson spun around, "Leland, let's get our protective gear on. Remember, on the way out, don't touch anything."

Keith Poole sighed as he clicked his phone closed. It seemed that Wilson once again requested his services. Apparently, there had been a shooting out on Goose Creek Pike. Keith scratched his head and looked around the office. He was busy as usual, but he had been the one that had accepted the position of County Coroner. He had no one to blame but himself for that decision. He thought about things that needed to be done. He had an eighty year old lady to prepare for burial. Her funeral was in three days. There was a seventy-five year old man to be dealt with. The lady had succumbed to natural causes, the man hadn't been so lucky. Keith recalled how the old man had passed and shook his head. *Why would a seventy-five year old man try to cut down such a big tree? Especially one that was located on such a steep grade, covered with ice?* Keith surmised that the old man must have heated his home with wood, had probably run out, and desperately needed wood.

Keith took a seat. He had to get a handle on what needed to be done. He needed to prioritize things. Obviously, his number one priority was the issue out on Goose Creek Pike. Some of the personal things that he'd planned for later in the week might need to be rescheduled. Keith didn't like things to interfere with his private life. But, he had accepted the position of Coroner and the responsibilities that went with it. Sometimes, Keith felt some of his Coroner duties seemed to intentionally interfere with his plans. But, he realized that was impossible. He stood and snatched up his keys from the desk. He walked out the door as his aide approached. Keith called over his shoulder, "Duty calls. I'll be back later today."

After he finished the call, Wilson slipped into his booties. Leland stood on the porch. Leland was anxious to get back inside. Wilson studied his Deputy.

"Leland, where the hell is the note pad that I asked you to get?"

"Oh, I must have laid it down when I was putting my gloves on. I'll get it."

Wilson frowned as Leland jumped from the porch and ran to the truck. He watched Leland close the truck's door. Wilson was surprised to see that Leland had had enough sense to get a pen.

"Ok, Leland, let's have a look at that door frame and try to figure out who might have kicked it in."

Leland scribbled away as Wilson spoke.

"There's a pretty good scuff on the door. It's definitely from a boot kick. It's hard to tell the exact size. However, I'm willing to bet it's the same size Padgett wears."

"What makes you think that, Sheriff? Why do you think that whoever kicked in the door wears the same size shoe as Padgett? Are you thinking Padgett had something to do with this?"

Wilson disgustedly stared at the Deputy. "Leland, in case you haven't noticed, I suspect Padgett of damn near every crime that's committed in Nicholas County. In case you've forgotten, he's the one that recommended that we come out here this morning?"

"But, Sheriff, you don't like Padgett. That's not a reason to suspect him."

Wilson could feel that he was getting angry. He didn't like being questioned, especially by his Deputy. "Leland, let's get back to work. You just worry about writing down what I tell you. Let's see, back to the door. It appears the door was only kicked once. So, it must have been a pretty good kick. You got that deputy?"

Leland nodded in agreement as he scrawled away. When they finished, they moved inside the trailer. Once inside the trailer, Wilson surveyed the room.

"It looks like there might have been a party going on."

"What makes you think that, Sheriff?"

"I'm basing it on the number of beer cans lying about."

Leland looked around the room and counted to himself. "Sheriff, it looks like there's about twenty beer cans in here."

"What's your point, Deputy?"

"All I'm saying is I've got buddies that drink a case of beer by themselves."

"Alright, Leland, just write this down. There may have been a party, or the victim may have been drinking a lot. Does that satisfy you?"

"Yes, Sheriff."

Keith turned off Route 68 and made his way southeasterly along Stoney Creek Road. He hadn't been out this way in some time. It was really wild looking country. He thought how glad he was that he didn't live out here. Poole didn't care for many of the more remote parts of Nicholas County. He had spent several years living on a farm, when he was a child. That was years ago, and he never wanted to live on a farm again. He liked having neighbors nearby, and the feeling of security that neighbors provided. It wasn't as if he was afraid to be out here, it was just that he'd never felt comfortable being out in the boonies.

As he pulled into the driveway, Keith could see Wilson standing just inside the trailer's front door. He climbed out of the van and made his way to the porch. He paused, and then slipped his booties and gloves on. Wilson pushed the screen door open, allowing room for Keith to step inside.

Keith glanced around the room and then asked, "What do we have, Sheriff?"

"We have a male victim in his early twenties. Looks like he went and committed suicide."

Keith stepped further into the room and turned to face the victim. Based on what he saw, it would be nearly impossible to determine the victim's age. Keith wondered if Wilson knew the guy. "Sheriff, you said that the victim was in his early twenties. Might I ask, how you can tell that? Did you know him?"

"Yes, Leland and I questioned him about something a while back. That's how I know his name, it's Lonnie Eldridge."

Tom watched as Bella wandered around the building site. He had plenty to do, but he also realized that he'd been neglecting her. "Hey, Bella, do you want to go for a walk?" With Bella, that was always a silly question, and she bounded off in the direction of her favorite trail. A long hike would do them both good. Tom knew that once he began working on the house, walks might be few and far between. He thought about what August had said, about installing a second wood stove. The idea made sense; the only problem might be a source of wood.

As they walked along the trail, Tom looked at their surroundings. Lately, he hadn't been paying much attention to the number of downed trees. He now realized that there were many. Maybe he could locate the property owner and get permission to remove some of the dead wood. A huge branch cracked as a turkey took flight. Bella watched as it flew away. Tom was curious about whether or not Wilson had taken his advice and gone to talk to Lonnie. *Probably not. Wilson doesn't like anyone to give him advice, especially me. Hopefully, Wilson will act on the lead he's been given and go bust the guy. One less thief living in Nicholas County would be a good thing.*

Keith was finished with what he had to do. The only thing that remained was getting the body moved to Carlisle. He sat on the sofa and watched as the Sheriff and Deputy milled about. He wasn't sure what they were doing. But, that was of little concern to him. He didn't aspire to be Sheriff. He mused about that a moment. *Wearing three hats; Funeral Home Director, County Coroner, and Sheriff. Wouldn't that be something?* Keith needed to talk with Wilson before he left.

"Excuse me, Sheriff. You said that you knew the deceased. Do you happen to know any of the relatives that live around here? He probably has parents or siblings that are still living. There's the matter of notifying the next of kin, remember?"

"Shit, I'd forgotten all about that, Keith. I'll try and find that out for you."

After the Coroner left, Wilson felt better. He didn't like other people to interfere with his investigations. He was trying to piece things together in his head. *Why would the guy shoot himself? For that matter, why did anyone shoot themselves? Drunk, maybe; depressed, maybe.* He and Leland had thoroughly searched the trailer and found nothing else. The gun, which was a 38, was found lying on the floor directly in front of the recliner. It must have recoiled that way after being fired, and then ended up there. Other than all the beer cans and a messy house, nothing odd seemed to stand out, except for the busted door frame. *Why had the door been kicked in? Could this actually have been a murder that was made to look like a suicide?* Wilson lost his train of thought as he noticed Leland crawling about on the floor. Leland slid his hand underneath the coffee table.

158

"Leland, just what in hell are you doing?"

"Well, Sheriff, the way I see it, the gun kicked this way." Leland used his hands to show the gun's path. "Why couldn't something else follow along with it, you know, because of the recoil?"

"Deputy, you're not making a damned bit of sense. What are you looking for under that table?"

Leland finally grasped what he'd been reaching for. He was still on the floor, but now he was kneeling. He studied the paper closely, and then reread it slowly to himself.

"Leland, is this some kind of secret? Do you mind letting me in on it? Leland, what the hell's written on that paper?"

"Sheriff, it says," '*If you want to find who did this, if you want to solve this crime, you need look no further than Tom Padgett. He is the person responsible for this. He is the bastard that caused this.*' "Sheriff, it's signed," '*Lonnie Eldridge.*'

He couldn't believe what Leland had just read. Wilson snatched the paper from the Deputy and laid it out flat on the coffee table and read it. Leland hadn't made any of it up. He'd read it word for word. Wilson smiled, possibly the broadest smile he had in years.

"Deputy, this changes things. By God, this definitely changes things."

After Tom and Bella finished their walk, he planned to go to Maysville. He needed some more tools for the upcoming project. As Tom drove along, he was preoccupied. He needed to talk with Nick. He should let him know that he would be moving soon. He wanted to get settled in his new home before winter had a chance to set in. Tom knew that Nick wouldn't be happy about that. But, he couldn't rely on Nick's generosity forever. Once Tom moved out, their relationship would return to the way it had been, before they'd become roommates. Tom worried that Nick actually liked the way things were and probably wished that things would stay the same.

Tom entered Lowe's and went directly to the hardware section. He studied the cordless tools on display. He really liked Dewalt tools, but they were out of his price range. It didn't matter if he was in Lowe's or Home Depot, he always bought power tools that were either lower priced or on sale, tools like Porter Cable or Ryobi, especially in light of his limited budget. Tom had never required the most expensive tools, not like many men did. He was frugal. As long as the tool did the job, he was satisfied. Tom had never been much of a brand name shopper, anyway. As he looked everything over, Bella wagged her tail and expected everyone that walked by to pay attention to her. She loved to come to Lowe's. After he finished shopping, he decided to pick up more beer. Tom was afraid the evening's conversation with Nick could last a while.

Theresa Walker sat at her desk thinking. She was toying with the idea of returning to private practice. Theresa was the Nicholas County Attorney. She'd been elected two years earlier. Now that seemed like an eternity ago, and she was only halfway into her first term. Sometimes the pettiness of county government nearly drove her crazy. Lately, she felt that she'd been doing way, way, too much hand holding. Didn't anyone around here know how to do their job? Being employed in Nicholas County, miles from her ex-husband Bob was definitely a plus. Now he couldn't drop in on her anytime he felt the urge. Still, she missed many of the things that they used to do.

When she had first left Lexington, it had been quite difficult. The house that she and her ex had shared, down in Chevy Chase, had been really nice. But that was behind her now. She was on her own. Besides, the little place that she bought in Carlisle and now lived in was just fine. However, entertaining her ten year old daughter, April, was a challenge whenever she visited. There wasn't anything to do in Carlisle. At least that's what her daughter claimed. After their divorce, Bob and April moved to Georgetown. They now lived less than a mile from the Toyota plant, which was where Bob worked. April had adjusted to the town and had found plenty of new friends. Theresa wished she had a better relationship with her daughter, but with her chosen profession, making time for a young girl could at times be difficult.

There was a knock on the door, which startled her.

Wilson poked his head inside. "Theresa, are you busy? Do you have a couple minutes?"

Theresa wanted to moan out loud. "What is it Wilson? I'm pretty busy right now."

"I just wanted to run something by you, about my suspicion of Padgett, and his possible involvement in the Lonnie Eldridge case."

"Sheriff, let's wait until we have the Coroner's report before we jump to any conclusions."

"But, I have evidence which shows Padgett's involvement."

"That's fine, Wilson. But, like I said, let's wait for the Coroner's report."

Wilson pulled the door closed behind him and then stomped down the stairs. He didn't like asking for help on cases. Just recently, he'd been given a talking to by the County Attorney. That hadn't been any fun. Theresa had made it clear that his habit of continuing to go rogue on cases constituted entirely unacceptable behavior. She had told him that he needed to advise her before he went after suspects. After all, she was the one responsible for handling the prosecution. But, Wilson didn't need her telling him how to do his job. He didn't need to wait for Keith Poole's results, either. He had results of his own. Wilson knew one thing for sure. Tonight, he was going to have some Jim Beam. He'd earned it.

Tom sat at the kitchen table and nursed his second beer. He was awaiting Nick's response.

Nick took a long pull from his beer before speaking. "Why are you in such a damned hurry to get into your house? I've told you that you can stay here as long as you like."

"I know that, Nick. Besides, I won't be moving out right away. I just need to get started on my house. It will take a long time to finish it, anyway. You had to realize that I couldn't rely on your generosity forever."

"Why not? I'm perfectly content with you staying here. I was getting lonely before you and Bella moved in."

Tom went to get two more beers. He could see that Nick was getting upset. It seemed Nick was going to get more upset than he had imagined. He placed another beer in front of Nick and took a seat.

"Tom, there's more to it than you just staying here. I want more than friendship. I want a partner. Do you understand?"

Tom realized his suspicions had been correct. He took a large swallow and looked across the table at his friend.

"Nick, I understand what you're saying. But I'm not the man for you. We can continue doing the things we enjoy doing together. But, I don't have the same kind of feelings that you do. Do you understand?"

Nick wore a pained expression as he sipped his beer. He stared down at the table and said nothing.

"This doesn't have to change our relationship. I'm sorry I don't feel the same way you do. But that doesn't mean we can't still be friends."

"Alright, but promise me one thing?"

"What's that?"

"That you won't go and put your building plans into high gear, now that you know about my feelings."

Tom had to laugh. "Nothing has changed, I'll be working on the house during the day, and then come back here in the evenings. We can still hang out at the Gyp or O'Rourke's or wherever, just like we always have."

Nick smiled at Tom and then got up and went to the fridge. They each needed another cold one.

CHAPTER 17

Keith finished the task he'd been working on. He picked up the phone and dialed a number. After he hung up, he took a long swallow from the Ale 8 that he had allowed to get warm while it sat on his desk. He figured it wouldn't be long before Wilson arrived. He might be mistaken, but it seemed that the Sheriff and his Deputy had been looking for something else at the shooting scene. The evidence that Keith had found clearly indicated a suicide, no question about that. He shook his head and chuckled to himself at the thought of Wilson. The guy just couldn't let go. He was like some relentless pit-bull when it came to his dealings with Padgett.

Wilson's pulse quickened. He turned his truck around and headed back toward town. He was optimistic that the Coroner would have good news. Anything that could tie Eldridge's death to Padgett would be an added bonus. Up ahead, a couple of cars were driving slower than Wilson cared to. He switched on his light bar and hit the siren as he blew around them. He glanced in the rear view mirror to fully appreciate the look of fear that he so much enjoyed creating. He was in pursuit. This was an emergency. He was going to make sure that the threat to Nicholas County finally received the punishment he deserved. *Padgett, I'm coming for your ass. No doubt about it and you're mine this time.*

Tom sipped on his coffee and thought about the previous evening's conversation. Nick had eventually calmed down, but it wasn't until well after midnight before he had done so. Through the course of the evening, they had managed to drink quite a number of beers. Nick had left for work ten minutes ago. Tom laughed to himself as he recalled the time he had asked Nick if Walmart allowed him to work drunk. Tom looked over at the overstuffed chair where Bella lay. She was all curled up and she looked quite comfortable. Bella appeared to be asleep, but every time Tom raised his coffee cup, her eyes opened. She was probably dreaming about a long hike.

Keith scowled at Wilson as both men tried their best to calm down. "Sheriff, I don't understand why you're so damned convinced that my report is inaccurate. Is there something you know that you're not telling me?"

Wilson didn't like candid questions thrown his way. He looked around the room before his eyes once again settled on the Coroner's. "Keith, there are things pertinent to the case that I haven't mentioned. Padgett was the source of info which led us to Eldridge. There is also evidence of foul play that I'm confident involves Padgett."

"Have you talked to the County Attorney about this? I seem to recall that you recently got into some hot water with Theresa over some of your heavy-handed law enforcement techniques?"

Wilson hated it when anyone mentioned anything about his mistakes. *Who the hell did Keith think he was talking to anyway?* Wilson almost whispered, "Yes I have. She suggested that I wait until I have your results before I consider going after Padgett."

"So, that's why you're upset with the results? You wanted to hear that Padgett was in some way involved? Sheriff, all indicators point to a suicide, and there is no evidence to make me believe anything different."

"But, why would Padgett suggest that we pay a visit to Eldridge? And, what about the forced entry into the trailer? What about the boot imprint on the door? Don't you think that indicates something?"

"It might, Sheriff. But, it does nothing to change the fact

165

that Lonnie Eldridge shot himself. If you think that Padgett forced the guy to do this, then that's an entirely different scenario. And, to be perfectly honest with you Sheriff, I feel it's a stretch, and I also believe it would be very difficult to prove."

Wilson slammed the door as he left the funeral home. Why is everyone in the damned county constantly covering for Padgett? Was he the only one that could see through Padgett's cloak of deceit?

Tom was nearly to the home site when his phone rang. It was Andy. *Had it already been two weeks? Had Andy and his new bride returned from their honeymoon? Where did the time go?* Tom slowly pulled over onto the shoulder of the road and stopped. He hoped he had reception, especially being so near the Licking River.

"Hello, Andy. How's married life? How was your honeymoon?" Tom listened and heard no response. He looked at the phone and noticed that he still had an alright signal.

"Andy, are you there? Can you hear me?"

"Yes, Dad, I can hear you. Our honeymoon was fine."

Tom waited another beat, but his son said nothing. Andy had never been overly forthcoming, especially when it came to talking on the phone. Tom listened to the silence on the line build. He reluctantly decided to try a more direct approach.

"Is everything alright, son?"

"No, it's not alright."

Tom wondered what he had done now. Why did it always have to be so difficult with Andy? "What's the problem? Is Nancy alright?"

"No, Nancy is not alright. She's not happy at all. Last night, she called her mother when we returned home. Nancy was totally shocked to learn that her mother knew nothing about her pregnancy. You were supposed to tell Mom. Why didn't you?"

Tom wanted to laugh at the situation, but found himself getting angry.

"Wait a minute, Andy. What do you mean I didn't tell your mother? Is that what she told you?"

"Yes it is. Are you claiming that you told her? When I mentioned the baby's due date, Mom was shocked. She claimed she had no idea."

Tom waited a few more seconds before replying. "Andy, I told your Mother. I also let her know that it was her responsibility to inform Nancy's parents. I didn't feel right doing that. Personally I didn't think it should be her responsibility to do your dirty work. But, I did as I was instructed. If she wants to put the blame on me, so be it. If you choose to believe her, I guess that's your decision. Now, if there's nothing else you'd like to talk about, I'm really kind of busy."

Tom severed the connection.

Theresa had not been having a good morning, and now Wilson wanted to talk with her. The petty issues had been many today. The thought of leaving Carlisle and returning to private practice, was stronger than ever this morning. She was already aware of the Coroner's findings. She realized that the Sheriff probably wanted to argue his point, one more time. She thought to herself, *if Wilson would pay half as much attention to the things happening in the county as he did to his obsession with Padgett, there might be far fewer crimes.*

Her thoughts were interrupted as Wilson stuck his head through her door and timidly entered.

"Come on in, Sheriff. What's on your mind? Whatever it is, let's get it done. I've got a busy day ahead of me, and I don't have a lot of time to waste."

Wilson was immediately on the defensive since the County Attorney had insinuated that he was simply a waste of time. He cleared his throat, "Theresa, I assume you received the Coroner's report?"

"I have. Do you have a problem with it?"

"Yes, I do. Even though the report states that Lonnie Eldridge killed himself by his own hand, I can't help but believe Padgett was involved."

"Wilson, haven't we already been down this road? I thought I told you not to go off on one of your wild goose chases after Padgett."

Wilson hung his head as Theresa chastised him. He wanted to defend himself. He wanted to blurt out the reasons for his suspicions, but he'd already done that. He'd wait for Theresa to come around to his way of thinking.

Theresa realized that she was lecturing, and then softened. "OK, Sheriff. What is it that you are suggesting? And, it had better be good."

"I'd like to bring Padgett in for his involvement in Eldridge's death."

"We were just discussing that very issue, Wilson. Keith said that the suicide was self inflicted. What makes you believe you have evidence to dispute that?"

"There's the matter of the suicide note; the note that implicates Padgett."

"Wilson, this is the first I've heard about any suicide note. Exactly what are you talking about?"

It was Wilson's turn to smile, and he did just that.

Tom found himself wandering around his home site, lost in

thought. The conversation he'd had with his son had been quite upsetting. He'd known better than to agree to do his son's dirty work. He was already the *'bad guy'* in both his son's and his daughter-in-law's eyes. And now, Darlene was contributing to the mess. Luckily, Bella was content to wander around the edge of the woods while her master wrestled with his thoughts. Tom was frustrated with his relationship with Andy. It seemed it would never improve. It wouldn't improve soon enough for Tom, anyway.

He decided to forget about his problems with Andy for the moment. He needed to concentrate on what he'd come to do. Today, he planned to install his wood stove. August had been right about the change in the weather. A winter storm was brewing. The mild winter was going to take a major turn. Luckily, August and his crew had finished. The rest of the project was up to Tom. With a utility knife, Tom removed the cardboard that covered the stove. Next, he needed to empty the contents of the stove. He stacked the firebrick off to one side, which greatly reduced the stove's weight. Now he could easily move the stove around and position it exactly where he wanted.

He grabbed his sawzall and began to cut though the exterior wall. He had two fully-charged 18 volt batteries. They should provide more than enough power for today's task. After finishing the hole, Tom stepped outside to mount the double-wall stainless steel chimney. Bella watched curiously as Tom climbed up and down the ladder, carrying sections of pipe. After he had attached the chimney cap, he climbed down and caulked around the hole's perimeter. Satisfied with the job, he moved inside to position the stove and finish connecting the interior sections. Lastly, he replaced the firebrick. *Let the bad weather come, I'm ready.*

Wilson whistled as he walked to Garrett's. He was going to have a hearty meal. He wanted to have a full stomach when he headed out to arrest Padgett. Wilson was quite proud of the way he had handled Theresa. Maybe there was hope for them yet. *She's quite the looker and she really has a nice set of tits.* Wilson slowed as he descended the steps. *I wonder what Theresa looks like naked?* He caught himself and stopped his hormone-driven thoughts before he entered the restaurant. He didn't need another incident right in the middle of town. Later this afternoon he would have the warrant in hand. *I'm going to thoroughly enjoy delivering the news to the big man.*

Theresa had just returned from a late lunch. She entered the courthouse and noticed the Deputy. He was at the end of the lobby, studying wanted posters. She walked over to him because she had a couple of questions.

"Deputy, were you with the Sheriff when Lonnie Eldridge's body was discovered?"

"Yes, ma'am, I was."

"Could you come up to my office? I'd like to ask you a few questions."

Lonnie excitedly followed Theresa up the steps. He had never been in the County Attorney's office before. *Why does she want to talk to me? Maybe I'm going to receive an award or something.*

Theresa entered her office and sat behind her desk, then asked Leland to have a seat. "Deputy Leland, I'd like to hear your take on the investigation that took place at Lonnie Eldridge's. I like to hear if your story is the same as that of the Sheriff's."

"Am I going to get in any trouble if it's different than the Sheriff's?"

"No, Deputy. I just need to have some of my doubts satisfied before I proceed with the arrest warrant for Mr. Padgett."

What the hell is taking so long with Padgett's arrest warrant? Wilson was confident that Theresa was firmly in his court. He was chomping at the bit to deliver Padgett the news. He was excited as he jogged up the steps, taking them two at a time.

The Attorney's secretary wasn't at her desk. Wilson straightened his hat, hiked up his pants, and then tightened his gun belt as he got ready to knock on the door. Suddenly, the door opened and out stepped his Deputy.

"Hey, Boss, how's it going?"

"Leland, what in the hell are you doing here so early? And, why are you talking with the County Attorney?"

"Oh, I was bored, so I decided to come in early. I was downstairs looking at the wanted posters and the County Attorney said she wanted to talk with me."

Wilson had no idea what this meant. He watched Leland walk out of the office and down the stairs. He heard a voice yell out. Wilson began to get nervous.

"Sheriff, have you got a few minutes?"

Tom relaxed on a lawn chair and popped open a beer as he observed his handy work. The installation of the stove had gone extremely well, which was quite unusual. Sometimes, even the simplest jobs require nearly every tool from the toolbox. But today, everything had gone smoothly. Bella was even satisfied and hadn't been pestering him all day about a walk. But, as Tom looked around at his shell of a house, he knew that many difficult tasks lay ahead. His utilities were stubbed in. First, he planned to do the electrical, and then he'd start on the plumbing.

Wilson left the County Attorney's office at quarter-past-five. To say that he was unhappy was an understatement. Theresa had read him the riot act. He had not gotten the arrest warrant that he'd expected. It didn't appear he was going to get it, either. He muttered to himself as he left the courthouse. *The damned attorney lectured me for the past hour about how the legal system worked.* He had zoned her out after about five minutes, but she prattled on. *'Not following procedure, tampering with evidence, vindictive*

171

behavior, prejudice, letting responsibilities slide because of an overzealous attitude toward Tom Padgett'. She went on and on. *So much for us becoming an item. I don't give a damn how nice her tits are, she's definitely off my list.*

Tom had picked up The Mercury and the Carlisle Courier and was reading them at the table, when Nick arrived home. Nick appeared to be in good spirits, which pleased Tom. He wasn't up for another stressful evening; one spent talking about relationships. Nick threw his blue vest over the back of a chair and walked down the hall to change. Tom was totally enthralled with the article he was reading. Lonnie Eldridge had committed suicide. He hadn't expected anything like that to happen. *Had I really been that hard on the guy? There had to be an underlying cause to make Lonnie do that.* The article went on to say that the Sheriff was investigating, but the Coroner's report claimed it had been a suicide.

CHAPTER 18

Wilson topped up another large glass. It was to the rim, full of Jim Beam. To hell with the County Attorney. Bill Wilson is still the law around here. He was going to continue his quest to get Padgett. *All that shit that Theresa had been rambling on about, was nothing more than a bunch of mumbo-jumbo. I'd like to know what the hell Leland told her to make her do a complete one-eighty?* Wilson took another long swallow of whiskey while he stared down at his phone's display. He browsed through his list of contacts, and then he hit send.

Nick brought two beers over to the table and sat facing Tom. "So, how was your day, Mr. Padgett?"

"Mr. Padgett? What's up with the sudden formality?"

Nick laughed and drained about half his beer. "I'm just messing with you, Tom. I just want you to know that there are no hard feelings."

"That's good, Mr. Mitchell. Did you happen to hear about the suicide over in Nicholas County? Lonnie Eldridge shot himself."

"I didn't hear anything about a suicide. Wait a minute, isn't that the guy that you suspected of robbing your trailer?"

"The same. I wonder what made him do something like that?" Tom's phone bounced around as it vibrated on the table. He picked it up and noticed a missed call and voice mail. He hit play and switched it to speaker phone.

"Padgett, this is Wilson. You're not going to get away with murder in my county, and sure as hell not on my watch. I know you were involved in Eldridge's suicide, I know you're dirty and I'm going to prove it." The message ended.

Tom stared at the phone, but said nothing.

"Tom, I think he sounded drunk. I'm sure of it, I'm sure he was drunk. Don't listen to what he said."

Tom still said nothing. He stood, went to the fridge, and then grabbed two more beers. He handed one to Nick before he stepped out into the back yard.

After gaining entrance, he quickly glanced around the room. He shook his head as he noticed that nearly every light in the house was on. He didn't require many lights, not for this evening's task. He switched the lights off as he moved about the house, all except for the one hanging over the kitchen table. He listened to the irritatingly loud snoring that came from the living room. He thought how easy it would be to make the annoying sound go away, snuff it out forever. But, that wasn't his intention. Not yet, anyway. He turned and then silently made his way down the hallway. He couldn't believe how slovenly the owner of the house lived. He felt it was absolutely disgusting that anyone allowed themselves to live this way. He found nothing of interest in any of the rooms. The guy was a loser.

After a bit, he made his way back into the darkness of the living room and paused. He tensed slightly as the noisy snorer nearly woke. From the shadow, he watched as the slob of a man moved about on the recliner, in an attempt to get comfortable. Once the loud snoring resumed, he returned to his search. He rifled through the miscellaneous videos. What perverted garbage. This guy needed to get a life. And the music selection, it was something someone twice his age would listen to. He was tiring of the game. It was time to make a decision. It was time to determine his fate. Did he deserve to live, or did he deserve to die?

Fortunately, for the snorer, tonight, he had decided on the former. It was then that he noticed the pad of paper which lay on the kitchen table.

The Next Morning

Wilson quickly shook his head back and forth in an attempt to wake up. Once again, he had fallen asleep in his recliner. That was becoming commonplace. It hadn't been his intention to tie one on the previous evening, but the damned County Attorney had left him little choice. Wilson scanned the room and felt the familiar throbbing begin to build in his head. He untangled his feet from the recliner's foot rest and made his way to the kitchen. He looked at the wall clock and shook three aspirin from the plastic bottle into his shaking hand. It was only five o'clock, but there was no point trying to go back to sleep.

Wilson scooped more coffee on top of the previously used grounds, added some water and then switched on the machine. He opened the fridge's door, but saw nothing that he thought was worth cooking. He'd have some coffee and then head to Garrett's to have breakfast. Something bothered Wilson, even though as usual, he remembered little from last night. But this feeling was strange. It felt as if he hadn't been alone last night. Wilson looked around the room again before he allowed the thought to fade. He noticed the list of ideas he'd written to get Padgett. It was still lying on the table. He wasn't in the mood to look at it. He pulled the carafe out from beneath the dripping coffee maker and poured half a cup. He hobbled down the hallway. He could smell his own body odor. Obviously, he needed a shower.

Tom woke from what must have been another fitful night. He and Nick had both been tired last night. That should have insured that it would be an early evening. But no, ever curious Nick wanted to discuss the suicide. He also wanted to talk about the accusatory voice mail from Wilson. Tom finally had to put his foot down and said no way. They were in bed before ten. He looked at his phone, it was five-fifteen. He'd had plenty of sleep.

175

Why did he feel so tired? He remembered having a dream, but it had been vague; not nearly as vivid as some he'd had lately. Regardless, it had been an odd dream. He would almost describe it as being dull. The only aspect of the dream that he had any recollection of was one of Wilson. In the dream, he remembered seeing Wilson. He was sleeping in his underwear as he lay curled up on a recliner. Tom stood and stretched, wandered into the kitchen and turned on the coffee maker. Bella stood waiting at the back door. He let her out.

Wilson finished his shower, and studied his reflection in the bathroom mirror. For once, he thought he looked even worse than he felt. But, that wasn't his fault. He had grand plans and he planned to rid the county of its number one problem, until the damned County Attorney interfered. Wilson convinced himself not to worry about that now. He wrapped the towel around his waist and cursed. The damned towel barely reached. Back in the kitchen, he looked at the coffee maker. He'd left his cup in the bathroom, so he pulled a dirty one from the pile in the sink. He poured himself more coffee, and then glanced over at his note pad, which was lying on the table. He carried his cup to the table and ripped the sheet from the pad.

Wilson was shocked at what he saw and nearly spilled his coffee. There was writing on the pad underneath the sheet that he'd just torn off. But, it wasn't his handwriting. He studied the pad. The handwriting was incredibly neat, neater than any Wilson had ever seen. All the sentences were written individually, with the first word of each sentence beginning with a larger capital letter. The remainder of the sentence was also in caps, but the letters were smaller. The letters were perfect, almost like fonts that he remembered from computer courses he'd taken in high school. The note wasn't long, but the message was clear.

YOU CHOOSE TO LIVE YOUR LIFE OF FILTH LIKE ALL SWINE.

IF SOMEONE HAS WHAT YOU WANT, THEN YOU TRY TO TAKE IT.

YOU HATE ANYONE THAT YOU FEEL MIGHT BE BETTER

THAN YOU.

NOTHING MAKES YOU HAPPY, SO YOU TRY TO KEEP OTHERS DOWN.

WILSON, I'VE READ YOUR NOTES. BE CAREFUL WHAT YOU WISH FOR.

THE NEXT TIME YOU BADGER MY BEST FRIEND, I WON'T BE SO NICE.

Tom sipped his coffee and stroked Bella's back. He didn't know what to think about the voice mail that Wilson had left last night. Was it just another typical Wilson maneuver? Tom had no idea what Wilson went on about. This morning though, the more he thought about it, the less he was bothered by it. Wilson was a blowhard, and someday he was going to get what he had coming. Tom thought about Lonnie Eldridge's suicide. He tried to understand why Eldridge would have done what he did. Was he really afraid that Tom would return and shoot him, or could he have been just worried about going to jail? Whatever the reason, killing himself wasn't the answer.

Wilson wasn't sure what to think as he re-read the note. He didn't understand what it meant. Was it from Padgett's other self? Had he managed to rattle Padgett? One thing was certain, whoever had snuck into his house and left the note, had sure as hell rattled him. Wilson tried to control his shaking hands as he poured more coffee. Maybe he needed to take the day off in order to think things through. Should he call the police for help? What good would that do? They'd just think he was imagining things. What Wilson really needed was a plan, but wasn't that what he'd been working on?

If the police came out and saw the ideas he'd been formulating to make Padgett crack, they would assume he got what he had coming. Maybe he needed to get rid of the list of things he planned to use against Padgett. That probably wouldn't work. If he did that, then the threatening handwritten note that was addressed to him would have no point of reference. The city cops would want to know about the so-called notes. All of a sudden, Wilson felt sick to his stomach. Once again, it seemed he had managed to get himself into another spot.

Tom knew that he needed to work on the house, so why was he here? He didn't know why he was walking through the woods with Bella. He was wrapped in his thoughts and had no idea what Bella was doing. The deeper they walked into the woods, the more of last night's dream Tom remembered. He thought it odd that his memories of dreams were getting stronger over time. Usually, they faded and tended to disappear quickly. Tom could clearly see Wilson. He was lying on a recliner sleeping and he snored loudly. He remembered that all the lights in Wilson's house had been on, but then a moment later they were off. He could see Wilson's stuff strewn about the place. It was a mess.

Tom paused as a group of deer were spooked and bounded away. Bella tilted her head and watched Tom. *How could I see inside of Wilson's house? Was that really what it looked like?* Tom had never been to Wilson's and he had no idea where he even lived. Tom noticed that Bella was giving him a very concerned look, so he resumed walking. *Maybe it was just an odd dream, and it wasn't really Wilson's house. Maybe it was just some dream details that had been created in my state of sleep. That was probably it.* But as hard as Tom tried, he couldn't shake the memory. His dreams had been getting more vivid since he'd been living in Nicholas County. But, he didn't remember ever having a dream where he could not only hear a person snore, but he could even smell the person's body odor.

Wilson disconnected the call. He had arranged for Leland to cover for him today. A three day weekend might just be what he needed in order to decide what to do about the two Padgetts. Yes, Padgett and his brother; the one that lived inside Padgett's head; the one that only came out to create havoc. Wilson had finally calmed down from the initial fright of seeing the note. He was quickly getting back to his old self. He wasn't going to let that tired old law-man frighten him, even if there did happen to be two of him. The way Wilson saw it, his chances of getting Padgett had just greatly improved. As a matter of fact, they had doubled.

Tom had finally been able to forget about the dream he'd had and even called Woozy to ask her out. So tonight, they were doing that, going out. Woozy didn't get many nights off, so tonight would have to do. Tom picked her up at her place and drove to downtown Maysville. Tom didn't believe that they would have needed reservations, but he was wrong. Chandler's was their first choice and they were told that there was an hour wait. Woozy suggested trying deSha's, which was close by. Once they were seated, Tom found himself once again at a loss for words. Actually, he could have blurted out just about anything and it might have sounded beautiful to Woozy. Her life with Jimmy probably hadn't lent itself to a great many compliments. But, as Tom sat at the table across from Woozy, he was silent.

Wilson studied the handwritten note as he sipped his coffee. He then reread the list of ideas that he had written down, the list that he had intended to use in an attempt to get under Padgett's skin. He looked from one to the other and tried to make sense of things. *If Padgett had been there last night, what prompted him to come?* The precise, handwritten note indicated that Wilson's notes had been read, and that he should be careful what he wished for. It went on to say that the next time Wilson badgered his friend, the mysterious note leaver wouldn't be so nice. *It was definitely a threat, but who was it from?*

Wilson couldn't believe he had sat there all day long and stared at that damned piece of paper. He picked up his phone and noticed the time. *Damn it's six o'clock. Where the hell had the day gone?* Suddenly he had a thought and clicked on his most recent calls. He stared at the display and tried in vain to remember the call. *So, I had called Padgett last night?* He futilely tried to remember. *Did I talk to him? Did I leave a message?* The length of the call on the display was for only a minute. *What could we have talked about that only took a minute?* He poured out the rest of his coffee into the sink, and then pulled a glass and bottle from the liquor cabinet. He needed to concentrate.

For a long time Tom had been meaning to ask Woozy something. He remembered an old saying, 'there's no time like the present.'

"Woozy, how did you get the name Woozy? It's quite an unusual name."

Woozy's expression saddened somewhat before she replied, "It's a long story, Tom. Are you sure you want to hear it?" Before Tom could answer, Woozy continued, "My father was an alcoholic, and to make matters worse, he was also abusive. On the day my mother gave birth to me, as usual, my father was drunk. By the time I was born, my mother already had a name picked for me, but my father was insistent, he was insistent that I be called Woozy. My parents fought often over the years. Many of their fights were arguments about my name. One time, my father punched my mother quite viciously. At the time, he was in one of his drunken rages. They were arguing over my name again. At the time, I was seven years old. My mother died from the injuries she'd gotten from my father punching her."

Wilson walked around the house and sipped from his Jim Beam. There was nothing out of place and nothing appeared to be missing. If last night's visitor had been Padgett, then something drastic should have happened. *Wasn't that his modus operandi?* Wilson still believed that Padgett had been the one that found the two meth labs. The explosions resulted in one person being seriously injured and another person killed. *He was most likely the one that had caught Fugate raping the Mexican girl. End result, Fugate's death. Padgett's other self wasn't likely to give a warning, so why would he warn me? To be honest, if I was Padgett, I'd be the last person that Padgett should give a warning to. This sure is a mystery. That's what Padgett's ex-wife said, 'There are many mysteries that surround Tom Padgett.'*

Wilson put on a coat and carried an armload of stuff with him out onto the back porch. It had turned cold, but armed with his writing pad and whiskey, Wilson didn't care. He poured a generous glass of Jim Beam and held it up to the light that filtered through the kitchen window. He loved the color of whiskey. He wondered what he said to Padgett over the phone. *What could I have said that was so damning that provoked last night's response? What could it have been?* He took a healthy swallow and hoped that the whiskey would aid him in remembering the conversation.

Tom sat quietly as Woozy took a sip from her wine, and then continued. "After my mother died, my father was sent to prison. He wanted me to forgive him. He asked me to legally change my name to the one my mother had chosen for me, but I refused. To me, the name Woozy represents defiance; my defiance of my father, for what he did to my mother and defiance for the name he saddled me with."

Tom wasn't sure how to respond, he wasn't even sure if a response was necessary. Woozy seemed to momentarily be in another place as she stared at the table. Finally, Tom got the nerve to speak. "That's terrible, Woozy. I had no idea. I'm sorry I asked."

"No it's alright, it feels good to talk about it every once in a while, anyway. It actually helps me keep things in perspective."

"Where's your father now, Woozy?"

"You know, after he was released from prison, he just disappeared. I haven't a clue where he is. I haven't had contact with him for at least thirty years."

Tom felt he needed to change the subject. Thankfully, their dinner arrived. They ate in silence, only occasionally smiling at one another. Tom wondered, *since Woozy has been so open about her relationship with her father, maybe it's time I shared some of my past.* He'd always had difficulty talking about his past, but Woozy seemed to be a good listener.

"I had some father issues too, Woozy. Don't get me wrong, I learned a great deal from the man, but some of the lessons were painfully difficult. My father was one of those men, you know, it was either his way or the highway. He could be quite abusive, especially if he'd been drinking. He could come unhinged quickly, sometimes only because of a simple thing. But, he never touched either of my sisters. He always seemed to save his pent up frustration for me."

"That's terrible, Tom. What about your mother? Was he abusive to her?"

"Sometimes, but as he got older he seemed to mellow, but there was always something mysterious about the man. He had some secret, I know it. But, my mother refused to talk about it. I would have loved to talk to her about my dad, to find out more about the man, but the right opportunity never came up. She spent her entire adult life with him, they were inseparable. My parents were both killed in an auto accident years ago."

Woozy sat quietly as she listened. When Tom finished, she said, "We seem to have a lot in common."

Wilson believed the whiskey was helping. He studied his phone's display. So, he'd made an outgoing call that had only lasted a minute. He desperately wondered, *did I talk to Padgett or just leave a voice mail?* Either way, it seemed the message had been effective. Wilson laughed as he thought back to how nervous he had initially been this morning when he read the note. He was really rattled, but not now. He had nothing to fear from Padgett. He had the guy just where he wanted him. At least, that was what he believed in his current state. He took another rather large sip of whiskey, swirled it around in his mouth, and then swallowed.

CHAPTER 19

Friday Afternoon

Becky Adkins had been living in Clinton, Tennessee for several months. The move here hadn't gone quite as she had planned. The job front had been an absolute failure. The pill mill was rapidly becoming less and less productive. The most important lesson Becky had learned though, was the message of a statement she heard quite often, 'You're not from around here, are you?' It carried a lot of weight, especially in Tennessee.

She carefully applied more color to her hair, making sure to get it evenly distributed. She was going back to her natural color, red. She never gave much thought to her Irish ancestry, but suddenly she felt that having red hair was important. The Tennessee slogan, *America at Its Best*, had not worked out for Becky, and now she was going home. She was leaving the great state of Tennessee and traveling back to her roots, back to Kentucky.

Becky Adkins had grown up in Morehead, Kentucky. It was the largest city in Rowan County. She lived at home with her parents while she attended Morehead State University. After she graduated from college, she finally moved out of her parents' house and into an apartment, sharing the apartment and expenses with her boyfriend, Adam. She and Adam had met at MSU and shortly after graduation, they married. That had been a mistake. Luckily, there were no children. Prior to becoming an Adkins, her maiden name had been McEntire. She wondered, *what has Adam had been up to?* She was also trying to figure out, *who had walked out on whom? Am I still legally married?* She never received any divorce paperwork. When she left Fleming County last year, she had done so abruptly. She had just packed up and ran. She ran from the Sheriff and she ran from Adam. *Maybe, I even run from Tom Padgett.*

Tom was at O'Rourke's, nursing a beer as Nick strolled in. Nick clapped Tom on the back. "How's it going, partner?"

"It's going alright. How was your day?"

"It was great. The Walmart Regional Manager visited our store today. He told us that our store was doing wonderfully. He said that we should be extremely proud of our performance. We are in the top twenty-five percent of the nation."

"That's great news, Nick. Did you guys get raises? Since you're doing so well, I believe that should entitle you to a raise."

Nick laughed, "No, we didn't get raises. But, our stock price keeps going up. Why today, it was up fifty cents." Nick ordered another round.

Tom glanced around the bar. It wasn't busy for a Friday afternoon, but it was still early. The door opened and a couple of men wandered in. The pair sat next to Tom, and ordered whiskey shots and beer. Woozy served their drinks and the pair quickly downed their shots, and then almost as quickly, they downed the beer. Tom laughed under his breath as he listened to them order another round. *Looks like trouble waiting to happen.* Once again, they quickly downed their drinks. Tom wondered if they were having some kind of competition.

She found a place to rent in Paris, Kentucky. Luckily for Becky, it was reasonably priced. That was fortunate, because she was low on cash. She wasn't selling nearly as much Oxycontin as she had in the past. That was mainly due to changes in the manufacturing process, which had made the capsules nearly tamper proof, so that they couldn't be smashed and made easily into powder. The addicts wanted a quick high and powder was the only way to achieve that. So, she had began to transition to alternative drugs, such as cocaine and heroin. Becky was optimistic that she could reclaim much of her original territory, but she had to be careful, especially in and around Nicholas County. She hoped that all the history with Wilson and Padgett was behind her. She would find out soon enough. She planned to return tomorrow morning.

Tom was half listening to Nick and half listening to the guy on his right. He had ordered another round of boilermakers and he and his buddy were getting wound up. As Woozy turned to help other customers, one of them asked, "Hey baby, what do you say about you and I getting together? What time you get off?"

Woozy continued to make her way to the other end of the bar as she called over her right shoulder, "I'm sorry, but I'm not interested."

Tom couldn't make out what they were talking about, but now they were sharing a laugh. Woozy returned carrying two more beers that Nick had ordered.

The guy called to Woozy again, "Hey baby, maybe we could have a drink after you get off tonight? Do you live around here?"

"I said I'm not interested."

More laughter; now Tom ignored Nick as he attempted to hear what the two guys were talking about. He was starting to have a very bad feeling about things. He felt that Woozy could take care of herself, especially in a public place, but he couldn't sit here and ignore the situation much longer. He didn't want to get involved and he hoped he wouldn't need to.

Her car was loaded. All she needed to do in the morning was get dressed and hit the road. Becky loved road trips, especially in her hot black Mustang. She loved rolling up the interstate in it. She especially enjoyed seeing the expressions on the faces of men as she blew past them. Tomorrow was going to be a good day. Becky hoped that the house she rented in Paris was as nice as the one she had in Clinton. Unfortunately, the Paris house was a two-family and was located in town. She was concerned that privacy might be an issue. But, it was furnished and had off-street parking. It should be okay. Now that all the trivial stuff was taken care of, she could relax and do a line of coke. She felt she'd earned it. She glanced approvingly in the bathroom mirror at the redhead she saw in the mirror, and then she wiped the powder from her nose. *Yes, Becky, your hair is longer, and now it's red. Nobody will ever recognize you.*

Woozy really didn't want to go to the other end of the bar. She tried not to listen as the obnoxious guy called for another round. Maybe she should refuse to serve him. He was definitely getting drunk. She reluctantly decided otherwise. She didn't need to have a complaint lodged against her. After she set the drinks down, the guy was even more aggressive.

"Hey baby, what you say we go out back for a little fun?"

Woozy was getting angry, so she ignored him.

Tom turned, "Maybe you didn't hear the lady? She said she's not interested."

The guy casually glanced Tom's way, as if sizing him up before replying, "I wasn't talking to you." He then turned his attention back to Woozy, "Come on baby, we could have a really good time."

Tom was getting angry. "The lady said she's not interested."

"Who the hell asked you, old man?"

Nick had been listening, while watching things develop. He decided to intervene. "If I were you, I wouldn't call him old man. He's an ex-cop. You better watch what you say."

"I don't remember saying anything to you, fat ass."

Amazingly quickly, Tom reached around and grabbed a handful of the guy's hair and then slammed his head against the bar. Then, he relaxed and finished the rest of his beer. Woozy and Nick both stared at Tom, but neither one said anything. After a minute or two, the guy Tom had roughed up groggily raised his head and looked around the bar.

Quietly, Tom said, "I suggest you apologize to the lady and to my friend here, for the remarks you made."

He painfully pushed himself upright and staggered to his feet. "I'm sorry for what I said." After that he and his buddy left the pub.

Woozy wasn't sure what to think. Should she be flattered? After a moment, she decided that she was not flattered. She was angry.

"Tom, I don't need any more possessive men around me. I've lived my whole damned life around possessive men, and I never plan on doing that again." She spun on her heel and walked to the other end of the bar and asked someone else to tend the bar for a while. Woozy didn't want to be around Tom or anyone right now. She needed time to herself.

Nick was at a loss. He watched Woozy walk away. He didn't say anything. He watched as Tom stood and look in the direction of the front door. But, then Tom walked to the bathroom. When he returned, he paused behind Nick's stool. "Nick, could you take care of Bella? I've got some thinking to do."

"Sure. What are you going to do?"

But, Tom didn't hear what Nick said. He continued to walk out the door.

Saturday Morning

Becky exited the interstate on the outskirts of Lexington and then followed Route 68 northeast en-route to Paris. Her new home was located on West 8th Street, near the corner of Lylesville Street. The house was similar in style to shotgun houses that are common in the South. Oddly though, it had an upper level. The off-street parking wasn't quite what she had expected, but the furniture was okay, so it would do. The more she thought about it, the location was actually quite good. It had quick access to both Route 68 and the Paris By-pass. Further out of town, West 8th became Georgetown Road. Becky believed that Georgetown would be a good area to explore. Cynthiana and Mt. Sterling were all about the same distance from the house. She hadn't had any idea that the proximity would be this good.

He woke with a hangover. His back ached and he was cold. Tom looked around the pitch black room and for the moment, had no idea where he was. He could feel warmth near his feet, which helped clarify things. Now he remembered. After he left O'Rourke's, he stopped and picked up a twelve-pack of Bud. He probably didn't need any more beer, but then again, maybe he did. He hadn't slept very well in the fold up lawn chair in his barn. He stumbled over to the front door of the soon-to-be living quarters and opened it. This allowed a small amount of light to filter into the room, so at least now he could see. He opened the wood stove's door, jostled the ash, and then threw a small piece of wood on the embers.

Saying he hadn't slept well was an understatement. He probably only slept a couple of hours. He couldn't stop thinking about Woozy's reaction. *Why did she act like she did? She hadn't behaved that way the last time I dealt with someone that was giving her trouble. She'd actually thanked me for taking care of Jimmy that night at O'Rourke's. Granted, maybe I did over-reacted last night, but something needed to be done. There wasn't going to be a nice outcome, not with that guy. What was Woozy talking about? Possessive men?* Tom was confused by the whole thing. *I reacted the way I should have, didn't I? I could have ignored the guy and expected the whole scene to just peter out. I could have talked to him and try to peacefully solve the issue, but would*

188

Woozy still have considered that possessive? He needed to stop stewing and head to the house. He needed a coffee. He knew a girl in Flemingsburg that would be glad to see him. Bella was always happy to see him.

Woozy sat thoughtfully at her kitchen table. She stirred her coffee. She tried to come to terms with what had happened last night. *Sure, that guy was getting out of hand, but what makes Tom believe he always has to be the one to remedy situations? Is it his former life as a lawman that makes him that way? If that's so, how is he any different than Jimmy was? Did I give Tom a mixed signal with my reaction?* She thought about that, back to how she had behaved after Tom had taught Jimmy a lesson. When they'd gone to dinner the other night, she told Tom the story of her childhood. *Surely he could see the correlation?*

The more Woozy thought about the story of her childhood, the less she believed that it was similar to Tom's reaction. Her father was an abusive alcoholic. *It's not the same thing as being overly possessive, is it?* Woozy had strong feelings for Tom, but she wasn't ready to be in a serious relationship, especially in light of last night's performance. *If Tom had pulled the same stunt a week ago before we'd gone to dinner, and I'd explained things about my childhood, would I have reacted differently?* Woozy wasn't sure, but, now another thought invaded her consciousness. She remembered her visit with the Sheriff of Nicholas County and the accusations that he had made about Tom. She had seen first-hand what Tom was capable of. She didn't want to face the question that bubbled to the surface, but she couldn't help it. *Could he have shot Jimmy?*

Becky Adkins had a productive day. Not only had she visited Georgetown, she'd also checked out prospects in Cynthiana and Mt. Sterling. Her new home, with its fantastic location, might help solve her recent drug selling woes. Much to Becky's surprise, the new two-family shotgun house was great. It would work well as her center of operations. She felt surprisingly optimistic. *Should*

I consider getting another car? Something a little less conspicuous? She could decide that soon enough; right now she needed an afternoon fix. She unlocked the door of her Paris rental and had another look around. The furnishings were minimal, but that was okay. Becky didn't plan to spend a lot of time here, anyway.

Today, when she was out and about, she had mostly been on a reconnaissance mission. She was hoping to get an idea about what the population was like around the area. Now that she was home and she sat in the living room, she felt satisfied. There seemed to be plenty of potential users in each of the towns she'd visited. All she needed to concentrate on was establishing relationships. That shouldn't be a problem. Now that she was once again a wholesome-looking redhead, Becky felt quite good about her chances at success. Besides, she had always been good at selling drugs. It didn't matter if it was for a major pharmaceutical company or at a local high school basketball game. She was a natural.

It had been a very long time since she'd been out and about. Miranda Johnson was nervous about going out with her friends later that night. She painfully recalled the last time she'd been out with friends. That fateful night, she had been enjoying herself at the Nicholas County High School football game. She was just a few months away from graduation, and Miranda enjoyed herself a little too much. She now had legs that no longer functioned with the constant companionship of an electric wheelchair to get her from place to place. She had learned her lesson. She hoped the same could be said for her friends.

Miranda thought, *maybe I'm over-reacting. My friends will definitely be on their best behavior. Besides, tonight we're all riding to the ball game together.* None of her friends' cars could accommodate an electric wheelchair. Luckily, her mother had agreed to be the evening's chaperone. Miranda was sort of okay with this. Miranda had been quite reclusive the year after she'd become a paraplegic. She assumed that was probably normal. Most of her friends had enrolled in college, gone away to various universities, and they were now home on break. Miranda eventually finished her senior year studies being schooled at home. She wanted to go to college, and hoped to enroll for the fall semester.

Tom moved slowly. He wasn't functioning very well. He hadn't felt this bad in a long time. He drove to Nick's house. Nick wasn't home, but Bella was. She jumped up on Tom as he walked in the front door. "Down Bella, let me get a cup of coffee, and then I'll see about taking you on a walk." Luckily, there was a partially warm pot of coffee in the kitchen. Tom turned on the microwave to heat up his cup and then let Bella out into the back yard. As he sipped his coffee, his thoughts returned to Woozy. *She's probably right. I was out of line, but I'm not sure how to keep my reactions in check. Sometimes I don't know how to just suck it up. Should I call her, or should I give her more time?*

She had managed to waste her entire Saturday morning. Woozy was in the bathroom getting dressed. She had just showered, and was due at work at four. She had calmed down somewhat from the previous evening's events and she had almost forgiven Tom for his actions. *He obviously cares for me. Tom can't help himself from exhibiting chivalrous behavior. He is a man, after all.* Woozy smiled as she remembered the look of surprise on the obnoxious guy's face as his head made contact with the bar. *Tom is protective of me that's all. It's not the same as being possessive. He would never hurt me. I'm sure of that. He was doing what he thought was right.* Woozy was coming to terms with what Tom had done at O'Rourke's, but she thought about what the Sheriff had said about Jimmy's death. Woozy sighed as she finished buttoning her blouse. *I hope Tom comes to O'Rourke's tonight.*

It had been a long painful morning. Wilson was glad that the afternoon had finally arrived. Most of his Friday, which he'd taken off from work, was a blur to him. He did remember some of the events that had led him to take Friday off - the handwritten threatening note and the fact that Padgett (or one of them) had possibly entered his house. When Wilson had gotten up earlier, he followed his usual regimen – some aspirin and then a return to bed. Fortunately, last night he had slept in his bed, and as a result, he hadn't woken up with his feet tangled in the recliner. That was the only positive thing, though. Wilson threw his head back and swallowed four more aspirin that he held in his hand. He looked up at the kitchen clock. It was three-fifteen. He turned and headed back down the hallway, back to the sanctuary of his bedroom.

Saturday Late Afternoon

Becky had just awakened from a refreshing nap. She had been worn out after her drive up from Tennessee and getting adjusted to her new place. All the running around she'd done added to her state of tiredness. But, as she took in a last bit of coke, she now felt energized. Becky had plans for the evening. She was going to find out what Paris had in the way of potential. She smiled. She was probably only ten or twelve miles from Carlisle, as the crow flies. And, old dumb-ass Sheriff Wilson had no idea that she was back. She allowed herself a chuckle as she recalled the conspiracy that she and Wilson had been working on when they were trying to entrap Padgett. She wondered if Tom missed her? She sort of missed him. She dismissed the thought. *There are plenty of fish in the sea, and I need to find me some new drug using customers.*

Miranda hadn't put on make-up or attempted to fix her hair for months. She realized that she had let herself go, but tonight she wanted to look nice. She thought that it's extremely important for a girl to look pretty, especially one that's stuck in a wheelchair. Miranda felt that having make-up on might be the only way the guys would notice her.

Her mother had always been there for her, especially after the accident. Miranda hated how she snapped at her mom sometimes. And, her father didn't like it when she was short with him. She just felt so angry sometimes. She couldn't help it. She knew that her attitude had put a strain on their relationship. But, her mom never complained. She was much more understanding than her dad. She had heard her parents argue about her going out tonight. Or as they referred to it, discussing things. But, her mother prevailed and agreed to take her and her friends to the ball game. The basketball game was going to be played in Paris, between rivals Bourbon and Nicholas Counties.

CHAPTER 20

Saturday Night

Becky couldn't believe her good fortune. Tonight, there was a basketball tournament in Paris. Who would have thought? There should be plenty of potential clients out and about. She'd heard that tonight's game was between Bourbon and Nicholas Counties. Becky thought back to the night when she'd sold Oxycontin to that high school girl over in Nicholas County. She whispered, *how ironic*. Becky had put the girl's unfortunate plight out of her mind. She had just delivered the drugs. She wasn't responsible for the way they were administered. *And besides that, if I allowed myself to suddenly become compassionate, respectful and caring for all the people that misused drugs, would anyone do the same for me? I really doubt it.* She had a living to make and she needed her drugs, just like everyone else.

It was halftime. Miranda was really enjoying herself. It definitely lifted her spirits with the game tied at 37, all. She had a really good seat, at court level, with a perfect view of the basket in the comfort of her electric wheelchair. Her friends and her mother were all seated nearby, a few rows up in the bleachers. The Nicholas County bleachers were practically full, and school spirit was everywhere. The half was over, and the players took up their positions on the court. Once the ball was tipped, Miranda anxiously watched as the teams wrestled for possession of the loose ball. The ball got kicked out of bounds and play was temporarily halted. Miranda watched intently as the ball was thrown back into play. Just then, Miranda saw her, over by the hometown bleachers; a lady with long red hair. Who is she? She looks so familiar. Miranda tried unsuccessfully to get her mother's attention. When she turned back around and looked across the court again, the lady wasn't there.

Becky was seated in the safety of her Mustang. She was parked way out, on the fringe of the school's lot. The parking lot was packed. Becky believed that everyone around the area must have driven to the game. Becky managed to locate the game being broadcast on a local radio station. There were still ten minutes remaining. She wanted to follow the kids from the winning team to wherever they'd go to celebrate after the game. She knew nothing about basketball, but still, she thought it surprising to hear that Nicholas County was winning by three points. She rolled down her window and allowed the sound of the radio to carry outside in order to satisfy the curiosity of the inquisitive police officer that patrolled the lot. At the moment, he was just outside her window. Becky pretended to act like a concerned parent waiting for her child. The officer nodded in her direction, then carried on with his patrol.

Nick had to hold his tongue. He didn't want to say anything that would upset Tom. But, he was dying to find out, *what had Tom done last night?* Finally, he couldn't contain himself any longer. "Where did you go last night, after you left O'Rourke's?"

"Nick, why do you care where I ended up last night? Is not knowing where I went really worrying you? It's not that exciting."

"You know how I am; it's just that I like to know things. You have to admit, it was kind of weird the way you just up and left the bar last night."

Tom had recovered from the pain of his hangover. He and Nick had just finished dinner and were now sat at the kitchen table talking over a couple of beers. "You know what, Nick? You should have been a reporter. Why'd you ever decide to become a bean counter, anyway?"

"Why do you think that? Why should I have been a

reporter?"

"Because of your insatiable interest in knowing every little thing that's going on. If you must know, I spent the night in the barn over at the home site. I spent it alone. It was far from exciting."

Nick looked puzzled. "But, you don't have electricity or water out there. So, how'd you manage to do that?"

"I can be resourceful if I need be."

It took a moment for Nick to reply, "I'm sure you can be."

The game was over. Nicholas County had upset Bourbon County 80-73. This was a cause for major celebration. Becky watched as the cars that carried the jubilant Nicholas County fans pulled from the parking lot. It was quite easy to tell the winners from the losers. All Becky needed to do, was follow the people in the cars that were honking their horns as they rolled along. She waited for much of the hysteria to wane before she pulled her Mustang into the flow of traffic. Much of the Nicholas County crowd were stopping at Taco Bell and the nearby Long John Silver's for their post-game victory celebration. She pulled into the adjacent shopping center's parking lot and stopped. She'd wait in her car, allowing time for more kids to arrive.

Miranda and her group had finally gotten their order and were starting to settle down. They were in the Taco Bell/Kentucky Fried Chicken dining area. It was crowded and noisy, but Miranda and her wheelchair were safely situated next to a corner booth and out of harm's way. Miranda was still trying to figure out who the redheaded lady was. She had been quite a distance away, so Miranda wasn't sure whether her eyes were playing tricks on her or not. She had mentioned something about the woman to her mother on the drive over from the school. Miranda told her mom that she couldn't be sure, but something about the way the lady moved, was familiar. She kind of reminded her of the lady who had sold her the drugs at the football game, the fall of her senior year. Miranda's mother assured her that it probably wasn't her, that it probably just looked like her. She told her to forget about it and try and enjoy the rest of her evening.

Nick studied Tom at the kitchen table while he bent down to grab two more beers from the fridge. *Why did Woozy react the way she had last night at the pub?* He wondered if he could get Tom to open up and talk about it.

"Tom, what do you think Woozy meant by what she said last night, about not wanting another possessive man?"

"I don't know. That's what I spent most of the night trying to figure out. I guess I must have misunderstood some things about our relationship. Maybe I wrongly assumed she was more interested in me than she actually is."

Nick listened patiently and then added, "You know what? I might not be the best judge of character, but I can tell Woozy is definitely interested in you. I think she just got scared when she saw what you did to that guy last night. Maybe it made her think about some of the abuse she's suffered."

Tom hadn't considered that. Although, he didn't feel he was in anyway similar to Jimmy, he guessed he could see the connection. "Maybe you're right. I have to admit that sometimes I let my emotions get the best of me. I thought I had calmed down and was able to handle my temper better, you know, as I've gotten older, but sometimes I'm not so sure."

"Tom, if I was you, I would give Woozy a call, and I think the sooner the better. You don't want her to get away."

She worked the group of kids that were hanging out in their cars in Long John Silver's parking lot. She was having limited success. Becky knew that trying to get established in a new area might be a slow process. She looked around the parking lot and realized that her exposure here was fairly high, probably why she wasn't doing as well as she'd like to. She glanced over at the Taco

Bell lot and realized it had more kids hanging around. She decided to cut her loses here and try there. Becky quickly wandered from car to car and asked if anyone was interested in what she was selling. Again, she had with limited success. She was getting frustrated. She decided she might as well go home and sample some of her unsold product.

Miranda chewed her bean burrito in silence and watched the activity around her. She felt odd as she sat there in Taco Bell. Being practically unable to participate didn't help at all. Her friends occasionally made an effort to talk with her, but Miranda still felt very isolated. She listened to her friends share conversations about school and all the things they'd been doing. She definitely felt like the odd man out, so Miranda just stared out the window. Her mother watched Miranda from a table nearby, and could see the difficulty she was facing. One of her friends addressed Miranda, then turned her head and re-engaged in her conversation, quickly becoming absorbed in the other, more exciting conversations that were taking place elsewhere.

Miranda found she was staring longingly out the window into the parking lot, where groups of people were talking, messing around, and having a good time. Her mother had gone to the bathroom. Miranda quickly turned around, desperately excited, looking for her mother. The redhead she thought she'd seen earlier was outside the window chatting to some kids from her school. Miranda couldn't believe it. It was like a terrible dream. Miranda turned her head and scanned the dining area. *Where could Mom be?* Finally she saw her mother. Apparently, she'd been waiting in line for the restroom.

It seemed as if her mother was crossing the dining room in slow motion. She was really anxious to tell her what she'd seen. Her mom gave her a puzzled look as she sat down at the adjacent table. "What is it Miranda? You look like you just saw a ghost."

Miranda could hardly speak. She was agitated and scared at the same time. "Maybe I did see a ghost, Mom. But, I'm pretty sure the woman is real."

"What woman, Miranda? You're not making much sense."

"The redheaded woman that I saw over at the high school. She's out there." Miranda turned and pointed out the window, but the redhead was gone. "I swear, she was right there a minute ago. She was right there. The woman that sold me the drugs at the football game last year in Carlisle. She was right out there. But, she looks different now, she's a redhead."

"So you think I should give Woozy a call? If you were in my shoes, what would you say to her, Nick?"

"I'm not sure, but how hard can it be? All you have to do is talk."

"Sometimes, at least for me, talking to women can be quite difficult. It's almost like I haven't gotten over being married all those years."

"Yeah, you're probably right about getting over an ex-spouse, that is. Look at me, twelve years a widower and I guess I haven't gotten over my wife being gone either, but how do I explain my sudden attraction for men?"

They both laughed, "Nick, if I were you, I wouldn't worry about trying to explain it. Besides, it's nobody's business anyway, so what does it matter?"

Nick liked that rational. He jumped up from the table, went to the fridge and grabbed two more beers. When he returned, he noticed that Tom was contemplating something. Nick sat and waited for his friend to speak.

"Back to what you said earlier, about how hard talking can be. I guess it's not all that hard, unless you've managed to make a total ass out of yourself, like I have.

Becky decided she would find out what her new neighbors were like. She hadn't lived next to people for years, not since she'd shared an apartment with Adam in college. She hoped that her neighbors were nothing like some of the ones she'd had while living in Morehead. As Becky unlocked the door and entered her house, she realized that her neighbors weren't the quiet types. The walls were thin, unfortunately, and the television next door was cranked up loudly. It sounded like a man and a woman lived next door, because Becky could hear them arguing. Becky had hoped to plan her activities for the following day. She wondered if it would be wise to knock on their door and ask them to keep it down. She decided that it probably wasn't an option since she heard something crash against the wall.

She carried her Kentucky map upstairs. Hopefully, it would be quieter. The noise from downstairs was diminished somewhat. Now, maybe she could think. After she had taken her pick-me-up, she spread the map out on the bed. Becky was excited to see that her proximity to both Lexington and Winchester were good. That meant that there were lots of potential customers nearby. She had a plan of attack for tomorrow almost worked out in her mind, but she was quickly losing the ability to concentrate. She pushed the map off the side of the bed and stretched out. She would reference the map again in the morning. Suddenly, she was in no mood to deal with the stress that thinking required.

After Miranda and her mother had dropped everyone else off, they drove home. Once inside, Miranda was still incredibly agitated. Her mother tried to talk Miranda out of her idea of calling the Sheriff. Maybe she should wait a while before she provided the Sheriff with information about what she'd seen tonight. Miranda's mother knew her daughter was right, but she didn't want Miranda to deal with anymore ordeals, like having to go to court. She wanted Miranda to forget about the woman she'd seen earlier. Her mom even suggested that it might not be the same woman. Saying that was the wrong thing to do, because Miranda dug in her heels. She wasn't one-hundred percent certain that it was the same woman, but when her mother doubted her recollection, Miranda decided that she was absolutely positive, after all.

It was after seven on Saturday evening, before Wilson finally dragged himself out of bed. He had convinced himself that it hadn't been the whiskey that led to his memory loss the previous night. Maybe he had a touch of the flu. He felt okay now, so he ambled over to the liquor cabinet. After a couple glasses of Beam, Wilson felt as good as new. He picked up his phone and once again studied his recent calls. He still hadn't come up with anything regarding the conversation he had with Padgett. Someone had broken into his house, though, and left a threatening note. Wilson was convinced it was Padgett. He corrected himself - the house hadn't been broken into. It couldn't have been, because the back door wasn't locked.

Wilson looked at the phone's display again, and willed the phone to give up some information about his recent call to Padgett. He scrolled through the recent calls and realized that most of the calls he'd made lately had been to Padgett. He laughed to himself when he recalled the first time he'd said, *Padgett; I've got my eye on you.*

Wilson jumped and dropped the phone as it rang. It had vibrated in his hand while he had been staring at the display, scaring the hell out of him. *Damn it.* He snatched the phone up from the floor and studied the number, Carlisle. Wilson didn't recognize the number. He wasn't sure whether or not he should answer. He glanced up at the clock.

It was late and it was Saturday night, but Miranda didn't care. She listened to the phone ring as she waited for Wilson to pick up. The phone just rang and rang, before it went to voice mail. She listened to the Sheriff's greeting, but she didn't want to leave a message. She wanted to talk to him. After the greeting ended, Miranda decided to leave a message after all. She said what she needed to say. After she hung up the phone, she was frustrated. She would keep calling. She wanted to call the Sheriff again and again until he picked up and spoke to her. Miranda laid the phone on the table and rolled her wheelchair over to the refrigerator. She was thirsty. After she had seen the woman at Taco Bell, she couldn't stop thinking about her. She saw her long red hair over

201

and over in her mind.

Wilson listened to the message a second time while he savored his whiskey. *Miranda Johnson, huh? Is that the girl that had bought the pills from that woman,...what was her name? Oh yeah, Becky Adkins. Old run away and hide Adkins. Miranda said Adkins was hanging out in Paris. That's interesting.* Wilson took a drink and envisioned Becky's face. He tried to recall exactly what she looked like. Wilson was definitely feeling the effects of the whiskey. He continued to think about Becky. *So, now she's a redhead. No doubt, she'd look good as a redhead.* He again glanced at the clock. *It's almost midnight, too late to return calls, especially on a Saturday night.*

Tom was ready to go to bed, but Nick wasn't. Nick seemed to have found his second wind. *The guy could talk all night.* Tom already knew that, but each time he experienced it again first hand, it continued to surprise him. Although the topic of conversation had changed course several times during the night, Nick preferred to talk gossip. He loved anything that had a gossipy feel to it. Tom was fading. He watched Nick return from the fridge for what must have been the sixth or seventh time.

"Last one, Nick. Don't you have to work tomorrow?"

Nick smiled, "No, as a matter of fact, I don't."

"Does that mean then, that you don't require sleep?"

Nick could tell his friend was fading, but he hated to go to bed early. It wasn't even midnight yet. But he knew that Tom was exhausted, especially after he'd spent the night in the barn. Nick understood, although it didn't mean he had to like it. He reluctantly submitted, "Ok, I'm ready to call it a night if you are."

CHAPTER 21

Tom was awakened early Sunday morning by whom else, but Bella. She licked him repeatedly in the face. That was a common occurrence, especially if Tom slept on his side. To Bella's way of thinking, if his face was reachable, then it was fair game. Her tongue had been effective. She had gotten Tom's face good and wet before it dawned on him what was happening.

"Ok Bella, I'm getting up. You know that it's Sunday. Obviously, you remember that I promised you a hike in the woods."

Tom knew how silly it seemed to give Bella credit for being so smart, but she was smart. He planned to do some electrical work at the home site today. He had gotten a lot of the rough-in done already, so he hoped to be able to finish it today. He had promised Bella a hike and she was just reminding him that she hadn't forgotten.

Nick loudly snored away as they passed his room. Tom thought about how Nick would have happily stayed up half the night talking and drinking, but today, he would undoubtedly spend most the day in bed. Tom opened the kitchen door and Bella went out to do her business. Tom poured a cup of coffee and sat down at the table. He had plenty of work to do today and he wanted to give Woozy a call. He knew she'd be off work. Maybe he'd call her later this afternoon, when he'd finished working. He really wanted to give her a call now, but he was well aware of how easily he could put off any conversation that might prove challenging or could be difficult.

Miranda got up early. She wasn't happy. The Sheriff hadn't returned her call and she didn't understand why. When she rolled her wheelchair into the kitchen, her mother was busy making breakfast. Her mother assumed, based on the look on her daughter's face that the Sheriff hadn't called.

"Good morning, Miranda. Are you hungry? Would you care for an omelet?"

"No thanks, Mom. Do you think it's too early for me to call the Sheriff?"

"Maybe, honey. It's only eight o'clock. Why don't you wait until at least ten? It is Sunday, you know. The Sheriff might be in church this morning."

"Really, Mom? Don't you remember that video I showed you? The YouTube video when the Sheriff only had on his underwear and his hat and he was singing karaoke? I don't believe Sheriff Wilson spends a lot of time in church."

Miranda's mother couldn't argue with her daughter about that. She tried not to laugh out loud at the memory of the video.

"You might be right, Miranda, but it would still be nice for you to wait a while before you called."

Miranda reluctantly decided to eat the omelet that her mother had prepared. She continually checked her phone, just in case there were any missed calls.

Wilson was awake surprisingly early for a Sunday morning. Maybe it was because he'd slept fifteen hours or so on Saturday. He drank his second cup of coffee and tried to determine whether or not he wanted to call that girl. Miranda was a snippy little thing and he never had cared much for her attitude. He listened to the message again and had a better feel for the situation. He recognized a sense of urgency in her voice. Maybe he should call her, even though it was Sunday. He had given Miranda instructions to call him if anything that had to do with Becky Adkins ever came up. Obviously, something had. But first, Wilson had to think about how he needed to play this. If Becky Adkins was once again in or around his county, he wanted her. He wanted her for more than just the Miranda drug deal - that was just the tip of the iceberg.

She was on the road early. Becky was aware that trying to sell illegal drugs on Sunday morning could be difficult. But, that wasn't her only reason for being here. She was also on a relationship-building mission. She had heard some recent statistics about drug use. Her target audience was generally the late-teen to the thirty-something crowd. And, the drug mix was shifting. Cocaine and heroin use were once again gaining in popularity. Becky was one step ahead of the curve. This morning, she was trolling the streets of Georgetown. She knew that school would be in session again on Monday morning. She parked her Mustang on Main Street and walked two blocks to the center of the campus of Georgetown College.

Becky had done her homework. She knew that Georgetown College was a liberal arts school. She felt that might just be a plus for plying her trade. But, a liberal arts school with a Baptist foundation committed to the Christian faith might be a little more challenging. She couldn't let that stand in her way, because even God's children need a boost every now and then. She walked the two blocks to the center of the campus and stopped. She stared up at the John L. Hill Chapel. Becky planned to play the old alumni card, with hopes to forge some new relationships around campus. She had memorized where most of the classrooms were located and had also committed their names to memory. She felt that she was prepared to meet some of the current students.

Tom pulled into the driveway and climbed out of his F-150. He opened the rear door, and as expected, Bella bounded outside. She was ready for a romp in the woods. Tom had wanted to get some work done before taking their hike, but quickly realized those plans probably wouldn't work. Today he wore a sweatshirt with a vest. It was cold this morning.

"Ok girl, let's go for a walk." Bella was through the gap in the fence quickly and was in pursuit of a squirrel that happened to have been standing on the trail. Tom always had a good laugh when he watched Bella chase squirrels. He imagined the squirrels had a good time, too. They always fooled with her. They'd allow her to get fairly close and then jump onto a tree and climb to safety. Bella was proud of how close she had gotten to that last squirrel. She ran toward Tom with her head held high and her tail resembling a flag, waving side to side.

"You almost had that squirrel, Bella." Bella loved hearing that she'd almost gotten something, whether it was true or not, it helped to boost her confidence. This walk would have to be shorter than Bella would like, because Tom needed to finish a task today. After Tom fired up the wood stove, he opened one of the barn doors to bring in some natural light. Soon, he would have electricity and after that, he could finish the plumbing and the drywall. Tom was anxious to have a place of his own again. He was grateful for all that Nick had done for him and Bella, but that didn't change things. He wanted to be out of the city and back in rural Nicholas County.

Miranda watched the clock as the minutes slowly clicked by. Nine-fifty-five, that was close enough for her. She pulled the Sheriff's number up onto the screen again and pressed call. Again, the phone rang multiple times. Miranda couldn't believe that the Sheriff wouldn't answer her call. But, what should she expect? When the recorded message ended, Miranda left her message. She wasn't as polite as she had been the previous evening, and she felt justified in this. Her mother was in the next room and could overhear what her daughter had said. After Miranda finished leaving the message, her mom entered the living room. She could see that Miranda was quite agitated.

"Honey, I don't think leaving the Sheriff a nasty message is the best way to receive a return phone call."

"What do you mean nasty message, Mom? Do you still believe that the Sheriff is sitting on his butt in some pew singing hymns this morning?" He's probably ignoring the phone because he doesn't want to talk to me."

"You can't be sure of that, Miranda. The Sheriff is probably a very busy man. You know, he's the only Sheriff in Nicholas County."

"Don't remind me about that. It would be nice if there was another one, one that did his job."

Wilson got out of the shower and wrapped a towel around his waist, then began to shave. He had big plans for today. He glanced down at his phone and noticed that he had a missed call as well as a voice mail. He hit play and listened to the disrespectful message that Miranda Johnson had left. Even if Wilson had planned on calling the poor little girl that was held hostage to a wheelchair, he wouldn't do it now. *That girl needs to be given a lesson in respect. I'm the law around here and I'm the only one that can, or will, help her.* Wilson returned his attention to the mirror and proceeded to shave. He was worked up because the message that Miranda had left him had really angered him. He nicked his chin. That didn't help matters.

The big plans Wilson had centered around Becky Adkins, and what she could do for him. Wilson had let Adkins off on another occasion, but not this time. So, if what Miranda Johnson had said was true, Becky was back, supposedly now a redhead, and was hanging out in Bourbon County. That was just a county away from Wilson's turf, but Wilson had no plans to ask for assistance, not from anyone in Bourbon County. It was his problem, and he'd deal with it his way. Wilson buttoned his thigh length wool coat and pulled a sock hat down over his head before he pulled on a pair of black leather gloves. He glanced approvingly at his reflection in the hall mirror. *Wilson, you old sly dog, you look good. Becky Adkins will never know it's you.*

Things hadn't worked out well in Tennessee. And now, it seemed as if they weren't working out so well around here in

Kentucky, either. Becky had tried her old alumni approach on a few of the students that were out and about in Georgetown. She'd been unsuccessful and was totally baffled as to why. Could there really be something to all that religious commitment stuff? Well, Becky was not a quitter. *If at first you don't succeed, try, try, again.* She'd heard that long ago. She wasn't sure it was applicable in her chosen vocation, but what the hell. She stopped at a coffee shop and got herself an espresso. She needed to think. *Could these kids be that committed to their school creed, all that religious stuff?* That confused Becky because the only thing that had that type of hold over her was her drugs.

And, if Becky couldn't find some converts soon, she'd be out of business. After a while an idea came to her. *Maybe the problem is the day of the week? Maybe Sunday is such a presence in these kids' heads that it's almost like an impenetrable force.* Sunday was definitely not the day to try and do what Becky Adkins did best. *What day would be?* Becky knew the answer, Friday. After the first full week back at school, the students would need to let off some steam. She had a plan, but it was for later in the week. Now, she needed to go back to Paris and unwind. Some days, the illegal drug trade could be really trying.

He was impressed with his morning's progress and took a break. Tom wrestled with whether or not it was a good time to call Woozy. He threw another log in the fire and sat down to pet Bella. Bella had been sleeping all morning. She was still tired after their morning hike. Tom had done well on the wiring and was nearly finished. He dialed the number and waited. Luckily, he didn't have to wait long. Woozy picked up after two rings. Suddenly, Tom felt revitalized. Now all he needed to do was start a simple conversation.

"Hello Woozy, hope I didn't wake you?"

"Why would you wake me Tom? It's nearly one o'clock."

"Oh, I guess I lost track of time."

Neither Woozy nor Tom were great conversationalists.

Both felt as if they were walking on eggshells. At the same time, they realized how silly they both sounded and began to laugh. They struggled to think of things to say, when in actuality, they had tons to talk about. Finally Tom got to the point, "Woozy, would you like to go out to dinner with me, later this evening?"

"I would love to. That would be wonderful. What time?"

It probably wasn't one of Wilson's better ideas. He waited in his truck in the parking lot of Walmart in Paris. He watched people as they entered and left the store. His grand plan had seemed simple enough, but what were the chances of Becky stopping by here today? Wilson initially thought his thinking was sound because of what had been on Miranda's voice mail. Miranda had said that Becky was at both the high school and Taco Bell last night, so Wilson assumed, why wouldn't she stop by Walmart? After he had sat in his truck with the engine running for a couple of hours, Wilson figured that he was just wasting his time. How could he find Adkins without drawing attention to himself? If his intentions were on the level, Wilson could have flashed Becky's photo around to the local law enforcement personnel to seek their assistance.

But, like many of Wilson's policing techniques, his motivation wasn't one-hundred percent legit. He needed to come up with a better plan to track down Adkins. He put his truck in gear and slowly rolled toward the exit, onto the Paris by-pass. As he waited for the traffic light to change at the intersection of Georgetown Road, a black Mustang flew by. It was heading into town. Wilson couldn't believe it. The woman driving the car looked a lot like Becky, and she even had red hair. Unfortunately, he wasn't in the turning lane. When the light changed, he had to follow the by-pass nearly half a mile before he could do a u-turn. After he'd gotten turned around and then turned left onto Georgetown Road, Wilson felt excited. Up ahead on the right, the black Mustang had parked. He pulled up behind it and checked the license plates, Tennessee. So, that's where Ms. Adkins had gone to hide.

After Becky arrived home, she fixed herself a little snack before she did a line of coke. She only needed a bit, because she wanted to take care of business later this afternoon. She studied herself in the bathroom mirror after she snorted her afternoon hit. Becky could tell that she had been losing more weight lately. That was one of the obvious downsides to cocaine use, but so far, the loss hadn't been too noticeable. She would start eating better as soon as business began to pick up, or so she told herself. She immediately felt better after her little hit, but Becky knew the effects of the drug in small quantities would be short lived.

She felt the initial euphoric rush and for the moment, she wasn't interested in lying down. She was tired. Maybe she should have delayed doing that line until after she had had a little rest, but it was too late for that now. She laid the Kentucky map out flat onto the table and considered possible routes. Should she concentrate on some of the nearby cities, devoting an entire day to each? Or, should she hit multiple cities and spend a shorter amount of time in each? Becky laughed to herself as she considered similarities between selling drugs legally and selling them illegally. A legitimate sales person had to work hard to establish a territory, same as the illegitimate one did. And, they were both totally affected by the whims of their customers. So, the jobs were quite similar. However, one was legal and the other was not. Becky laughed at the thought that they were both commission-based.

Tom was happy to finally be finished with the electrical rough-in. It was a big accomplishment. Now, all he needed to finish was the plumbing, and then he could start doing the interior finish work. He had showered and left Bella in Nick's care for the afternoon. Bella liked Nick, but she didn't like the fact that Tom had gotten dressed up and was going someplace without her. Tom thought it was ironic that Bella was being possessive of him. *Wasn't that the same thing that Woozy said she didn't want?* He knew that he shouldn't bring anything like that up tonight. His dinner plans with Woozy felt a lot like a first date. He parked his truck in front of her house, then climbed the steps and knocked on her door.

Woozy was waiting just inside the door and she quickly opened it. Tom smiled at her and she smiled back. Tom felt the first hurdle was behind them. He thought to himself, *one step at a time Tom, one step at a time.* They were going to Applebee's. On another occasion, Woozy had told him that she liked their happy hours. Once at the restaurant, they picked a table in the bar area, and then ordered a couple of drinks.

Tom was nervous. On the drive over, it had been just a little too quiet for him. He wanted to get the conversation started. He didn't like awkward situations, and silence made him feel awkward.

"Woozy, I'm sorry about how I behaved the other night. I was out of line."

"You don't need to apologize, Tom. That guy was the one that was out of line. You just reacted, that's all."

"No, that's not all. I seem to react that way much more than I should. Sometimes I wonder if I need medical help."

Woozy was silent. She wasn't sure how to respond, so she sipped her drink. Tom also took the opportunity to have another drink of courage before he continued.

"Woozy, being a cop most of your life, definitely takes a toll on a person. I know it did on me. Being a cop might even be comparable to serving multiple tours of combat duty. It changes you, it has to. I'm not sure how it's changed me, but sometimes I feel different. It's hard to explain sometimes, but it seems like there are things that I've maybe done, that I'm not even aware of."

Their dinner arrived and Tom was thankful. He thought about the things he'd just said. He wasn't sure where he was headed with that line of conversation, and Woozy seemed content to let him talk. Maybe he should just shut up and talk about the meal. Yes, change the conversation back to food. People enjoyed talking about food, don't they?

It began to feel like another damned waste of time to Wilson as he was parked behind the car that he thought belonged to Becky Adkins. He had no idea which one of the houses she lived in. He hadn't seen one person out on the street and he'd been parked there for over two hours. *What the hell do people do all day long, just sit inside their houses?* He had plenty of information to start with. He had her vehicle, so he could run a DMV report. He had a possible address. It was either West 8th Street, or Lylesville. Wilson figured he should cut his losses and call it a day. He could return first thing in the morning for a little bit more detective work. *Yeah, I'll get here bright and early and catch Ms. Adkins before she goes out for the day to do her business.* As he was about to pull back onto 8th Street, a Paris police cruiser rolled by. The cop gave Wilson the eyeball. It was time to leave.

Dinner was a success. At least Tom felt it had been, anyway. He thought that Woozy seemed to enjoy herself. He managed to stay away from divulging more information about his past. *It shouldn't matter anyway, should it?* After the initial rough bits, he and Woozy had some good conversations, and even shared a few good laughs. Woozy had a good personality and a great sense of humor. After he dropped her off at home, he asked her if she'd like to go out again sometime. She quickly agreed. That lifted Tom's spirits. He felt he'd nearly blown it the other night. He was quite happy that Woozy hadn't wanted to revisit the events of Friday night.

Woozy watched from the front door as Tom pulled away from the curb. She felt that tonight had been a lot of fun. She hadn't been on a real date for years. This was quite a change from her life with Jimmy. Tom managed to lighten up as the evening progressed, and seemed much more at ease. To Woozy, he seemed to be a man of secrets. He had almost shared some of them. Woozy knew exactly the moment that Tom had changed the subject, when he realized that he was possibly opening up a little too much. But, that was ok. They had time to talk about things. She'd love to help Tom through any issues he might have. Woozy looked forward to their next date.

CHAPTER 22

Monday Morning

Even though it was only seven-thirty, Wilson was already on West 8th Street, watching houses. He hoped to learn which one Adkins called home. As much as he hated it, all he planned to do this morning was validate that the woman he'd followed yesterday was Becky Adkins. After he verified that information, he would come back to visit at a time of his choosing. He was dressed casually. He wasn't wearing his uniform. After Adkins crawled out of bed and showed herself, Wilson would head back to Carlisle and go about his Nicholas County business. He hoped she wasn't a late sleeper. He didn't feel like waiting here all morning. Wilson was just about to call it a day, when the door of one of the two story shotgun houses opened, and out stepped Adkins. Wilson clearly recognized her, aided by the binoculars he held, as he studied her face.

Wilson smiled as he thought of the missed opportunity he had last fall. *That's not going to be the case this time, Ms. Adkins. I have plans for you, and this time, you're not going to run. I guarantee it.* Becky climbed into her Mustang, fired it up, and pulled from the curb. She appeared to be heading into town. Wilson followed at a comfortable distance. He was surprised when she turned left on Main Street, Route 68, and headed north, in the direction of Maysville. Wilson thought, *maybe she's going to Nicholas County, back to her old stomping grounds.* He was disappointed when she turned left on the by-pass. Since he'd been following at a distance, he was caught by the light. Frustrated, he watched as Becky's black Mustang sped off to where ever she was going. *See you soon Becky. I'll see you real soon.*

Miranda was unhappy, maybe even more upset than she'd been yesterday. The Sheriff hadn't returned either of her calls. *Why won't Sheriff Wilson call me?* Miranda Johnson called the number she found listed in the directory.

"Nicholas County Sheriff's Department. Can I help you?"

"Yes, is the Sheriff in?"

"No, he hasn't made it into the office yet this morning. Would you like to leave him a message?"

Miranda considered and decided that it would be useless to leave the Sheriff another message. "Is Sheriff Wilson working today?"

The clerk tensed at the question. "Of course he is. Is this some kind of an emergency? Do you need the Sheriff's cell number?"

"No thank you, I've already left him two messages. I can't understand why he doesn't return my calls."

"He must be busy. I'm sure he'll return your call when he has a chance."

Miranda reluctantly thanked the clerk and then disconnected the call.

Tom felt good. Bella was relaxing in front of the wood stove. She watched him as he glued pieces of PVC drain and vent lines together. She wasn't sure what he was up to, but any time Bella was with her master, it was a good thing. Tom was in a good mood. He was pleased with how his date with Woozy had gone. He stopped daydreaming for a moment because he had water lines to run. Tom was using a product he was unfamiliar with, and installing it was simple enough. The water line was Pex, far less expensive than copper. Tom knew better than to use copper, because if you used copper, it was almost like sending out an invitation to be robbed. Lately, copper had become a hot item for thieves. They would go to unbelievable lengths to rip the copper out of a construction site, and then sell it at a scrap yard.

Pex wasn't very expensive. Tom had enough of people screwing with his property. He still had painful memories of the fire. He thought about what had happened to Lonnie Eldridge. It was terrible, but it wasn't his fault. Lonnie took his own life. Whether or not Tom's threats played a part in that, he wasn't sure. Tom snapped back from his thoughts. He needed to concentrate on what he was doing. The water lines were easy to cut and the connectors were simple to install, so the job proceeded quickly. Tom added another log to the wood stove. Bella suddenly wasn't happy because she had to get up from the comfy spot that she had directly in front of the stove. "Bella, I had to load the stove. Sometimes, you can be the biggest baby."

Wilson rolled up Route 68. He was a mile or so south of Millersburg, when his phone rang. He recognized the number and grumbled to himself. *Why won't that annoying little girl leave me alone?*

"Wilson... Uh huh... Because I was out of town this weekend... Yes, I got it. I got both your messages. I got them this morning... Yes, I'm working on it right now. I'm working with the Paris police. We're trying to determine if the person you saw is the one that sold you the drugs... How can you be so sure?... Uh huh... Well, I'll let you know as soon as I have something concrete."

Wilson clicked off and accelerated out of Millersburg. Now he was angry. He didn't like the way Miranda talked to him. *Who does she think she is? Just because she got herself in trouble and is now an invalid, that sure as hell wasn't my fault. Why does she always take her frustration out on me? And besides that, I don't need anyone else giving me advice on how to do my job. Especially some teenage girl that screwed up her own life, trying to issue orders from a wheelchair.*

Miranda stared at the phone. Had the Sheriff hung up on her? She frowned. She guessed it didn't matter. Miranda didn't buy the Sheriff's story about being out of town. She was convinced that Wilson probably didn't do much traveling. He was most likely sitting at home on each occasion that she'd called, over the weekend. He probably sat on his butt while he listened to the phone ring. She thought back to last year and her dealings with Wilson. *I identified the woman, and supposedly Wilson knew where to find her, so what had happened? Why hadn't the Sheriff gotten back to me? Why was the woman still out there?* I don't trust Wilson, not one bit.

Later That Morning

Wilson sat at his desk, stewing. After he returned from Paris, he went home to change into his uniform. When he got out of his truck, his nosy neighbor yelled at him. It was freezing out, and the old woman stood outside in her front yard in a bath robe. She asked 'why he wasn't at work, doing what he was paid to do? She was a taxpayer and she wanted to see him doing his job.' If he wasn't Sheriff, he might have enjoyed going over to her house to give her a good working over. Wilson smiled, *yeah that might actually be satisfying, smacking that old woman a time or two.* Wilson's smile quickly faded as his deputy entered the office.

"Morning, Boss, where have you been?"

"Leland, how many times do I need to remind you about calling me Boss? And where I've been this morning, is none of your business. What are you doing in here this early, anyway?"

"Oh, I don't know. I was just sitting around the house, thinking."

Wilson wanted to tell Leland that he seriously doubted that, but decided against it. "And what was it that you were thinking about?"

"Well, I know the Coroner's report said Lonnie Eldridge's death was a suicide. But what I can't figure out is why there was a boot mark on the door; the boot mark you stated was the same size as Padgett's?"

217

"I did say that, didn't I? The County Attorney warned me to stay off Padgett's case. Do you happen to remember what you and she talked about that day?"

"If I tell you, you'll get mad."

"What in hell are you talking about, Leland? Of course I won't get mad."

"But, it sounds like you're mad already."

"I just want to know what you two talked about."

"She just wanted to hear my take on what happened at Eldridge's. She wanted to hear my version. She wanted to be sure that we both saw the same thing."

"Of course we saw the same thing. What did you tell her that was different that might have made her change her mind about giving me that arrest warrant for Padgett?"

"I told her about the boot mark on the door, and how you said it was Padgett's size, and how you believe Padgett is involved in most crimes that happen in the county."

Wilson could feel a headache coming on. "Deputy, why don't you run over to Garrett's, and get me a cup of coffee?"

"Sure thing, Boss."

Early Afternoon

Dave Daugherty sat alone at the bar at The Scoreboard. Dave had been there since it opened at eleven-thirty. He was thinking about his life. He'd been doing that a lot lately. He had grown up in Versailles, Kentucky, but today that seemed a lifetime ago. Even though Dave was only thirty years old, for some reason, he felt he carried the weight of the world on his shoulders. He had his share of ups and downs lately, but it seemed the downs were becoming more commonplace. *Maybe I should have been content to settle for an undergraduate degree. What made me believe that having a master's would open so many more doors?* He motioned to the bartender for another beer. *My grades were average when I graduated from UK, seven years ago. What was the compelling reason to go back to school last fall? Was it because of potential promotion opportunities?* Unfortunately, he couldn't remember.

The University of Kentucky master's program hadn't worked as well as Dave had hoped, and now this. He'd been placed on academic probation, all because his GPA had dropped under 3.0. *It doesn't seem right. It wasn't really my fault.* He'd been working a full time job while he also attended class. But, he was fired from his job and was trying to find another one. *That was what caused my grades to slip. Why should UK punish me with probation?* Making matters worse and adding fuel to the fire, his former employer had agreed to pay his educational assistance. Now, they refused to pay for the fall semester. They claimed that since he'd been fired, the educational assistance automatically ended. *Damn, random drug testing. That's what did it. How was I supposed to know?*

Becky spent most of the morning working in Cynthiana and felt she'd been successful. But now, she was tired from all the running around. On top of that, she needed a boost. Becky thought about her cash reserves as she drove toward Paris. She figured she'd be ok until the end of the month, maybe a little longer. It felt as if things were beginning to improve. She thought about her plan. She would spend partial days in the cities on her list. She was confident that made sense. If she spent too much time in one place, she'd become too familiar. She worried about the cops, so abbreviated stints would prove best. She turned right at the corner of Main Street, heading southwest toward downtown. Becky glanced over her right shoulder and noticed a bar, The Scoreboard Sports Bar and Grill. *A beer might taste really good right now.*

Bella had been patient long enough. She began to pester Tom. She didn't care if he got the water lines installed or not. All she was concerned about was going on a hike. Tom had just finished lunch, so he was anxious to get back to work. But, Bella had other plans. She started to follow him from place to place, getting in the way as much as she possibly could. Tom told her to go lie down and relax. That only worked for a moment. Bella once again got in his face as he tried to finish the plumbing. It didn't help matters that Tom was on his hands and knees, working down on the floor. At that height, he was readily accessible to Bella and her tongue. Finally, Tom gave in. "Ok, Bella. We'll go for a hike, but only a short one."

Once again she'd gotten her way. Bella sprinted off into the woods. Tom walked along behind her and observed how much the woods had changed. The leaves had changed colors a few months back, and since then, most of them had fallen. Tom continued to walk and passed Bella as she slowed down to sniff something smelly on the trail. A moment later, Tom stopped. He heard a noise rapidly approaching from the rear. It sounded like horses running. Bella thundered past as she pursued some deer she had seen up ahead. As she blew by, she made quite a racket. Tom wondered if Nick had been feeding her more table scraps. Tom felt he probably needed to become the heavy and put Nick and Bella both on diets.

Dave glanced up at the mirror over the bar when he heard the door open. He thought to himself, *this really changes things*. He saw the reflection of a good looking redhead in the mirror, and she was smiling at him. She sat immediately to his right and ordered a beer. Up until now, Dave had been the only person in the bar all day. The redhead that sat next to him was definitely a welcome change. Before he could open his mouth to say something, the hot looking new arrival introduced herself.

"Hi, my name's Becky Adkins. I just moved to Paris a few days ago."

"That's great. By the way, I'm Dave Daugherty. I'm kind of new around here, too. But, I'm a lifelong Kentuckian."

They shook hands. "Nice to meet you, Dave, I'm a native Kentuckian also, but for the past few months, I've been living down in Tennessee. It feels good to be home."

"Glad to see you decided to come back," Dave replied.

Becky took a sip of her beer and looked around the room. "Not much activity in here this afternoon. Is it always this slow?"

The bartender looked over at Becky as if she'd insulted him. "No, it's not always this slow, but it is Monday, and Mondays are usually the slowest day of the week."

Becky was still curious, "So, are the weekends busy? What's usually your busiest day of the week in here? And, what are the ages of the people that hang out around here?"

The bartender looked closely at Becky. He was getting annoyed, "What are you doing, writing a book or something?"

Becky laughed, "No, I'm just naturally curious. Since I'm new in town, I'd like to know the best times to come out, you know, to meet people."

"Uh huh. We're usually busy on the weekends, but through the week it's hard to tell. People just kind of show up, when they do."

Dave was listening to the exchange and volunteered some information under his breath, "I've only come here a few times, and the bartender, Mr. Friendly, has never been much of a conversationalist. Would you be interested in joining me over at my place? I've got cold beer in the fridge, among other things, if you know what I mean."

Becky liked the sound of that. "Sure, let me finish the rest of my beer, and then lead the way."

Thank God, Leland had finally left. One of these days, his Deputy was going to drive him crazy. Wilson turned his thoughts over in his mind. *So, Leland had been the one that had opened his big mouth, and turned the County Attorney against me.* He wouldn't worry about that right now, he had to think. *How was he going to get Becky Adkins to cooperate?* He had learned where Adkins had run to when he did a check on her plates. The fact that she'd been living in Clinton, Tennessee, was of little significance now. *How am I going to approach that woman, and get her to do my bidding again? She's back, but how can I keep her here?*

Wilson looked at his phone display and noticed the time, four o'clock. It had been a long day. So what if most of it was spent working on his personal investigation? He tilted back in his chair as his thoughts churned away. He returned his concentration to his latest dilemma, which was to keep Becky from running again. That was his main objective, which would lead straight to Padgett, the real number one priority.

Wilson snapped upright in his chair. He had it. *Bill Wilson, you're a genius, an absolute genius.* He threw his coat on, and walked to the door. On his way out of the office, Wilson yelled to the clerk over his shoulder, "Goodnight, I'll see you tomorrow."

The plan Wilson had devised was simple, but he was positive Adkins would fall for it. Wilson gloated as he drove home. He proclaimed loudly, *Wilson, you've outdone yourself this time.* Once Wilson was inside his house, he quickly changed into some sweats and then poured himself a generous glass of whiskey. He laughed out loud as he took his first sip. The idea that had popped into his head was foolproof. It might have worked on Padgett, if he'd been in Adkins' predicament, but unfortunately Padgett wasn't.

All Wilson needed to have done was get creative, and he had been just that. He had a great plan in mind, and he fine tuned his strategy on how to trap Adkins. Once he had her, she would be at his mercy, and she'd do anything he asked of her. Wilson really liked the sound of that. He closed his eyes and enjoyed the taste of his whiskey and thought about Adkins. *She's a redhead now.* Wilson savored the thought as he swallowed. *I wonder if she's a natural redhead?*

CHAPTER 23

Tuesday Morning

Becky woke up early and felt refreshed. She could take her time this morning. There was no place in particular that she needed to be today. She had hit the mother lode last night when she had found Dave Daugherty. Initially, they'd gone back to his apartment and shared a few drinks, but then out came the drugs. Becky had no idea that Dave was a fellow dealer. He even sold many of the same drugs that she did. The biggest difference between their techniques centered on pricing. He had competitive prices on marijuana and various pills, but when it came to cocaine, which was the drug of choice for both of them, Becky felt that Dave was overpriced. She could act as the middleman or woman in her case, and become his supplier and still make a nice profit.

They had decided to go to Becky's place after they'd become better acquainted. At Dave's, they drank some alcohol, shared some coke, and then did a few pills. Neither of them was feeling any pain when they finally got to her place. The main reason they went there, after spending most of the afternoon at Dave's, was to complete one final transaction. Dave had recently cashed out his 401K, after he'd gotten fired from his job. So, he had quite a chunk of change at his disposal. Becky was quite happy to help relieve him of some of his cash. Naturally, she'd throw in a little sex session in order to sweeten the deal, but it was a win, win situation for both of them. Dave had been quite hungry for sex, and Becky, well; she was forever on the hunt. Lately, Becky's sexual appetite seemed stronger than ever. She wasn't complaining, but she used to have standards regarding who she slept with. Now, any warm body would suffice. Men, women, it had never mattered to Becky. It was sort of like what she expected from her drugs, as long as she got where she wanted to be and was satisfied, that was

223

all that mattered.

Tom was laughing to himself as he knocked on Nick's door to wake him up.   "Breakfast is ready. It's time to get up."

Nick grumbled, "What do mean breakfast is ready? What time is it?"

"It's late. It's six-thirty."

"Tom, what are you doing? Why are you waking me up so early?"

"I already told you, breakfast is ready, and come on, get up before it gets cold."

Tom was enjoying a cup of coffee, when Nick finally lumbered into the kitchen. Nick's eyes were half open as he peered down at the table and looked around for the hot meal that Tom had mentioned.

"I don't see what you're talking about. What did you mean breakfast is getting cold? All I see is a couple of bowls of fruit and two containers of yogurt. They're already cold, so where's breakfast?"

"This is breakfast, my friend. I'm putting you and Bella on diets. Sit down and eat your food. I'll get you a cup of coffee."

Tom returned with a steaming cup of coffee and placed it on the table in front of Nick.

"Hey, this coffee is black. What about my cream?"

"Cream is fattening. I know what I'm doing, stop complaining."

Nick made a face as he tasted the yogurt. "Can I put some sugar in this stuff?"

"It's already loaded with natural sweeteners. Eat you

breakfast and stop your whining."

Nick slowly worked on his fruit and yogurt as he sipped his coffee. He looked questioningly at Tom, "Ok, Tom, what's the deal? You think I need to lose weight, right? Is that what this is all about?"

"Partly, but if you're a good boy and eat all your food, maybe we'll go out to O'Rourke's later, to celebrate."

"You said something about Bella being on a diet, too. What does that mean?"

"She only gets a cup of food in the morning, and a cup in the evening. And, she doesn't get any more table scraps from you, understood?"

"Tom, sometimes you're worse than my mother used to be."

He had a serious hangover when he first got up, but he had fond memories from last night. Maybe it'd been fate, meeting Becky Adkins at The Scoreboard. It was the first really good thing that had happened to Dave Daugherty in quite some time. And, she had an excellent price for cocaine. He wondered, *where did she get it?* That wasn't something that he expected her to readily reveal, at least not until their relationship developed more thoroughly. He knew she felt the same way about him, otherwise, why would they have shared all those drugs and then slept together? He thought about potential conflicts, like he and Becky trying to attract the same clients. It might be advantageous to work as a team and share the rewards. *Yeah, maybe I'll run the idea by her.*

Dave had some of his own business to attend to this morning. He needed to submit some resumes. He might do that over at the library. Sometimes the bootleg Wi-Fi connection he used in his apartment could be spotty. He ventured another thought about Becky, *she was quite the catch. If I had a girl like her, I could be quite content.* Dave toweled off after he had gotten out of the shower. He examined himself in the mirror and liked what he saw. It was amazing what a little sex can cure. Yesterday, as he sat in the bar, he had actually been contemplating suicide. Now, that was the farthest thing from his mind. Hopefully, he could wrap up his business early, and then maybe he'd drop in on Becky, later this afternoon.

It was a few minutes after eight. Wilson's truck rolled to a stop. He was impressed. Padgett's place was looking good. He noticed smoke rising from the chimney. *Well, it looks like Padgett is moving right along on his project.* He climbed from the cab out into the frosty morning air, and then walked toward the only door that was open. He found Padgett and his dog inside. Padgett seemed to be working on some kind of plumbing. Bella barked as Wilson came in. Tom approvingly looked in her direction before he glanced Wilson's way.

"Morning, Padgett. It's been quite a while since I've stopped out to chat with you. Since it was such a beautiful morning, well, here I am."

Tom nodded, but said nothing.

"Looks like you're moving along nicely on your project. When do you expect to move in?"

Tom stared at Wilson as he poured himself some more coffee from his thermos. He wasn't sure he was even going to talk to the man, but he was considering it. He watched as Wilson expectantly stared back at him.

Tom sat his cup on a sawhorse. "Wilson, it's never been your style to just visit and carry on a friendly conversation. I know you're not about to turn over a new leaf. Why don't you tell me what's on your mind?"

Wilson smiled, at least he'd gotten Padgett to speak, "Yeah, Padgett, you're right about that. I never have been one for small talk. And, I haven't bothered you for, what has it been? Four or five days? In light of that, I surely would have expected a more neighborly greeting."

Padgett laughed, "Wilson, you're not my neighbor. As I recall, the last time you spoke to me, it was by voice mail. It was the most ridiculous, accusatory voice mail I've ever received. You probably don't even remember it, do you Wilson?" Tom saw confusion written all over Wilson's face. "I thought as much. You don't remember the night you left me that asinine message, about me being responsible for Lonnie Eldridge's death. For your information, Wilson, the guy committed suicide."

Wilson was pleased. He finally learned what his phone call to Padgett that night had been about. "You know what, Padgett? The Coroner's report agrees with you, but there's that boot mark on Lonnie's busted door that wasn't explained. While I'm on the subject of your extracurricular activities, why don't you explain your whereabouts the day Fugate was killed?"

"I don't need to explain anything to you. You're the law around here, as you aptly put it. Since that's the case, that puts the burden of proof squarely on your capable shoulders."

Wilson had about enough of Padgett. He turned toward the door, but then reconsidered. "One more thing; something you might like to know. Becky Adkins is back. I wanted to be the first one to tell you that."

"Why do I care one way or the other, if Becky Adkins is back? Is she back in Nicholas County, where you can get your hands on her?"

"Actually, I hear she's hanging out in Paris these days, I thought you'd like to know." Wilson stepped back outside into the cold January air.

She had wasted much of the morning, but that was okay. It was early afternoon and Becky had finally gotten motivated. She cruised through Mt. Sterling. She had done business here in the past but the city seemed busier than she remembered. *Yes, this is a bonus. Things are looking up.* The drive over from Paris was easy enough. It was a straight shot. All she had to do was follow Route 460. All the cities she had visited over the past few days were equally easy to get to. Becky pulled into a shopping center's lot to reference her map. Actually, Lexington was nearly as close to Paris as Georgetown, Cynthiana and Mt. Sterling were. But Becky wasn't sure if she was ready to jump into that market. Winchester was about the same distance from Paris, as the crow flies, but getting there was much more problematic.

Becky folded the map and then turned left onto Paris Pike, heading northwest. She was anxious to get home. She looked forward to some relaxation this evening. Becky ventured a thought about Dave Daugherty and laughed. She thought that they'd had a good time and all, but that was as far as it went. He wasn't her type, but as she thought about it, Becky wasn't sure what her type would be. Maybe her type didn't exist. Maybe she was some kind of freak, one that was willing to try just about anything. She laughed as she drove along. She was glad to have Daugherty as a new customer, but she didn't necessarily want to have sex with him every time they did a transaction.

Tuesday Afternoon

Nick was supposed to get off from the Mart at four o'clock. He and Tom had planned to meet at O'Rourke's at about that time.

Tom parked the F-150 and climbed out. He opened the back door and gave Bella a comforting rub. "Will you be ok out here, Bella? It won't be too cold for you, will it girl?" Judging by the length and thickness of Bella's coat, Tom was sure she would be. Bella had finally shaken all of the assorted ailments she'd wrestled with all last year. It had been an expensive journey, but it seemed that Bella was finally on the mend. After multiple visits to the vet, it was determined that the majority of Bella's ailments were food related. No more cheap dog food for Bella. No corn fillers, only the best for Bella. Tom reluctantly laid down big money for each and every bag, but his Bella was worth it.

Nick pranced around the bar when Tom entered. Tom noticed Woozy and gave her a wink. She looked good tonight.

Woozy approached and handed him a beer and smiled, "I

had a good time the other night, Tom."

"I did too, Woozy, I'm really looking forward to doing it again, soon. Just let me know what works for you."

Woozy had to attend to customers at the far end of the bar. Tom watched Woozy's bottom as she walked away. He might have watched it too intently. He caught himself and hoped that his tongue hadn't been hanging out of his mouth. It felt good to behave like a child in some ways. Nick finally came over to have a seat. He was out of breath. *Was he panting?*

"Nick, what are you so fired up about?"

Nick took a drink of his beer and attempted to catch his breath. Tom watched his friend closely until he finally settled down.

"How'd you make out at the home site?"

"Oh, I did well. I did have an unexpected guest though."

"Not Wilson? He didn't show up did he?"

"Yes, good old Mister Wilson seems to be getting back to his old self."

The county was in good hands, as far as Wilson was concerned. He left specific instructions with Deputy Leland for items that required attention before he left the courthouse and headed home. Wilson needed to switch vehicles. He was going down to Paris this afternoon, in an unofficial capacity. After he changed out of his uniform and jumped into his own truck, he left Carlisle; destination, Becky Adkins' new place. He was excited as he sped through Millersburg. He didn't pay any attention to the posted thirty-five mph limit. He wasn't even sure if Millersburg still had a policeman. If they did, he'd rarely seen him. After he arrived, Wilson turned off his ignition and studied the exterior of Becky's new home. He smiled to himself as he thought about his latest plan.

Becky excitedly opened the door, as if she'd been expecting someone. Her smile quickly turned downward as she stared back at Wilson. He smiled his classic smile back at her.

"Well, well, well, if it isn't my old friend Becky Adkins. I thought I might never see you again. But, since you're back from your Tennessee vacation, how bout inviting me inside for a spell?"

The last person Becky expected to see this afternoon was Sheriff Wilson. The fact that he wasn't in uniform did nothing to ease her mind. She glanced around outside her front door, and then indicated for Wilson to follow.

"I hope I didn't interrupt anything Ms. Adkins. You weren't expecting company were you? The door did open quite quickly, almost urgently if you'd ask me."

Becky had yet to say anything. She was in a state of shock.

"I know you're probably surprised to see me. Actually, I was kind of surprised to see you, too. After you moved away from the state, it seemed you must have forgotten our little arrangement. I'm so happy to see you. You have no idea how happy this little reunion makes me."

Becky was slowly coming around. She had a fairly good idea about Wilson's mood by just looking at the shit-eating grin he displayed. She still hadn't thought of an appropriate response, so she said nothing.

"You seem rather quiet today, Ms. Adkins. You don't mind if I sit down, do you?

Wilson looked around the room as Becky continued to glare at him. She was getting sick to her stomach just listening to Wilson gloat. He sat down and leaned way back in a recliner in order to get more comfortable.

"This place isn't nearly as nice as the one you used to have over in Fleming County. That place was actually pretty cozy. I'm guessing that maybe business has fallen off, or are you just, what's that phrase, oh yeah, downsizing?"

Wilson's phone rang and he glanced at it. Becky noticed that Wilson had stopped smiling. He quickly hit the silence button. He realized he had lost his smile, so he immediately put on another brilliant display.

Against her mother's advice, Miranda had made her mind up. She planned to call the Sheriff every single day until he did what he said he was going to do. She was going to leave another message for Wilson. That was another part of Miranda's plan. She was going to leave more and more obnoxious messages as the days continued to drag on. After his greeting ended, Miranda was ready.

"Hi Sheriff Wilson, this is Miranda Johnson. Do you happen to remember me? I'm that girl, the one in the wheelchair, the one that bought the drugs from that woman, you know, that woman that you showed me the picture of? Anyway, Sheriff, I haven't heard anything from you and I hope that you're alright. I'd hate for that woman, that redheaded woman down there in Paris, to get the jump on you or anything like that. I hope to hear from you soon. I know you're probably working very, very hard to try to find that woman. Good luck, Sheriff and don't forget to call."

He had submitted several resumes and Dave felt satisfied. Attempting to find a new job had been hard. He wondered if his former employer would go as far as blackball him in the workplace; they might. He had really screwed up when he tested positive for drug use. Dave thought he'd done his homework. He had done some research and found that cocaine was supposedly only detectable in the blood for 24 hours. He thought that all other testing techniques would yield similar results. Boy, was he ever wrong. The testing results could vary tremendously based on the techniques used. Who would have thought that cocaine could be found in saliva for up to ten days and in the urine for up to thirty days? Dave just hadn't factored in the possibility that they really did take random urine samples.

He couldn't worry about that right now, what's done was done. He combed his wavy brown hair and checked his

231

complexion in the mirror. He noticed that he had a pimple on his nose. Dave hadn't had a pimple in quite some time. Now that he was thirty he rarely got them, and even then, it was usually only after he'd had sex. That made him smile. He bent down closer to the counter and inhaled the first line into his left nostril and the second one into his right. He immediately noticed the increased intensity in his eyes. His dilated pupils always excited him. Dave sniffed the excess blow up his nose as he attended to the white rings around his nostrils. As he cleaned his nose, he gave the pimple a squeeze. That got rid of it. He threw on a coat and stepped outside into the cold afternoon air. Becky's house was only a half mile away. A walk would feel good.

CHAPTER 24

Tuesday, Early Evening

After he'd hung up, Wilson managed to force another faux smile.

Becky was ready. She looked at Wilson as a smirk appeared on her lips. "Alright, Sheriff. You've had your damned fun. If you think you can show up here dressed in your off duty outfit and threaten me, you've got another thing coming. I've got news for you. I'm not afraid of you. You've got nothing on me. Maybe you did way back when, but not any longer. You blew that chance."

Wilson continued to smile. He was enjoying this, and he liked the way Becky's lips twitched when she was angry. He enjoyed watching the way her breast moved up and down while she breathed. *Yes, this is nice. It looks like she's lost a little weight. I can't be positive, but I intend to find out.* Bill Wilson had been fantasizing about Becky for a long time. Since he was in control again, he was really going to enjoy this.

Becky paused and then looked expectantly at Wilson. He hadn't moved and his smile hadn't wavered. "Are you still with me, Sheriff? Or, have you died and gone to orgasmic heaven; sitting there all comfy while you fantasize about my tits?"

Yes, she's still the same. Becky's the same cocky drug running woman that I want so badly after all these months. Maybe she's right. Wilson tried to wake from the lustful daydream he was indulging in. He visualized her, stunningly beautiful with nothing on.

Becky was frustrated. Wilson continued to stare at her. "I'm going to the bathroom."

She walked down the hallway and Wilson enjoyed the view from his comfortable roost in the living room. Her ass swayed left and right as she walked angrily away. *Her ass still has plenty of life in it. Maybe she hasn't lost as much weight as I thought.*

In the privacy of her bathroom, Becky did a line and then tried to relax on the toilet, while she waited for the drug to take hold. She felt more in control now. Wilson listened from up the hallway. He knew she was giving herself a fix, but Wilson didn't care. He had a fix of his own in mind for Becky Adkins. After the door finally opened, Becky marched up the hallway. She had more assertiveness in her step and Wilson liked that.

"Ms. Adkins, I hope you feel better now that you've had your fix?"

"Yeah, I do Wilson. Mind telling me what's on your mind? I've got things to do, in case you've forgotten. I don't have a regular job like you. And now, you're screwing with my business."

Wilson chuckled softly. That wasn't all he planned on screwing with. "Becky, you do realize, don't you, that I could haul your ass off to prison just like that. It would happen so fast, that you'd never even know what hit you."

Becky laughed at him. "Why don't you do it then, big man? Why don't you haul my ass off to prison just like that?"

"I think you know Becky. I'm sure you know why. It's the only reason that you're not rotting in jail right now."

"Let me guess, does it have something to do with Tom Padgett?"

"Exactly; now we're beginning to understand one another."

The walk from his apartment to Becky's was farther than

Dave thought. But, he was almost there. That was good. He was freezing. There had been scattered patches of ice on the sidewalk. He had slipped one time and fallen. Finally, he was at Becky's door. Dave knocked lightly while he glanced around. Becky's car was across the street, so he was sure she was home.

Inside the house, Wilson jumped up from the recliner and quickly grabbed Becky by the wrist. "Get rid of whoever it is. We're not finished with our business yet. Becky, don't try anything funny or you're going to regret it."

Becky's wrist hurt where Wilson had grabbed her. He was surprisingly strong. She hesitantly ambled to the door as she massaged her wrist. She hooked the chain before she opened the door slightly. She peered through the opening in the door and saw Dave Daugherty standing there. It looked like he was really cold.

He smiled meekly. "Hey, Becky. I was in the neighborhood. Thought I'd stop by."

"It's not a good time, Dave. I'm really busy." She slammed the door.

He stood dejectedly on the step, wondering what had happened. Dave thought that they were friends. He had believed that they were possibly more than that, but it wasn't evident from the reception he'd just received. Becky looked pissed off when she peered through the door at him. What could she be angry about? He considered knocking again, but then decided against it. He was still cold, but the cold he felt now, was more emotional than physical. He turned and slowly walked back the direction he'd come from. As he walked along West 8th Street, he wrestled with his thoughts. *We had a good time together. That was only 24 hours ago, and now she acted like that. Was it because I showed up unannounced? Is there another man?*

As he walked home, though he was freezing, Dave did a lot of thinking. He'd lost his job and his prospects for another one looked bleak. He'd flunked out of school, although not really, but it felt like he had. The new woman in his life had given him the old heave ho. Dave felt that he was in the same predicament that he'd been in yesterday afternoon. *Am I back to square one?* He knew he was depressed and there was only one way to alleviate that tonight. He had hoped for another round with Becky, but that seemed like ancient history now. He looked back over his shoulder and gave one last thought to Becky, then resumed walking. Actually, he picked up his pace. All of the sudden, he was anxious to get home.

Wilson stepped out from hiding in the kitchen and motioned for Becky to sit.

"You did good, you did real good. Who was that anyway? Are you expecting anyone else?"

"No, not tonight. That was just some guy I met yesterday."

He was initially angry. He didn't want to be seen here. But, after the unexpected guest left, Wilson was back in control. He walked to the kitchen and went to the refrigerator.

"Do you have anything to drink?"

Becky didn't plan to give a damned thing to Wilson, but before she had a chance to reply, he returned holding a beer.

"Let me try and explain the situation to you, Ms. Adkins. Are you straight enough to comprehend what I'm talking about?"

"Wilson, as long as what you say makes just a bit of damned sense, I'll understand."

Wilson grinned. That's what he liked about Adkins, her cocky attitude.

Tom didn't know why he did it. He should have known better than to tell Nick about Wilson's visit. That was all it took.

"You believe Wilson's still out to get you? Why would you think that, Tom?"

Nick nearly drove him crazy, sometimes he was

impossible. "Let me try and explain to you what makes Wilson tick, what motivates the man. It's me. Why can't you see that? I'm not making any of this up."

Nick listened while he sipped on his beer.

"Why do you think Wilson would bother telling me that Becky Adkins was back? Because he's a matchmaker?"

"I don't know. Maybe he's trying to help, you know, to help you guys get back together again."

"There's no chance of us getting together. Nick, don't you remember? Wilson was using Becky. Together, they were trying to set me up. I can't imagine what Wilson's plans are this time. Oh, forget about it Nick, one last beer and I'm calling it a night."

"Okay by me. Hey, do you want to split a pizza? I've been starving all day, especially after only having yogurt and fruit for breakfast."

Tom had forgotten about the health food regimen he'd served Nick and Bella that morning. He had done it more as a joke than anything.

"No, I don't want a pizza. I'll eat something when we get home. But, if you want one, go ahead. You've been starving all day after that skimpy breakfast. Didn't you eat lunch?"

All of a sudden, Nick looked embarrassed. "I had a foot long Subway, and a large soft drink."

Tom realized that was a fairly big meal, but Nick had probably been starving.

Nick continued, "And, I also had another six inch sub after I finished the first one."

"Nick, sometimes you're impossible."

Wilson reclaimed the recliner, took a large gulp of beer,

and stared hungrily at Becky. Becky returned the stare. She was accustomed to men looking at her that way, so it wasn't any big deal.

"Becky, let me make one thing perfectly clear. You will not be running again. Escaping isn't an option."

Becky considered what he'd said, "Escape from what, Wilson? My sworn duty to help you on your mission to trap Tom Padgett?"

"Yeah, that's right, something like that." Wilson drained his beer and got up to get another. "Just so you know, I've been in touch with the authorities in Tennessee. Clinton, Tennessee, as well as the rest of the state, is no longer a refuge for you. I've communicated my wishes with the pertinent law enforcement agencies throughout Kentucky, and they're on board as well."

Becky felt like laughing out loud as she watched Wilson's performance, with his full of shit demeanor, but she didn't. She decided she might as well listen to what he had to say. She was anxious to learn what his plans were.

"I know you're thinking I'm full of shit. Think what you may. Let me warn you, Ms. Adkins. Try and run out on me again and you'll wish that you were rotting in a jail cell. There won't be a repeat performance of last year. You'll be here the whole time I'm laying the Padgett trap. You're instrumental in my plans, you and that hot little body of yours. Yes, you'll play a critical role in the game of getting Padgett. I expect you might even enjoy parts of the game. But, make no mistake, Becky, no one will be able to save your ass if you try and cross me. You'll need to save your strength. Your sexual exploits with Padgett are critical for the plan to work. But, don't wear yourself out, because your new master, Bill Wilson, expects payment, too."

Becky couldn't contain herself any longer and let out a giggle. Wilson didn't appreciate that, especially after he finished his long winded, well thought out speech.

When Becky, finally stopped giggling, she wanted to know, "Ok, Wilson, I realize that I'm a critical part of your plans, and apparently there is a lot of sex involved. Other that a bunch of sex, that I may or may not want, what's in it for me?"

Wilson's smile was absent. "Remember that girl you put in the wheelchair? What's in it for you? How about if you get out of this mess with your life, Becky?"

Dave Daugherty was nearly home. Fortunately, he hadn't had any more spills along the way. He hurriedly unlocked the door. He felt cold as hell. Once inside, Dave pulled a bottle of water from the fridge and stripped off his coat. He rarely drank water. It rarely occurred to him. Sometimes, his body let him know that dehydration was looming. He thought about the random drug test. The morning of it, his urine had been bright yellow. If he'd made a point to occasionally drink some water, maybe they wouldn't have found the cocaine in his system. But, that was just the way things went lately. Luck wasn't on his side.

He started down the hall toward the bathroom, but then paused. He wondered if maybe things would work out with Becky. Maybe she had been in the midst of a major transaction when he had dropped by. Probably not. If that had been the case, she wouldn't have been angry to see him, would she? Dave convinced himself otherwise. It was probably another man. Everything had been difficult lately, and now one of the bright spots in Dave Daugherty's life seemed to have faded. The education mess, the job loss, and the prospects for finding another job sucked. Things had turned to shit. After entering the bathroom, he felt the familiarity of the room quite soothing. He quietly pushed the door closed behind him.

Becky was relieved when Wilson finally left. Yeah, she'd had some pretty rough sexual encounters in her life, but she wasn't in the mood tonight. She wasn't up for a night of being slobbered and pawed on by Wilson. She'd been in worse situations before, but Becky wanted to be the one in control when the action started, as well as when it ended. Wilson was really pumped tonight. He would have been a handful. She thought about Wilson's threats.

Was there really anything to them? She wasn't sure. It could have been a bunch of Wilson bluster, but she wouldn't put anything past him. *Would he really have talked to the other police agencies? I doubt it.* But, that last threat he laid on her seemed credible. *So, he had the girl, Miranda Johnson.* She had identified Becky, and Miranda was ready and willing to testify.

A drowsy Bella blinked several times in Tom's direction as he unlocked the truck. "Sorry girl, I didn't mean to wake you." He'd been in O'Rourke's longer than expected. Thankfully, it hadn't been too cold for Bella. Bella laid her head down when Tom started the F-150. She hadn't appreciated the interruption and was going back to sleep. He had managed to convince Nick to come home and forget about the pizza. Tom told Nick he'd whip something up at home. They'd have pizza another night. He knew that if it was up to Nick, junk food would rule. He laughed when he remembered what Nick had eaten for lunch. The guy could pack it away and it was really starting to show.

Wilson whistled to himself as he sped northeast away from Paris. He was in a good mood. The night worked out exactly as planned. Adkins was going to cooperate. Did she really have a choice? She might be volatile, but Wilson planned to keep an eye on her by visiting often. He'd drop by every couple of days. Wilson decided to wait before he made her his sex slave, though he desperately wanted her. Tonight, he had heaped a lot onto her plate. After Becky had done her drugs, her high intensity quickly began to fade.

Wilson eyed the liquor cabinet when he arrived home. Nine o'clock. Why not? He'd have one glass of good old Jim Beam. *That should help take the edge off.* As he took a sip of whiskey, he felt a sense of tremendous satisfaction. *I did well tonight. I've definitely made a transition. Wilson, you've become a force to be reckoned with.*

CHAPTER 25

The Following Morning

Today, he planned to have lunch at Garrett's. It had been a while since he'd been there. Earlier in the morning, he had wired some outlets and light switches. Now, with his big shop lamp, Tom could see what he was doing, and at the same time, keep the cold January winter outside. Bella wasn't bothered one way or the other because she was close to the wood stove. She continued to love her creature comforts. He would leave a light on for her when he went to town. Tom assured Bella that he'd return soon. She didn't care how long he'd be gone, as long as the stove was warm.

Tom drove along Route 68 and shook his head as he passed the eyesore, the place that had so much junk around it. It was covered with it, acres and acres of old broken down, worn out equipment. Tom had read in the paper that the county was going to start to enforce a no junk ordinance, sort of similar to homeowners' covenants. The article stated that the Sheriff would be the enforcer. He'd have to ask Wilson about it.

Wilson had just finished eating and was drinking coffee with some of the Carlisle cops when Tom entered Garrett's. Tom nodded, and then sat at the counter. As he placed his order, he heard a chair slide away from a table. Without looking behind him, he knew it was Wilson. A moment later, Wilson joined him at the counter.

"Padgett, you haven't been in town for a while. What brings you out today?"

"I don't know, Wilson. I just felt like socializing. What's new in police business?"

241

"Not much. I've got some good leads I'm following. I should know soon if they're going to yield fruit."

"I read something in the paper, something about a no junk ordinance. It said you're the person responsible for enforcing it."

"Yeah, what about it?"

"If I read it correctly, it said that if a resident of the county considered something to be an eyesore or offensive to them, they can file a complaint. It also said that you'd be the one responsible to serve the offending party. Have you received any complaints?"

"Nope, not yet."

"So, if I filed a complaint, you'd be obligated to go visit the offensive place?"

Wilson began to fidget on the stool. He hadn't expected Padgett to come in today, especially with a work request.

"Technically, Padgett, as long as the complaint is valid."

"And, I can remain anonymous if I was fearful of repercussions?"

"I imagine, though I'm not sure, since no complaints have been filed."

"That's good news, Wilson. I'll keep it in mind. I've got a place in mind that's offensive to me. I'll let you know if and when I'm ready to complain."

Tom's lunch was served, so Wilson used the opportunity to slip out the door. He wasn't happy with Padgett's suggestion. He wasn't happy being an ordinance enforcer, either. The new task could interfere with his primary objective.

Tom watched Wilson cross the street. *He's probably heading back to his office to check out his new job responsibilities. It feels great when I can silence Wilson, throw him off guard.* Tom paid his tab and left Carlisle. Before he quit for the day, he wanted to finish more of his electrical installation.

Wilson pulled out the specifics of the ordinance when he returned to his office. *Damn, Padgett is right. Let that SOB submit his complaint.* The amount of time allowed for a response to a complaint was unclear, especially if the complaint was filed by an anonymous person.

Even though Becky had a good day, she was still on edge. She had spent most of her morning in Winchester, but decided it was time to head home. She had no idea what Wilson had up his sleeve. For all she knew, Wilson might be sitting on her doorstep right now. Becky hadn't given much thought to Wilson's plans. The only thing that concerned her was Miranda Johnson, the girl in the wheelchair. She didn't feel pangs of regret for her, but without her, Wilson's hold on Becky wouldn't be much. But, it didn't matter to her. She could tolerate being used as a ploy, especially if she got some time alone with Padgett. That would be a good thing. Becky figured that if she helped Wilson get Padgett, Wilson would be grateful and would probably uphold his end of the bargain and let her go. But with Wilson, one could never be sure.

As she entered Paris, Becky wondered, *what happened to Dave last night? I did send him away rather abruptly, but given the circumstances, it was necessary. I needed to make a point for Wilson and sound impressive.* She pulled her Mustang over to the curb and got out. Dave's car was out front. She'd see what he was doing and might even apologize for her behavior last night. She didn't need to alienate any of her customers.

She ran a brush through her hair before she rapped on the door. After a bit, she knocked again. No answer. *That's strange. Maybe he walked down to The Scoreboard, it's not too far.* She drove to The Scoreboard but when she got there, the place was empty. No Dave.

The bartender glared at her. "Looking for more information about the partying habits of people here in Paris?"

Becky slammed the door and got back in her car. *Dave was*

243

right about one thing, that bartender has an attitude.

She said she was disgusted. So what? So was he. Wilson deleted the messages that Miranda Johnson had left. *If that smart ass little girl expects my help, she needs to learn some respect.* Miranda probably had a legitimate gripe, but what she failed to realize was that Wilson was addressing the bigger picture. He was willing to forgo the small, relatively minor crimes, in an effort to solve the larger one. It was the will of the people. *Who knows? Maybe with Adkins' help, I could not only trap Padgett, but turn the tables on Adkins at the same time.* It might prove tricky, but Wilson wasn't one to give up without a fight. He couldn't rush it, though. Before the shit hit the fan, he wanted plenty of time alone with Adkins. He'd hate to lose that opportunity.

As he sat in his office, he imagined what Becky would look like naked. He was sure she would be hot. The thought of her long red hair and the opportunity to determine whether or not it was natural, nearly drove him insane. *Can I wait two more days before I pay Becky a visit? Hell no! Wilson, there's no time like the present. Let's go see Ms. Adkins tonight and start to work on the Padgett plan.*

Wilson allowed himself a mischievous grin. He thought about Padgett's earlier comment about being the ordinance police. *Padgett, go ahead and file your complaint about whatever you want. I'll just file it away. It'll be in my file cabinet a long time. Before I look at anything signed by a person named anonymous, it'll be a long time, a damned long time.*

Bella raised her head slightly when Tom came home. Apparently, she hadn't missed him. Tom managed to get the stove open and was throwing a log on the fire before she had a chance to get excited. Bella was getting more jumpy the older she got. The slightest things seemed to set her off. He'd heard it was a trait of Goldens, but he had hoped that her Yellow Lab traits were dominant. Unfortunately, it didn't seem to be the case. As he was trying to close the stove door, she jumped again. It seemed the door had nearly touched her leg. Bella gave him a pitiful look, one that she used when she felt that she'd been unjustly disturbed or had her feelings hurt. He sympathized with Bella's pained expression for a moment, and then his phone rang.

"Hello,... yes, this is Tom.... Yes, I remember you. How are you Miranda?... Yes, I understand, but I'm no longer a policeman. I'm retired now.... I don't know why the Sheriff doesn't return your calls.... You're positive it was her?... And, what did the Sheriff say he was doing about it?... He said he'd get back to you? And how long has it been?... Did you say nearly a week?... The lady was in Paris at a basketball game and then later you saw her at Taco Bell, on the Paris Bypass?... What?... She has red hair and its longer now?... Miranda, I can't guarantee anything. I'll do some poking around in an unofficial capacity. ...Yes, I'll get back to you. Goodbye, Miranda."

As she rolled back into the living room, Miranda thought, *that was satisfying*. She hadn't wanted her mother to hear the conversation.

"Who'd you just call, Miranda?"

"Oh, I left the Sheriff another message," she regrettably lied. "Of course, he didn't answer."

Miranda's mother resumed reading her book. That gave Miranda time to think. She regretted keeping anything from her mom, but her mother sometimes preferred to let bygones be bygones. But given the circumstances, that was entirely unacceptable. Miranda had some regrets of late. One of them was failing to snap a photo of that red headed woman when she'd had the chance. Granted, taking a picture at the basketball game would have been tough, but at Taco Bell, Miranda felt she should have been better prepared. Another thing she wished she done sooner, was to tell Tom Padgett about the woman she'd seen in Paris. But she'd done it now. The thing she regretted most though, was telling the Sheriff. That had been a waste of time. He was useless as far as Miranda was concerned. The Sheriff was some kind of weird, twisted man. She didn't care for him at all.

It was four o'clock. Wilson felt that he'd put in enough hours today. He had big plans for the evening, but first he needed to run home and change before he went to visit Ms. Adkins. He'd been thinking of nothing but Adkins since about one this afternoon. He'd gotten tired pretending to be doing paperwork. As he trudged out the door, he yelled to the clerk that he'd see her in the morning. Then, Wilson was gone.

After he changed clothes, he felt a sense of relief. He climbed into his truck and started it up. Now, he was a normal guy in his personal vehicle, totally inconspicuous. He glanced up at the rear view mirror as he backed from the garage. He was nearly to the street when he saw movement behind him. He slammed on the brakes, just in time. The nosy neighbor stepped from behind the vehicle and glared at him through the driver's window.

"Why don't you pay attention, Wilson? You almost ran me over."

He said nothing. He watched the old woman walk back in the direction she'd obviously come from. *Where the hell had that old bitch been hiding?* He put the truck in gear and sped off toward town. *Maybe I should have run her ass over. I could have claimed it was an accident. No, that wouldn't work. I was home from work early and driving my personal vehicle.* Wilson thought that he'd have to come up with a way to get her, but he'd worry about that later. Once he crossed into Bourbon County, he relaxed. Now, he was out of the danger zone. He didn't have to worry about law and order. He could do what he wanted to do. He was a free man.

It was nearly five o'clock. When Becky had gotten home earlier, she took a power nap and got up an hour ago. She did some coke and was in a good space. *Maybe Wilson isn't coming.* That would be great by her. She didn't feel up to listening to his conspiratorial bullshit. She leaned back in her recliner and enjoyed the rush. *What was that? No, it couldn't be a knock on the door. There it is again, a friendly seven knock signal. Who the hell could be so cleverly annoying? It had to be Wilson.* She wanted to ignore him. Reluctantly, she drew herself upright and padded over to the door. She looked through the peephole and saw an eyeball staring back at her.

"Who the hell is it?"

"It's yours truly."

Becky unhooked the chain and unlocked the door. Wilson could do the rest. He wasn't handicapped. She reclaimed her recliner as Wilson waltzed into the room.

"Hello, Ms. Adkins, and how are you this lovely afternoon?"

She felt like saying something derogatory, but knew that would be a waste of time. She said nothing. She was sure Wilson would talk enough for both of them. She was right.

"Did you have a productive day, out there pushing your stuff? I hope you did, because once we get started on my project, your customers will be put on the back burner. You'll need to focus on the top priority, and that's Tom Padgett."

"Yes sir, Mr. Wilson."

He liked the sound of that. He loved the way her lips moved when she said sir.   "Yeah, Becky, I've got big plans for you, and big plans for Padgett, too. Are you ready to hear some of them?"

"I'm as ready as I'll ever be Wilson."

Tom had been parked outside, when Wilson left the courthouse. He figured it was time to see what Wilson was doing after he had received the call from Miranda. Tom didn't want to be spotted, so he followed at a good distance. He wasn't worried about Wilson checking his rear view mirror, and he felt it unlikely Wilson would even consider that he was being tailed. But, Tom didn't want Wilson to know he was behind him, or that he was trying to find out where Becky lived. Tom allowed a few cars to move in front of him as they entered Paris. He continued to follow Wilson as he turned right on West 8th Street. Miranda was right. Tom slowly passed the house that Wilson had entered. He hadn't actually seen Becky. He didn't need to. She was there. He saw her Mustang. It had Tennessee plates. So, Becky had gone south when she had left Kentucky. Tom was curious, *why'd she return?* He pulled his truck to the curb and stopped and kept the engine running. It had turned quite cold. Tom wondered, *what's Wilson up to?*

Last year, before Becky fled, she and Wilson had been actively conspiring to frame Tom by making it appear that he was a drug dealer. That hadn't worked out. Now, Becky was back and Miranda Johnson had seen her. Miranda had let the Sheriff know that the woman who sold her the drugs had returned, but Wilson chose to ignore it. It seemed that once again, Wilson wasn't worried about bringing Becky Adkins to justice. He has his own personal agenda.

Tom considered the possibilities available to Wilson. *He probably has a personal interest in her.* Tom could understand that. *Becky is a nice looking lady.* Tom again considered, *why'd Becky returned to Kentucky? Maybe she hadn't been successful in Tennessee. Maybe she had another drug deal go bad and someone else got hurt or killed. Maybe her choice drug was out of favor.* Tom had heard Oxycontin was losing some of its appeal. Tom wondered, *does Becky still sell drugs for a living?* He was quite sure that she did.

CHAPTER 26

Wednesday Evening

They had discussed different ways of getting Padgett for the past two hours and Becky was getting tired. Wilson had some ideas that he wanted her to employ, but Becky felt they were utterly ridiculous. She stared blankly across room and Wilson stared back. The whiskey that Wilson had been drinking obviously wasn't helping him become creative. He had brought three bottles of Jim Beam with him. Becky hoped he wasn't planning on drinking all three. He was already nearly incoherent, and he'd only had three glasses. The last idea he'd come up with had about done it for Becky. She stood and walked down the hall.

"I'm going to the bathroom, Wilson. I hope you can create a more feasible plan by the time I return."

His eyes longingly followed her as she walked away. *Yeah, I'm going to come up with a plan, but tonight's plan won't have anything to do with Padgett.* He sat and sipped his whiskey as he waited. After several minutes, Becky still hadn't returned. Wilson walked down the hall and pounded on the bathroom door.

"What the hell are you doing in there?"

"I'm using the toilet, damn it. Do you mind?"

Wilson found his way back to the living room and poured another rather large glass of Jim Beam. He was going to enjoy this. As soon as Adkins' stoned ass found its way out of the bathroom, he planned to sample some of it. Wilson had waited long enough and she had given him plenty of trouble. That was ancient history, though. Now, they were a team. He was just about to yell again

249

when the bathroom door swung open. Becky strolled up the hallway. She wore very little.

Wilson's mouth uncontrollably gaped open. "What's that thing called? He wasn't sure what Becky was wearing, but he'd suddenly forgotten about his whiskey. The glass slipped from his hand and onto the floor.

"It's nothing special. It's a lace halter. Do you think it will be effective against Padgett?"

"I'm sure of it. Why don't you bring your sweet little ass over here, and see if it's effective on me?"

Tom planned to put Bella in the back yard as soon as he got to Nick's. She'd been a good girl while he'd been spying on Wilson and his co-conspirator. Bella had been very patient, as she lay on the floor of the truck. She was glad to be out, though, and finally able to stretch her legs. So was Tom. He led Bella through the house. As he passed the fridge, Tom grabbed a beer, and then went out back with Bella. Nick sat at the kitchen table. He watched them come in the front door, and then walk out the back door. Tom had managed a simple hello, but that was all. Nick drank a beer while he read the paper. He wondered, *what the hell is going on?*

After a couple of minutes, Nick came outside. He found Tom sitting on the steps, petting Bella. "Hey, Tom, is everything all right? You don't usually blow through the house, like you did tonight. Is there anything I should know about?"

Tom hadn't realized his level of preoccupation. As he had walked through the house, he'd barely registered that Nick was even there. He had been thinking while he rubbed Bella's ears.

"Oh, I'm sorry. I wasn't paying any attention. I guess I was preoccupied. I didn't mean to ignore you."

"Are you sure you should be sitting out here? It's pretty darn cold."

"I'm ok, Nick. We'll be in a few minutes, and we're ok, really."

Nick stepped back inside, into the warmth of the kitchen. He could see that distant look was back in Tom's eyes. Something wasn't right. But, at least Tom didn't seem to be in that intense state, the intensity he'd witnessed on a couple of other occasions. Nick closed the door behind him and then sat back down at the table to finish the paper.

Fifteen minutes later, Tom and Bella came inside. Nick had just reached into the fridge, to get another beer.

"Would you like a cold one?"

Tom grinned, "Why not? A cold beer on a cold night should hit the spot."

Bella moved over to the register when she heard the furnace kick on. Tom shook his head as he watched Bella get comfy. *Still loves her creature comforts.* Nick placed the beer on the table and studied Tom for a moment.

"Are you sure everything's alright? You seem quieter than usual. Did you have anything to eat? If not, there's leftover pizza in the fridge."

Tom smiled, "Thanks, everything's fine. I'm wrestling with a few things in my head, that's all. I'm trying to figure some things out."

Nick looked at the table and said nothing. It seemed that Tom wasn't in a volunteering mood tonight. Nick knew he might just have to coax the info out of him.

Tom sensed Nick's dilemma and chuckled, "Nick, don't worry about me, I'm fine. There are a few things I need to sort out, and only I can do it. So, stop worrying about me."

The twenty minutes it had taken Becky to totally zap him of

251

his energy were wonderful. Wilson was absolutely spent. He lay on his back panting, like some wild dying animal. He reached over for his glass of whiskey on the nightstand. Becky had climbed out of bed as soon as they finished, and went to take a shower. Wilson probably needed a shower, too, but at the moment, he was too damned tired. *Becky might just have to put up with a little man scent for the evening.* He thought for a minute. *I wonder if all that moaning she did was genuine?* He'd had a few women in his day, and Wilson was well aware that they could fake orgasms. *I wonder if I've ever really satisfied a woman? It doesn't matter. If they can't get their act together and enjoy the moment, that isn't my problem.* All he knew was that he was happy and content, and in Bill Wilson's book, that was what mattered. He smiled as the realization dawned on him, *Becky Adkins; she is a natural red head.*

He took a sip of Jim Beam and then excitedly turned his head as he heard Becky return from the bathroom. He was disappointed because she was now wearing sweats, big baggy sweats.

"What happened to the nice outfit, that halter thing that you were wearing? Why are you all covered up in those baggy ass sweats?"

"This is what I sleep in, Wilson. Since it seems you've invited yourself to spend the night, I figured I needed to stay warm while I'm downstairs, sleeping on the couch."

Wilson watched as Becky headed downstairs. *Well, if she wants to sleep on the damned couch, so be it.* It wasn't going to change one a damned thing. She was still his prisoner. He had plans for her, whether she liked it or not. First thing in the morning, they were going to figure out the next step, for Padgett. If Wilson was late for work, that wasn't a problem. And, he'd already explained to Adkins, that her customers were no longer a priority.

It had been a long day. Working as a cashier at the Paris Walmart, hadn't been Sharon Walters' dream job, but it paid the bills. She unlocked the front door of her tiny apartment and entered the living area. She looked around the room before throwing her coat on the couch. Once in the kitchen, she opened the fridge and pulled the leftovers out. They would be just fine for dinner. She set the timer on the microwave to *reheat plate.* That should do it. She hit start, and then headed to the bathroom. She was exhausted tonight. She planned to put on her pajamas and climb into bed and hoped to finish the book she'd been reading. As Sharon pulled her sweater over her head, she heard that painful, familiar noise. She loathed that sound, the sound of dripping water. She looked up and sure enough, there it was, the ceiling was dripping. The guy in the upstairs apartment had left the sink on, again.

She put her sweater back on before she stepped outside into the cold evening air. She knocked on Dave Daugherty's door. There was no answer. She waited a moment and then knocked again, this time much harder. Still no answer. As she shivered, she glanced around and noticed that his car was there. Why wouldn't he answer? Maybe he was asleep. She stepped back inside and locked her door, just as the microwave dinged. Her dinner was ready. Sharon was starved. She quickly ate, and then looked at the clock. It was only nine-thirty, it wasn't too late. On another occasion last fall, Daugherty had left his sink running and it had overflowed. But that time when she knocked, at least he'd opened the door. How he could forget to turn off his sink was beyond her.

She dialed the landlord's number. After he answered, Sharon explained the situation. The landlord could be a pain, but sometimes he was exasperating. "But, I'm telling you, the water's coming through my ceiling. The sooner you get the sink turned off the better. ...Alright, I'll close the bathroom door.... Yeah, I'll see you in the morning."

Tom woke up when he heard Bella cry. He rolled over on his side. Now he could see her. She was lying on the floor next to his bed. The moon was full, so he could see her clearly. He watched her for a moment. She was dreaming. Bella's legs were pumping and she was whimpering. Was she running from something? Or, was she the one doing the chasing? Interestingly, Tom had also been dreaming. It had been a normal dream, if there really were such things. It wasn't as wild as some he'd had recently. In this dream, he saw Wilson and Becky. They were conspiring about ways to get him. Tom chuckled. He had been to Becky's new place earlier, so it seems the Wilson conspiracy plan is in play again. If that wasn't the case, why didn't he bring Becky in and simply charge her?

Tom fluffed his pillow under him, while thoughts began to churn in his head. He wasn't tired now. His mind continued to spin. *What could Wilson be doing, and why was he using Becky? Why had Becky come back, was it planned? How long would it be before Wilson started to drop him hints, hints about future events?* How long had he been living in Nicholas County, what was it, eight months? And Wilson had never given up, never stopped hounding him, *would he keep at it forever? He probably would.* Tom knew it was unlikely, but he needed to clear his mind. That way, he'd be able to get some sleep. He wasn't ready to get up, it was only 2am. Maybe, if he thought pleasant thoughts, he'd be able to sleep. Visions of Woozy filled his head. Tom smiled and closed his eyes.

The Next Morning

Wilson was pleased that his head wasn't pounding. Fortunately, last night he'd kept his drinking well under control. It was a little after six. He'd go wake Becky for the planning session. He smelled the coffee as he descended the steps. *Surely she can't be awake yet?* Becky was in the kitchen, holding a coffee in her hands, while she stared at the wall.

Wilson looked at her eyes. "Oh God, can't you stay away from that shit for once?"

"What the hell are you talking about, Wilson? Stay away from what?"

"That damned coke you're doing. I need you to be sharp this morning. We've got to come up with a plan for Padgett, and I need you running on all cylinders."

Becky laughed, "Right, Wilson, the same way you were running on all cylinders last night. You worry about yourself Wilson, I'll worry about me."

Wilson poured himself some coffee and sat down. He smiled, "Maybe you can whip us up some breakfast, so we'll be able to concentrate?"

"I can concentrate just fine. If you want some damned breakfast, then I suggest you whip it up yourself."

Wilson sipped his coffee and stared at Becky. She stared back at him. He could see that this might prove more difficult than he'd originally thought. He needed to be more subtle. He needed a gentler approach.

"How about I make us some scrambled eggs then. Do you like eggs?"

"I'm not hungry. In case you've forgotten, I've already had breakfast. You remember, the coke you just mentioned."

"But, you need to eat. You're going to need your strength, remember?"

"How could I forget about that, Wilson? Especially if you plan to stay here and expect to lie on top me half the damned night, slobbering and grunting. I know I'm going to need my strength."

Wilson opened the fridge and noticed only a few cans of beer. *What kind of diet is that?* He'd run over to McDonald's and get something when they finished. *The hell with the nice guy approach. It isn't going to work with Adkins. She's damaged goods.* He looked for his pad because he needed to write things down.

Becky watched. As he started to scribble, she laughed, "Enough of the child-like hand writing. Why don't we just talk about the plans, like two adults?"

Wilson didn't like her damn attitude. Maybe he'd drag her ass back to Nicholas County and bust her on the Miranda Johnson drug charge. No, he wanted more than that. The drug bust was small potatoes compared to the grand prize, the big enchilada, Padgett.

Sometimes, property management could be a real drag. Last night, Ted Miller had just fallen off to sleep, when his phone rang. Sharon Walters claimed that the apartment above hers had a leak, or whatever.

Morning came too quickly. Ted got into his truck and fired it up. It was cold today. He turned on the defroster, and then went back inside the house. He was fortunate. At least that's what his dad always told him. He was fortunate because he'd been left the family business. The family business consisted of six rental properties scattered around Paris. *Can I make it on the income from the family business? Hell no.* He also had a full time job, in addition to running the so-called family business.

When Ted arrived at the apartment, Sharon Walters was standing outside in front of the units. She was mad that Daugherty had ignored her when she'd knocked on his door last night. After he'd said hello to Sharon, Ted knocked on the door. No answer. Ted didn't like surprises. He didn't like to let himself into any of the rental units. He dialed Daugherty's number, and it immediately went to voice mail. He shrugged and then pulled his big key chain from his pocket. *Which one of the keys is it?* All the properties that the family business owned were old, and all the old properties had many keys. He unsuccessfully tried key after key, until presto. He finally had found the right one. Slowly, he opened the door and began to climb the steps. Sharon was at his heels.

Ted turned around and stopped. "What are you doing? What if he's up there and he's screwing a girl or something?"

Sharon grinned, "I don't know, but why should you have all the fun?"

He slowly sipped his ultra hot McDonald's coffee while he

enjoyed his Egg McMuffin. Wilson believed that he and Becky had finally formulated a decent plan. As a result, he'd given her the rest of the day off. Well, not really. But he wasn't planning to return to her place until the following evening. Yeah, he'd thoroughly enjoyed their little roll in the hay last night. He wanted her fresh for their repeat performance on Friday. Wilson had been pleased with his sexual prowess. It had been a couple of years since he'd actually had sex. Well, sex with anyone other than himself as he watched pornographic movies or visited internet porn sites. Wilson felt he'd been dominant and in total control. Becky probably was anxiously looking forward to their rendezvous.

The plan would commence on Saturday. The weekend was the best time for what they'd come up with. Padgett would be relaxed and in a receptive state on the weekend, at least that's what Becky believed. Wilson tended to agree with her, based on personal experience. But, if Wilson got a little too heavy into the Jim Beam, then weekends could be a problem. Becky assured Wilson that Tom Padgett wouldn't allow himself to lose control, just because it was Saturday or Sunday. Besides, he was retired and every day was a weekend. That type of thinking made perfect sense to Wilson. He couldn't wait until retirement. Even though it was more than thirty years off, Wilson was counting the days until he could call it quits.

Becky wasn't sure how much more of Wilson's shit she could take. *Wilson is so damned full of himself, and based on what? He's an utter clown. I'll be so glad when this Padgett bullshit is behind me.* One thing she planned to do Friday night was to get some dirt on Wilson. She needed something that would give her additional leverage; something that would prevent Wilson from turning his sights on her, as soon as Padgett was in the bag. She had no reason to believe any of the things Wilson said. He was only in this for himself. *Well, two can play that game Mr. Wilson.* All the while they'd been scheming together, thinking of ways to get Padgett, she'd been thinking of alternative ways to get the Sheriff, and Becky believed she'd come up with one. She felt it might even be foolproof.

Wilson told her earlier that he was giving her the day off. *That was awfully big of the bastard.* Becky had never liked taking orders, and she didn't like dangling like some puppet from Wilson's string either. She was worked up this morning. She wasn't in the mood to do any transactions. She'd wait until the Padgett Plan was behind her before she returned to work. Then, she'd be free to do as she pleased. She might even have unfettered access back in Nicholas County, when all was said and done. That would be nice. Maybe she could even have Wilson act as her page for a while. That would be perfect. She hoped to slip the shoe on the other foot, and if her plans worked out on Friday night, she'd do just that.

He couldn't believe what he found. Ted Miller nearly fainted when he found the body on the apartment's bathroom floor. He was sure it was Dave, but he wasn't going to touch the guy and turn him over. He wasn't about to turn the sink off either. He and Sharon might have already contaminated the scene. After he saw the unfinished line of cocaine on the bathroom counter, he quickly backed up and told Sharon to leave.

"Don't touch anything. Just go back down the steps; don't even use the handrails."

This wasn't part of the family plan. This wasn't part of what the family business was meant to provide. It was supposed to be a money making proposition, rental properties. Now it looked as if a tenant had died here. How was he supposed to rent this place again? He noticed that Sharon Walters wasn't as excited as she'd been earlier, now that they'd discovered the body.

"I told you to stay out, but you insisted on coming."

He dialed 911 because he didn't know what else to do. After he hung up, he and Sharon waited inside her apartment. He could still hear the water dripping, but it didn't seem to matter anymore. Sharon handed him a coffee. They both sat down at the kitchen table, and waited for the police.

A Force To Be Reckoned With

The police came and sealed off the scene. The name of the victim would be withheld until the Coroner finished his business. Ted watched from the warmth of his truck as the crime scene was worked. He already knew the name of the victim, and the cause of death. It was easy to tell. The unfinished line of cocaine that had been left on the bathroom counter top, the overflowing sink, obviously Dave hadn't been able to turn it off. All in all, Ted Miller would have to say that it had been a shitty day. He guessed he wasn't in a position to complain after he considered what Dave Daugherty had gone through. Still, he found he was complaining silently to himself.

He was aggravated that Sharon had left, saying that she was due at work. *Hadn't she been the one that started this whole ball rolling? Why wasn't she here with me, waiting until the police said it was ok for me to go? I haven't done anything. The only involvement I had with Dave was that I was his landlord.* He cranked the engine again, because the cab of his truck was getting cold. What would his father think about the family business now? He wondered whether he should call his dad and tell him about the latest adventures, then decided not to. He didn't want his dad going off on him about what had happened.

It looked like the police were wrapping things up. He hoped he'd be allowed to go into the apartment and clean up. He felt really bad about what had happened to Daugherty, but not nearly as bad as he felt for himself, because he knew how hard it was going to be to rent the place again. Especially, when someone had died from an overdose inside.

CHAPTER 27

Early Friday Morning

Judy, Miranda's Mother, replaced the handset onto the base. If she hadn't had a land line, her sister Jewel, would never have been able to reach her. It had been ten years since they'd spoken to one another. It had been such a long time that neither one of them remembered the real reason for the rift between them. But, a death in the family had a way of bringing families close together. Judy thought about what her sister had just told her. Her nephew, Dave Daugherty, had died yesterday. It was determined that he'd died from a cocaine overdose. He was Miranda's first cousin. It was unlikely that Miranda would remember much about him. Judy softly whispered, "A cocaine overdose, and it happened in Paris, Kentucky?"

Judy wasn't sure how to break the news to her daughter. She might not remember her cousin very well, but Miranda was smart. She would be able to put two and two together. First, there was the lady that Miranda had seen in Paris, the one she believed sold her the drugs. Now this, her cousin dead from an overdose, and it happened in Paris. That was too much of a coincidence. Judy was positive Miranda would make the connection. She was having a difficult time deciding what to do. Judy knew that Miranda would insist on action. She would hound the Sheriff until he did something. Judy wanted something to be done as well, but she didn't want her daughter to go through any more difficulties. If Miranda was forced to participate in a trial, it might have long lasting effects. But, the lady needed to be punished. Miranda had been one of her victims, and had a right to see that justice was served.

For a Friday, he was in the office early. Wilson almost felt pangs of guilt about all the time he had spent with Becky this week. Although he'd been negligent in his responsibilities, he knew the entire situation and understood the bigger picture. *Most of the small-minded people in this county, probably can't appreciate that.* Tomorrow, he was going to get Padgett, the big kahuna. He'd worry about the rest of the hoods running around loose in the county after that. He put his feet up on the desk and contemplated the near future. *Busting Padgett, how would it feel?* It had been a long time and the end was near. He sipped his coffee and smiled, Wilson was in a great space.

There was a light rap on the door, which startled Wilson. He swung his feet from the desk and glanced up at his visitor. Theresa Walker, the County Attorney, peered at him through the doorway.

"I'm quite surprised to see you here, Sheriff. It's not like you to come in early on a Friday. It's only a quarter to eight. I've noticed that you've been coming in late a lot lately. But, I'm sure you've got a good explanation for that?"

Wilson was suddenly frustrated. How was he supposed to answer that? Was it a question? "I've been busy tying up loose ends, Theresa. But I'm optimistic that I'll have some closure this weekend."

Theresa was confused. She had no idea what Wilson meant by any of that. "Well good for you, Sheriff, and if I don't see you again today, have a nice weekend."

"Same to you, Theresa."

He watched her leave. He wanted to say more, but what was the point? She couldn't understand police methods. She knew law, she had no idea about doing police work. Yes, Wilson planned to have a good weekend, actually a great weekend. He grabbed his coat and walked from the office. He started his engine. Maybe a cruise around the county was in order. It was starting to feel like casual Friday, except that he was in uniform. But later that afternoon, the uniform was coming off, and the Jim Beam Black was coming out. It was going to be a fantastic weekend.

It was a beautiful January morning, cold, but the sky was crystal clear. Tom had a nice hot fire going in the wood stove. Naturally, Bella was lounging, stretched out in front of it. Bella had no idea how close she was to getting her tail singed every time Tom threw a log on the fire. She wagged her tail back and forth, fanning the flames, while Tom attempted to load more wood. He warned her every time. He told her she was in the way. Bella didn't care. Her comfort was the only important thing. He watched her lay back down in front of the stove. She was only slightly miffed at him for having disturbed her. Tom needed her to sleep someplace else so loading the stove wouldn't be such a hassle. He had it, that old blanket he used for moving. It'd be perfect.

Once Bella was comfortable on the blanket and no longer in front of the stove's door, Tom went back to work. He'd done well this week. He was ready to begin to hang drywall. Drywall can be a messy job. It wasn't one Tom was looking forward to. He hoped to keep the rooms warm, which would allow the mud to cure. Earlier in the week, Tom bought a portable air mattress, which had a fold up frame. Now, if he was really involved in the project and didn't feel like going to Nick's, he could stay the night. There were many things undone, like plumbing and such. But, he could rough it, if need be. He had finished hanging the second sheet of drywall, when his phone rang. He looked at the display, recognizing the number. Tom wrestled with whether or not to answer since he had a lot of work he needed to get done.

Miranda's Mother had been right. Miranda hadn't taken the news well, and had quickly concluded that the red headed woman had a role in her cousin's death. Miranda immediately made a phone call. She didn't tell her mom who she had called. It really shouldn't matter anyway. Miranda wanted someone to do something. The Sheriff had obviously done nothing. After Miranda left her message, Judy tried to get her daughter to calm down. She tried to explain things to Miranda, in an attempt to defend Wilson's actions. Quickly, she realized that was a mistake. Miranda then told her mom that she hadn't even telephoned the Sheriff. She told her that she called and left a message for someone else.

Judy was shocked. "What do you mean you left the message for someone else? Miranda, there is no one else."

Mom, the Sheriff's not doing anything. He's not doing his job, I'm sure of it. Remember when that man came to talk to me last year? He came with the Sheriff?"

"Yes, but you said he used to be a policeman. He's retired, isn't he? There's nothing he can do. You'll have to tell the Sheriff."

"I have told the Sheriff, and what has he done? Why didn't he catch that woman before my cousin was killed?"

Judy knew that continuing to argue with her headstrong daughter would be pointless, so she decided to let it drop. They would wait and see who called first, the Sheriff, or Tom Padgett?

It had been a productive morning and Becky believed she was due a reward. She had found a camera shop in Lexington that had exactly what she wanted. The device was perfect for her plans. She got home and then plugged in the alarm clock to let it charge. She laughed to herself, as she thought of her latest plan. The clock she purchased was actually a spy camera. Tonight, she planned to record Wilson. That would give her ammunition if and when Wilson decided to turn on her. It was motion activated. Becky moved in front of the camera testing it to see how it worked. After her test, she plugged a card into her laptop and watched the video. It worked well. She had no idea when Wilson would show tonight, but he would, and she was ready.

Becky felt sad, which was unusual after she did a line of coke. She realized that she'd probably never see Padgett again, if things went as planned this weekend. She was sure Wilson would be around, which would provide some entertainment; the way he strutted when he walked, and how cocky and conceited he was. Actually, he was kind of funny. The video she planned to record tonight might come in handy, even if she didn't use it. Maybe she could upload it onto a porn site, and who knows? It might lead to a new career. She laughed at the thought that she'd probably have to crop Wilson from the video, but she knew plenty of tech guys that would be willing to do that.

It was a nice day for a drive. Wilson was west of Route 68. This was a part of the county that he rarely visited. He drove slowly to read road signs; Mt. Moriah, Saltwell, Butterville, Calcutta, Buffalo Trace. He didn't recognize any of the names. But, soon he would get familiar with this part of Nicholas County, after he'd put Padgett's ass away. If things went as planned, this weekend would be Padgett's last, as a free man. Wilson eyed the dashboard clock. He didn't want to be late, not for this rendezvous. After turning north on Route 68, he followed it to Old Maysville Road. He made a left and followed it over to Sugar Creek, and then another left on Bald Hill. He pulled over from the road and referenced the map. If he made a left on Sugg Road that would lead him back to Route 68. A quick glance at the clock, two o'clock. Time to call it a day.

Wilson was excited and filled with anticipation. He whistled a tune as he turned onto Lake Road, Route 1455. After Padgett was gone, he might have to take up fishing. He would have a lot more free time. Wilson wasn't sure if Lake Carnico was a pay lake or not. He didn't have a fishing license, but he was Sheriff, so nobody who would mess with him. He was about to turn and head into town, when a speeding truck blew past. The driver had to be pushing sixty, in a thirty-five zone. Wilson again looked at the clock, two-forty-five. He wouldn't worry about it. As he completed the turn, he mumbled under his breath, "Let's consider this a warning." Carlisle was peaceful afternoon. That made him smile. *Yes, peace in the county was coming at last, and Bill Wilson was the man that made it happen.*

He turned left onto Route 32 and then hit Send. Tom wasn't sure what Miranda would be calling about. He wasn't anxious to find out. She excitedly answered after only one ring. Tom listened as she rapidly explained the situation. He was attempting to understand what someone that had had a drug overdose might have to do with Becky Adkins. Miranda kept talking and talking. It sounded as if she was nearly hyperventilating.

"Miranda, slow down. Let me see, if I understand the situation. Keep in mind, just because I'm willing to listen, doesn't mean that I can help. There's one important fact, I'm not a cop anymore. Let me recap what you told me already. You claim you saw the lady that sold you the drugs, right?... You said you saw her twice, in Paris, and it was last weekend?... She was hanging around the High School and Taco Bell. You called Wilson and told him about it. He told you that he was working with the police in Paris, attempting to find the lady. Is that right?... And the last time you talked with Wilson, he told you that he'd let you know when he had anything, anything substantial."

Tom thought about the information Miranda had given him. *A man had died in Paris from a cocaine overdose. What was the connection to Becky Adkins? Even if Adkins was selling cocaine, it didn't mean she sold it to the guy. Something Miranda said didn't make sense. She mentioned the guy's name, the guy that overdosed. Why does she know his name?*

"Miranda, you mentioned the guy's name was Dave Daugherty, is that right? Why bother even telling me his name? Did you know him?"

Tom pulled to the side of the road and stopped.

"Miranda, I'm so sorry. This changes things, and I'll look into it." He clicked off.

Wilson parked up the block away. He didn't necessarily want the neighbors to see him. He'd yet to see anyone out on the street on any of his previous visits, but he didn't want to take any chances. He rapped his special rhythmic signal, and Becky annoyingly opened the door. He went inside, and then gently pushed the door closed.

"Friday night at last. Becky, you have no idea, how I've

waited for this evening."

Becky was feeling the effects of her afternoon fix, "Oh, I have a pretty good idea, Wilson. What's the plan? Are you taking me out?"

Wilson chuckled, "No, no, no, Becky, I'm a stay-at-home kind of guy. I don't want to share you. I want you all to myself."

Becky sat on the sofa. She curled her legs up underneath her and watched Wilson pour himself another whiskey.

"Becky, would you like a shot of Jim Beam? It'll do you good. It'll put hair on your chest."

Was that supposed to be a joke? "No thanks, I don't want anything."

Wilson leaned back in the recliner that he'd reclaimed and studied Becky. He noticed she was wearing her baggy sweats again. He wasn't worried about that. It would easily be rectified. He thoroughly enjoyed his whiskey as he stared at her. Neither of them spoke. Wilson assumed she was thinking about him, which felt pleasing.

On the opposite side of the room, Becky also studied Wilson. She was thinking that if he drank enough whiskey, the secret video could be more damning. She liked that. Contrary to what Wilson thought, that was all that was on her mind. Having no conversation with Wilson was good.

Wilson reached over and grabbed his whiskey. Becky wasn't exactly worried about the furniture in this place, but she still didn't appreciate the bottle sitting directly on the coffee table. Wilson again topped up his glass. As he did, he spilled some of it on the carpet, and that made him smile. Becky didn't find it amusing, but offered him a thin smile. Tonight, she would play along. Maybe, if she was lucky, he'd pass out.

"Becky, are you ready for the games to begin?" He smiled.

She wasn't sure what he was talking about, and was worried

what he meant by 'the games'.

He continued to smile, "Are you ready for the Padgett games?"

Oh, the Padgett game; that she was ready for. Hopefully, there wouldn't be any Wilson games. She wasn't sure if she was up for those. She nodded in his direction. She was content to be silent.

"Ah, the silent treatment. That's good. Soon, I'll have you moaning with delight, Ms. Adkins. You'll be begging me for more."

Becky stifled a yawn. She didn't need to antagonize the man. No tonight. She was going to go along with whatever he wanted. If she wanted her relationship with Wilson to end amicably, she'd need to stay on good terms with him.

They had been talking at the kitchen table for the past couple of hours. Most of the conversation had centered on going out. Tom told Nick that he wasn't up to going out tonight. That baffled Nick, of course, because it was Friday night.

Tom wasn't patient tonight. "Nick, just because it's Friday night, doesn't mean we have to go out. There's nothing wrong with taking a night off."

Nick didn't agree. "But, I was looking forward to going out. We always go out on Fridays."

Tom no longer listened. The more beer he drank, the more he seemed to block Nick's protestations. He was thinking about other things. His mind was whirling, and various thoughts flooded in and out. It felt as if he was about to have a migraine, and just as quickly, it passed. Nick observed his friend from across the table. There was a mysterious look in Tom's eyes. It was several moments before Tom seemed to return. It was as if Tom had been on a trip, inside his own head. Nick sensed that something was very different when Tom seemed to return.

"Tom, are you alright? You don't look so good."

Tom snapped, "Of course I'm alright. I told you, I've got a lot on my mind." He stood up and walked from the room.

The way Tom had spoken shocked Nick. In all the time that they'd known each other, Tom had never once snapped at him. Nick felt hurt by the verbal assault. He realized something dramatic was going on, but he wasn't sure what. He didn't want to upset Tom any further. He would remain quiet.

Several minutes passed before Tom returned to the kitchen. Nick was surprised because Tom had changed clothes. *He must be going out. Tom said he didn't feel like going out, and now this?* Tom gave Nick a distant stare and continued to walk through the kitchen. Nick heard the front door close, and shortly after that, an engine started.

He sat at the table, and tried sort out what had happened. Bella nuzzled Nick and gave him a smell. She was also confused.

Why was Tom dressed in black? Nick had never seen him dressed like that.

Becky was tired of waiting. *When is he going to stop drinking?* She had changed into her nightgown when she did her last line of coke. Initially, Wilson was excited when she walked from the bathroom, but that didn't stop him from continuing to drink whiskey. She wasn't sure if he'd even be able to climb the stairs. Becky was ready for bed.

"I'll see you in the morning, Wilson. I need some damned sleep."

Something clicked in Wilson's mind, as he watched her climb the stairs. *Yeah, Adkins isn't wearing that baggy sweat outfit anymore. One more glass and I'll get me some of that sweet ass.* Wilson struggled to pour another glass. Then he held the bottle up to the light and noticed it was empty. He threw his head back and swallowed what remained. He was ready.

"I'm coming Becky. I'm coming to show you what a real man can do."

The bedroom light was on. Becky had been in bed for ten minutes. There was still nearly ten hours of recording time left on the spy cam. She could tell that Wilson was close, because he stepped on the third step from the top, which had a noticeable squeak. She hoped she was up for another roll in the hay with Wilson.

Wilson was having a difficult time standing steady when he reached her door. He swayed back and forth, but smiled when he saw her nearly naked body lying on top of the comforter. *This will be great.* He flipped the light switch off.

"Hey, why'd you turn the light off? Don't you want to see what you're getting?"

"I've already seen it. Tonight, I can make my way by feel alone." He closed the door.

If she got up and turned the light on, it might make Wilson suspicious. She would wait till later. Wilson managed to remove his clothes and groped around, trying to get on top of her. Tonight she wanted to control the situation. She quickly straddled Wilson. The sudden move surprised him, but he seemed to like it. Wilson lay beneath her. Becky rode him, up and down, almost like a carousel. To Becky, it was a non-event. Every once in a while, she checked to see if he was awake. Unfortunately, he was.

The drive had been a blur, but he made it. The street where he stood was empty. But, why wouldn't it be? It was late. It was no more than twenty degrees outside, and the night sky was crystal clear. He loved the night sky. Why didn't he take the time to enjoy it more often? He slowly approached the house. He examined it while he did so. It was a traditional type structure. There would be no architectural surprises waiting for him; standard building principles and floor plan. The deadbolt was cheap and easy to pick, no resistance offered. Inside he paused and listened to the noise which came from the top of the stairs. He let his eyes further adjust to the dark. He listened to the bed springs continue to make a repetitive sound. Soon that sound would cease. He didn't like the noise. He never had liked the noise that old beds made.

He looked at the steps and noticed nothing out of the ordinary. One or two of the old stringers could be a problem. They might possibly squeak, but there was no way of knowing that. He would have to take that chance. But, he had a definite advantage, because he wasn't tangled in a compromising position. However, something didn't feel right and he wasn't sure what it was. He took the first step. It was solid. So were the second, and the third, and the fourth. He paused as the squeaking from above increased in intensity. He wanted to laugh out loud, but he knew how soon the noise would end. He was four steps from the top. So far his luck had held. He looked down at the step and wondered if he should step over it to the next one. No, that would require more effort, and it may not be necessary. He grimaced as his weight pressed down on the third step.

Becky instantly jerked the second she heard it. "Wilson, someone's here!"

Becky quickly dismounted and spun in the direction of the bedroom door. Becky had dismounted abruptly and Wilson was immediately jolted awake. He instinctively reached for his gun, which he had laid on the nightstand. The door flew open and the light came on. A shot was fired, and the light went back off. Then, two more shots were fired in rapid succession. Only the muzzle flash could be seen, then silence. The only noise was the sound that could be heard from downstairs, a loud car passing by the front door. The door stood wide open.

CHAPTER 28

Late Friday Night

The Paris Police were called to a disturbance on West 8th Street. Shots had been fired. An eyewitness reported seeing a man run from the scene. The witness wasn't positive, but he thought he'd also seen a pick-up speed away, heading in the direction of the by-pass. The house was cordoned off. Only police personnel were allowed in. The victim was a white female, between thirty to forty years of age. She'd received one bullet wound to the chest. She was DOA. Drugs and alcohol were involved. A domestic dispute hadn't been ruled out. No other information was available.

Saturday Morning

Wilson woke up incredibly disoriented. After a moment, it dawned on him that he had slept in his truck. His truck was parked in his garage. He opened the truck's door and fell out onto the garage floor. It took a minute for Wilson to stagger to his feet. He aimed his body in the direction of the back door. He searched his mind for a recollection from the previous evening. The last thing Wilson remembered was leaving work early. He believed his intention had been to visit Becky Adkins. Had he? Wilson remembered none of it. He grabbed a handful of aspirin and glanced around the room. Not a Jim Beam bottle in sight. This was a relief. He poured a half cup of cold coffee into a dirty mug and then choked the aspirin down. Why had he slept in his truck? Had he gone out last night?

Tom sat on the side of the bed. Why was he here? He was confused. Why had he slept on the air mattress? It didn't even have sheets or a comforter on it. He had more vivid dreams last night. They felt so much more real, as if he was actually a part of them. In his dreams, he saw things that he'd never seen. He seemed to be familiar with the inside of Becky's house, but he'd never stepped foot in the place. Had he told Nick that he was going out? Would Nick have known to take care of Bella? Tom was sweating profusely, even though the wood stove was out. He turned on the light and looked down at the clothes he had on. He was perplexed as he studied the black outfit he wore. And the balaclava, which lay on the floor, he'd never seen before.

Nick watched the Lexington news Saturday morning. He was shocked to learn that Becky Adkins had been killed. As he watched, he thought about Tom and the events of the previous evening. *Last night, Tom was more mysterious than ever. Why did he go out last night? We'd been talking about it and Tom was adamant that he wasn't going out, so why did he? Why had he been all dressed in black, and why hadn't he come home?* The news report said that Becky Adkins had been shot to death, last night in Paris. Nick didn't want to draw any conclusions, but between Tom's disappearance and Becky's death, but he just couldn't help it. After a while, Nick managed to convince himself that his friend would never have been involved in Becky's death. The fact that Wilson had given Tom a threatening warning about Becky's return, was suspicious though. Tom had been worrying about what they had up their sleeves, obviously for good reason.

Miranda hardly ever watched the news, so why did her mother insist that she watch it now? She rolled her wheelchair into position near the monitor, and then her mom clicked on the icon for the story. They both watched and listened while a reporter talked about the shooting that had occurred in Paris overnight. Miranda had no idea why her mom wanted her to see this, until the photo of the victim appeared on the screen.

"Mom! Hit the pause button. Hurry up! Hit it before she goes away."

Judy had a hunch that it was the same woman, the same one that Miranda had seen last week in Paris. As she watched her daughter's reaction, it appeared Miranda been right. Miranda couldn't stop staring at the photo of the woman on the screen. Judy didn't know why, but a woman dying in Paris from a gunshot wound, with red hair, seemed too much of a coincidence for it not to be the mysterious woman. She watched as her daughter continued to study the screen. Miranda had yet to say a word. Finally, a smile spread across Miranda's face, but she still said nothing.

Miranda wanted to call Tom Padgett to thank him, but she wouldn't do that. She didn't want anything to happen to Mr. Padgett. Besides, he might not have been involved in the murder, anyway. It was just a coincidence, just pure coincidence.

Nick sat at the kitchen table, behaving like an expectant mother, when Tom came in. Bella was there too, wagging her tail, and happy to see him. From the look on Tom's face, Nick knew better than to start in on him.

"There's some coffee in the pot. Would you like something to eat?"

"Yeah, that would be great, Nick. Just give me a few minutes."

When Tom walked in the kitchen, he was no longer dressed in black. He had put on jeans and a white tee-shirt. Nick was as good as his word. He had breakfast on the table, coffee and micro waved pizza.

"Tom, where did you go last night, when you left here?"

"I have no idea, but I ended up over at the home site, sleeping on an air mattress, without any covers."

"Did you hear anything about Becky? Did you by chance catch the news?"

"No, I didn't catch the news and what are you talking about, hear anything about Becky?"

"It all over the news. Becky Adkins was killed last night. She was shot to death, in her house in Paris."

Saturday, Early Afternoon

He picked himself up off the floor and stumbled to the bathroom. Wilson forced himself to stand under the shower, willing the pounding in his head to stop. What had he done last night? He walked around the living room after he had gotten dressed. There was no evidence that he had gotten out of control. Wait a minute, now he remembered. He and Becky were supposed to start the Padgett plan today. How could he have forgotten that? He was sketchy on what Becky was going to do, but that was her area of expertise.

Wilson microwaved a cup of coffee and checked his phone's display. He had one new message. The number on the display was blocked. Wilson didn't appreciate blocked numbers. *How's a person supposed to know if they want to answer the call or listen to the message?* Reluctantly, he pressed play. The voice was unfamiliar to him, but what the caller was talking about wasn't. Wilson disconnected and thought about what he'd heard. The message was short.

"Wilson, I'm sorry to hear about Becky. Looks like you're going to need to fine tune your plans if you ever expect to get Padgett."